CURSES & SMOKE
A NOVEL OF
POMPEII

CURSES & SMOKE
A NOVEL OF
POMPEII

VICKY ALVEAR SHECTER

SCHOLASTIC

Scholastic Children's Books
A division of Scholastic Ltd
Euston House, 24 Eversholt Street
London, NW1 1DB, UK
Registered office: Westfield Road, Southam, Warwickshire, CV47 0RA
SCHOLASTIC and associated logos are trademarks and/
or registered trademarks of Scholastic Inc.

First published in the US by Scholastic Inc, 2014
First published in the UK by Scholastic Ltd, 2014

ISBN 978 1407 14662 1

British Library Cataloguing-in-Publication Data.
A CIP catalogue record for this book is available from the British Library.

Printed and bound by CPI Group (UK) Ltd, Croydon, CR0 4YY
Papers used by Scholastic Children's Books are made from wood
grown in sustainable forests.

1 3 5 7 9 10 8 6 4 2

This is a work of fiction. Names, characters, places, incidents and dialogues are
products of the author's imagination or are used fictitiously. Any resemblance to actual people,
living or dead, events or locales is entirely coincidental.

www.scholastic.co.uk

TO MY MOTHER,
MARILYN STROUSBERG,
WHO TOOK ME TO POMPEII

CHAPTER ONE

—~~~—

Lucia

(One Month Before)

Lucia was sure that the white-haired gentleman reclining on the dining couch before her would make a delightful grandfather. As a future husband, though, he left a great deal to be desired.

The man's bushy eyebrows rose as he waited for her to speak. A breeze from the open atrium ruffled the leaves of the potted palms behind her. She stood frozen, staring down at him. "It is a pleasure to see you again, sir," she finally managed.

Lucia's father, Lucius Titurius, waved his dented bronze wine cup at her. "Do not call him *sir*, daughter," he chided from his own dining couch beside the old man. "In a matter of weeks you will be Vitulus's wife."

Her betrothed picked up his goblet — the one her father usually kept locked up, the silver one carved with tiny fighting gladiators — and held it up as well. "I would have us joined sooner — this very night, even — if I did not need to attend to my properties in Sicilia," Vitulus said, the loose skin from his upper arm waving slightly with the movement. His gaze moved languidly from her feet to her face and he added, "Then again, waiting for the wedding night only increases anticipation, does it not, my darling?"

Lucia suppressed a shudder and looked down. *Jupiter and Juno.* How could her father do this to her?

"Lucia, why don't you join your betrothed on his couch?" her father prodded.

She forced a smile. "I will sit," she said, thankful someone had left a chair near the dining couches. She pulled it closer to her father and sat.

The old man chuckled. "Ah. You have brought her up well, Lucius. She knows a woman's place. I have never believed men and women should share couches. Indeed, no one in my family has ever allowed it. I'm a great admirer of Cato and the old ways, you know."

Wonderful. Wait until he found out about her writings. He would probably ban that too. Would he even let her *read*?

Lucia smoothed her pale blue *tunica* over her thighs and looked at the sky through the atrium rain pool, seeing, in her mind's eye, the woods leading up the slope of Mount Vesuvius. The late-afternoon light would catch the gold and green flutters of leaves from the vineyards on the lush mountain's flanks. She could be *out there*, in the countryside, that very moment with her dog.

Just as the eggs poached in wine and fish sauce were being served, Pontius, the overseer of the gladiatorial school, entered the atrium. Her father's face darkened. He did not like to be interrupted when he was courting a wealthy guest.

Pontius gave Lucia a quick wink, and she smiled back at him as her father joined him at the other end of the room. The big man bent his head to speak urgently into her father's ear.

2

Titurius returned to their guest. "I'm sorry," he said with a slight bow. "My newest fighter has been injured, and I must assess the situation. Would you excuse me?"

"Of course," said Vitulus, waving a spotted hand.

When her father disappeared with Pontius, Vitulus focused his gaze on her chest, and her skin prickled with distaste. Keeping her eyes down, she hoped, would discourage him from trying to engage her in conversation. Maybe he would think her a dullard and cancel the betrothal.

"Are you sure you wouldn't like to join me on this couch, my girl?" Vitulus asked, smoothing the area beside him. "I don't mind the occasional break with old customs."

"Oh, no. Thank you," she said, suppressing another shudder.

"Ah, well. I've noticed girls from the country are a bit old-fashioned, which is part of your charm. Country girls are at least better bred than city women, who are much too modern and full of themselves." Vitulus gulped his wine.

"I would hardly call Pompeii the '*country*,'" Lucia said, bristling. "We have everything Rome has — not to mention a thriving port, and Rome's navy right across the bay."

Vitulus laughed. "Oh, child, you have not been to Rome yet, have you? When we are married, you will see the difference. Trust me. Pompeii is a backwater."

Backwater or not, Pompeii is my home. I don't want to live anywhere else.

An idea came to her. She stood. "I must inform the kitchen that they need to delay bringing the rest of the food out until Father returns," she said. "Excuse me while I attend to these matters."

He nodded, and she released a breath as she hurried out of the atrium, her bare feet skimming over the black-and-white geometric mosaic. The pits and cracks in the floor made her wonder if she should've slipped into her shoes, which a slave had left beside her chair. No, she just needed to get out of there.

Once in the colonnaded inner courtyard, she slowed. Her nurse, Metrodona, who had been waiting nearby, looked at her aghast as she approached.

"What are you doing, child?"

"Father was called away, and I am not staying with that man by myself. I told him I was going to check on the food."

"You've left a guest alone?" gasped Metrodona. "That is the height of bad manners. You cannot insult the man so. You must return right away!"

"But don't you think it would be highly improper for a young girl to remain in the same room with a man without supervision?" Lucia asked with exaggerated concern.

"It is not improper if he is your betrothed!"

Lucia continued her slow pace toward the back of the house. Metrodona huffed after her. Maybe if she walked toe to heel, she could make this trip last until Vitulus left.

The kitchen abutted the dusty courtyard housing the gladiatorial school's barracks and training rooms. A couple of slaves rushed past her toward the school's courtyard.

"What is happening?" Lucia asked as she watched them race away.

"Someone is getting whipped," a young slave cried, running toward the commotion.

Idly, she wondered if her father was having the gladiator who'd been hurt punished. Perhaps the man had shown terrible form, which caused the injury. Before she even got to the cook, a serving slave rushed back to report that the master had returned to his dining couch. She sighed. No point in telling them to wait now — she had no other choice but to return to the atrium.

Her father barely flicked a glance at her when she resumed her seat.

"So," Vitulus said to him, "did you tour Vespasian's amphitheater when you were in Rome last? No matter how many times I see it, the colossal size of that arena takes my breath away. Titus Caesar promises it will be finished within the year. Do you think it will happen?"

Titurius warmed to the topic, but Lucia's attention drifted away.

Suddenly, their wine goblets rattled. Somebody yelped as crockery smashed on the floor. Lucia's chair swayed. She gripped the seat with both hands.

Vitulus sat up in alarm. "What . . . what is happening?"

"Just tremors. They are quite common here in Pompeii," her father explained.

After another moment, the shaking stilled.

"They are common, yes," added Lucia. "But lately they have been stronger and more frequent. In fact, I have noticed quite a number of strange phenomena recently —"

"Now is not the time, daughter," Lucius hissed at her.

"Does that mean a big earthquake is imminent?" asked Vitulus, throwing his hairless, spotted legs over the side of the couch. "I do not want to pour money into your school if the city expects another major earthquake!"

"No, no," her father soothed Vitulus. "That disaster was seventeen years ago! This kind of trembling is *quite* ordinary."

"I have heard rumors," Vitulus persisted.

"One should not listen to the superstitious imaginings of farmers and fishermen, truly," Lucius said. "Once our houses are aligned, you shall see —"

But the earth trembled once more, cutting him off. A dog howled. Lucia shot to her feet. Poor Minos was chained in the back garden, and he was probably terrified. "Excuse me, Father," she said. "I must go and make sure all is well with the household."

Not waiting for permission, she raced out of the atrium, this time grabbing her shoes.

CHAPTER TWO

TAG

Tag mopped up blood from the warped wooden table. The new gladiator was all sewn up, and he'd done it without having to take out the man's eye. True, the stitches were more ragged than he would have liked, but the beefy fighter would just end up looking extra dangerous in the arena, which he'd use to his advantage. So, all in all, not bad.

Tag blew air out of his cheeks and rolled his shoulders, looking up every time a shadow flicked by the doorway. His father — Damocles, the head medical slave — had been summoned to treat the injured fighter, but he had never appeared. Tag had waited as long as he could, then stitched the man up himself. It was not like his father to dawdle when a fighter needed medical attention.

"I want a full report on my new gladiator," boomed a voice outside the room. "How bad was his injury, and when will he be able to resume training?"

Tag groaned inwardly. The stocky form of his owner, Lucius Titurius, loomed in the doorway. Despite knowing that it was unlikely, he had still hoped — prayed even — that he would somehow manage to avoid seeing the master after being away for three years.

"The injury was on the right orbital ridge, *Dominus*," Tag reported. "Though there is no damage to the eye, he received twelve stitches. If there is no inflammation, he should be able to resume light training within a matter of days."

The master looked at Tag incredulously. "And who in Pluto's world are *you*?"

He didn't recognize him? "Tag . . . er, Tages, *Dominus*. Back from training in Rome."

The master's face blanched as he stared at Tag with wide eyes. Tag tried to keep his expression impassive as images of the last time he'd seen the master flashed through his mind. Titurius's red face and bulging neck-cords as he yelled. His spittle hitting Tag's cheeks like tiny poison darts. The blows to Tag's ribs that followed. His absolute certainty — before he'd lost consciousness — that he would die at the hands of the man who owned him. Tag forced himself to push it all away.

"I called him back," Pontius the overseer explained, stooping to enter the small room. "He came yesterday."

Titurius signaled for the overseer to follow him back outside. Tag couldn't help but listen as his master hissed at the man, "I thought I made it clear that I did not want that slave boy returned yet!"

"We've gone over this, *Dominus*. We're gettin' a new group of fighters as soon as the little *domina* is married, and they will need a lot of attention in the beginning. The old man is barely keepin' up as it is. It's either him or we purchase a new medical slave."

Tag's stomach clenched. Was his father failing? He hadn't seemed himself when Tag had arrived the night before, but he just assumed Damocles had been tired from overwork.

"We don't have the money to buy another medical slave," Titurius said angrily.

"Then sell the boy and we will."

"You know I can't," Titurius said, lowering his voice. Tag sneaked forward to catch the rest. "The priest said the curse-bearer must stay part of the household."

The curse-bearer. Is that what Titurius called him now?

The overseer sighed. "Look, we need to put all that behind us. The kid can do the work and we need 'im."

Tag straightened to attention as Titurius reentered the room. Titurius narrowed his eyes, and Tag suddenly realized he was looking down at his master. He had grown more than he had realized in the years he'd been gone.

Bow your head. Look at the floor. He knew he needed to act subservient, but a sudden surge of defiance burbled in his blood. His neck stiffened.

Titurius bared his teeth. "Do not test me, boy," he said in a low and dangerous tone. Tag forced his eyes down. The master spit on the floor. "I don't have time for this. I need to return to Lucia's betrothed," he said, turning away from Tag. As he stooped to leave, he called over his shoulder to Pontius, "That boy needs to remember who his master is. Whip him for daring to look at me in the eye. *Now.*"

Gods. He'd been back in Pompeii one day — *one day* — and his owner was already having him whipped. Tag swallowed, steeling himself to show no fear. It only made them want to beat you harder.

"Strip," the overseer ordered, grabbing the handle of the black whip tied to his thick leather belt.

With great reluctance, Tag pulled the tunic over his head and tossed it on the table next to the bowl of blood.

But instead of taking him by the wrists and tying him to the whipping rope in the outside hall, Pontius crossed his hairy arms and examined him. The whip tip coiled onto the dirt floor like a cat's tail. "Ye have grown well, boy. Still skinny, but how did a medic slave get such well-formed muscles?"

"The gladiators in the Ludus Aemilius let me train with them."

The big Samnite's eyebrows rose. "Really? Why'd they let ye do that?"

"At first for fun when we got bored," Tag said. "Then because I'm actually pretty good."

Pontius grinned. "So yer good, are ye now?"

Heat rose up Tag's neck at his look of disbelief. "I could be. With some training."

The old gladiator shrugged his shoulders as if to say, *That's what everyone thinks*. "Did ye know that I am free now?" he said.

"*Dominus* freed you?"

He nodded, pointing to the wooden sword of freedom, his *rudis*, tucked in his belt. A wide smile broke through his woolly black beard. "I am now the school's highest-ranked freedman!"

"Congratulations," Tag said, frowning.

The Samnite laughed. "Don't look too excited for me now, boy."

"It's just . . . that you're free, and yet you are still *here*."

"Where else is an old gladiator gonna go?" Pontius pointed out. "Fighting is what I know."

"But you could have gone to another school. Maybe even your friend's school in Rome. You could act as a bodyguard anywhere. Why stay here?"

"Settin' off without the protection of my former master makes me look untrustworthy," the overseer said. "Why would I risk my reputation in such a way? I'd still have to find another patron."

"If I won my freedom in the arena, finding a new patron is the *first* thing I'd do."

"Sounds like ye've been thinking a lot about this. So lemme guess," Pontius said, his leathery face settling into disapproving grooves. "Ye want to fight in the arena so that ye can win yer freedom and get away."

Tag nodded. No point in lying.

"Achh! And here I thought ye were smart. Ye of all people should know most gladiators never make it out, boy! Ye have it easy as a healer. Titurius feeds ye, educates ye. Ye have an easy life."

Tag laughed bitterly. "Should I remind you that you are here to whip me for merely looking the man in the eye? I'd rather die on the sands. At least that has some honor."

Pontius sighed. "Well, if circumstances with the *dominus* were different, I'd consider trainin' ye. Turnin' a pretty, fancy slave into an arena fighter would be an interestin' challenge." He stared up at the ceiling, clearly imagining it. "I can see it now — 'The Scowling Young Apollo!' The ladies would love ye!"

Tag blinked. "So train me. *Dominus* doesn't have to know."

The hairy Samnite's laugh sounded like someone hopping up and down on a giant bellows. Tag clenched his fists.

"Ah, young'in, I meant no insult with my laughter. But 'twould be impossible to hide that. And *Dominus* would never allow it. Concentrate on yer healin', boy. That's what yer good at."

Tag swallowed his wave of disappointment.

"Now, don' look at me like that! I'm savin' yer life for ye."

11

A life forever owned by Lucius Titurius.

"But," Pontius added, uncrossing his arms, "I *can* teach ye one of the most important fightin' tricks every champion knows. One that ye can start using this very moment."

Tag lifted his head. "What's that?"

"Showmanship," the old Samnite whispered theatrically. "Crowds love the boys who know how to act their hearts out."

"I don't understand how that applies to me."

Pontius gave the whip a small snap in the air. "I *have to* draw blood, but I won't go so hard as to make ye pass out," he promised. Then, leaning in and lowering his voice even further, he added, "But ye can make it go faster by making it sound like I'm *killin'* ye, understand?"

Tag swallowed and nodded.

"Now. Into the hallway, and grab that rope over yer head."

CHAPTER THREE

Lucia

Once freed from his chain, Lucia's dog, Minos, raced to the corner of their property. Lucia scrambled after him, climbing over the portions of the crumbling old city wall that led out into the woods toward the slopes of the mountain.

Yet another tremor hit, giving her the perfect excuse to disappear for even longer. If her father even noticed her absence — which he might since Vitulus was visiting — she could just say that she was doing her duty by making sure the slaves weren't stealing from them in the chaos. She quietly thanked Poseidon, the Earth Shaker, for the tremors.

Once off the property, she swept up the long edges of her *tunica* and tucked them into the corded belt under her breasts to keep the fabric from snagging. Then she wound her way along her secret trail, amidst wild laurel bushes, spiky ferns, and cypress trees. Once far enough into the forest — when she could no longer see the wall — Lucia called for Minos. The dog darted out of a thicket toward her, panting hard. She stroked his head. "Good boy."

They headed for the small spring on the western edge of the woods. But when she saw it, she stopped cold.

What in Pluto's cave? Most of the water was . . . was *gone.* Disappeared. Maybe she'd made a mistake — maybe this wasn't "her" spring. But no, there were the large willow and the three poplars. . . . Yet the reeds and ferns that normally surrounded the spring looked parched and burned. She circled the shrinking pool and sniffed. The air was heavy with sulfur. Had Pluto reached up and stolen their water, leaving the telltale smell of the underworld as his signature?

The thought spooked her. She backed slowly away, holding Minos by his collar, then turned and ran toward her wooded hideout, the dog at her heels.

She relaxed only when the great tangled mass of vines and branches that made up her private woodland cave came into view. Crawling inside, she inhaled deeply of the soothing moist earth and pine scents. Sunlight filtered through tangled green and brown branches, infusing the cave with a mellow glow. Her secret hideaway had seemed enormous when she and the *medicus*'s boy had built it years ago. They'd been able to almost stand straight up in it then. Now she had to bend and stoop.

Lucia sat and moved aside the old blanket and the piece of wood that covered the hole where she kept her secret things. She opened the oiled leather pouch and pulled out a wax tablet and stylus. Quickly, she cut her observations about the disappearing spring into the wax: the circle of mud, the burned-looking reeds, and the strong rotten-egg smell.

But noting the phenomena did not tell her what it *meant.* What could have caused it? Had Pliny the naturalist ever written about such an oddity? She made a mental note to look through the third book of his *Natural Histories*, which dealt with local geography.

Minos suddenly jumped up and raced out of the cave. Lucia heard a rhythmic crunching of grass and leaves, which meant somebody was approaching. She froze. A young woman alone in the woods was vulnerable to all kinds of abuse. The footsteps drew closer. Why wasn't Minos barking? She shoved the tablet away in its hiding place and strained to hear what was happening.

Minos was whining. Gods, was the interloper hurting him? No, the voice she heard sounded more like murmuring than attacking.

She crawled out of the opening to see her fearsome dog on his back, having his belly rubbed by a dark-haired man.

"Minos!" she called, her mind whirring. Her dog was supposed to scare people away. Now she would have to command whoever this was to keep her presence here a secret. Hopefully, he was a slave and not a freedman — slaves were much easier to control.

"He remembers me," the squatting stranger said, curly head bent over the dog. Then he looked up at her and stood.

Lucia averted her eyes. The young man wore only a loincloth. Was he one of her father's gladiators? What was he doing way out here? Damn Minos for not chasing him off. "I am Lucius Titurius's daughter, and I will report you as off the property if you do not immediately return to the barracks." She hoped she sounded strong, because she didn't know what she'd do if the man was dangerous.

"I know who you are, *Domina*," the young man said. "And I am not one of your father's gladiators. You do not recognize me?"

She looked back at the young man, forcing her gaze to stay upon his face. After a moment, the name came to her. "Tages?"

He nodded.

The *medicus*'s boy. Her old childhood friend. She cleared her throat. "I thought you were in Rome."

"I was, *Domina*. And now I'm back."

Lucia stared up at him. Could this tall young man really be the same boy who helped her build her shelter in the woods? "Why are you dressed as a gladiator?" she asked, noticing cloth bunched up in his right hand. His near nakedness was highly improper. "You . . . you must put your tunic back on in my presence," she said.

"I am not dressed as a gladiator," he said. "I just need to keep my injuries open to air until I can find my father and get them treated."

She shook her head. "Your injuries?"

He turned his shoulders to show her. Lucia gasped at the sight of the raised, bloody welts. *He* was the slave getting whipped earlier? But why? What had he done? She grasped for something to say. "Do they hurt terribly?" she asked, realizing too late that it was a stupid question.

"The lashes? I've had worse."

Worse? Heat flooded her cheeks, as she knew that her father had likely ordered the punishment. Still, being whipped for disobedience was a reality for slaves, wasn't it? Why should she feel ashamed?

Except that she suspected — knew, really — that Tag had probably not done anything wrong. If her father was in a bad mood — or in this case, irritated at being called away from his rich guest — he would order a beating for the slightest real or imagined infraction.

An awkward silence grew between them. The young man shook out his tunic and draped it over his front. "Why are you out here?" she finally asked. "Did my nurse send you to fetch me?"

"No, *Domina*, she did not. I am here to visit my old hideout."

"*Your* old hideout?" She laughed. "It's mine."

He clenched his jaw and looked to the side. "My apologies. Yes, of course it is yours, *Domina*."

Her smile dissolved. She'd meant her response as a playful quip — a reminder of how they'd once teased each other. "Please don't call me *domina*," she said. "You never called me that when we were children, and I don't like hearing it now."

He nodded.

"And by the way," she continued, exaggerating her playful tone to see if she could draw out the mischievous boy she remembered, "I consider the cave mine because *I* did all the hard work. I cleared the spot and found the vines and . . ."

His head shot up. "Not so! I was the one who dragged all the heavier branches to make the walls and —"

There he was. She grinned at him as he continued.

"— piled up the vines to make the roof and did all the heavy lifting. . . ." He trailed off when he registered her grin. He smiled back at her, seeming to breathe out at the same time. "So, you still come out here. I thought you would have abandoned it by now."

"Oh, no," she said. "I make it out here as often as I can, especially when Metrodona is napping. She thinks I'm spinning wool when she sleeps." Lucia rolled her eyes.

He chuckled. They both knew she'd never been any good at the skills all Roman girls were supposed to master.

"You should come inside," she said, stepping away from the opening. "I'm curious what you think of our giant 'wooded castle' now."

When he bent over to enter, she averted her eyes again, not wanting to see his raw lashes up close. After giving him a moment to settle in, she crawled in after him.

"This place used to seem huge," he observed after draping his tunic over his front again. "Now look at us."

The cave did suddenly feel very crowded. Lucia hugged her knees, making sure her hem was tucked under her feet to cover her legs.

"I dreamt of this place while I was in Rome."

"What was Rome like?" she asked.

"Big, loud, crowded, smelly. Imagine Pompeii, a hundred times bigger and a thousand times smellier, and you've got Rome."

"Did you see the emperor?"

He chuckled. "Being in Rome doesn't mean you 'run into' Titus Caesar. It's a very big place. Although I did see Vespasian once before he died — from afar — as he toured the construction site for his great amphitheater."

She scowled.

"Why are you making that face?" he asked.

"Because I blame the amphitheater for Father's insistence on marrying me off. The man promised him money for new gladiators so he can break into the Roman market." As the owner of a gladiatorial school, her father often took his champions to Rome in a bid to rent them to Roman sponsors. He rarely succeeded, though — his school just wasn't big or famous enough.

"Still, if your betrothed is rich and noble, what is the problem?"

"Vitulus is *forty-five years* older than I am! His nose-hairs are longer than my eyelashes."

Tag barked a laugh and his face transformed. It made her want to make him laugh again. "Do you remember that summer we found a nest of baby hedgehogs?" she asked.

He blinked at the sudden subject change and nodded.

"Do you recall how they looked, those tiny, wriggling gray-tipped babies?"

He nodded again.

"Well, every time I see Vitulus's gray nose-hairs quivering, I think of those little baby hedgehogs. It is like they are trying to tunnel up his nose with every breath."

"Ugh." He laughed.

"Father is constantly going on about how rich he is. Surely the man owns a pair of scissors!"

"If he is that rich, he probably owns several — as well as people devoted to doing little else than cutting his body hair," he agreed, still chuckling.

"Yes, and they need to be whipped for forgetting about his nose —" Her hand flew to her mouth as if she could shove the words back in.

Tag's smile disappeared and he looked away.

"I'm sorry, Tag. I was just trying to be funny. I wasn't thinking."

He turned back to her, eyebrows up. "You apologize to a *slave*?"

"I apologize to an old friend."

He examined her curiously, and she forced herself to gaze steadily back. This was Tag, her childhood playmate. Their differing status had not mattered when they were children, and it shouldn't matter now in the place they'd built together.

"Thank you," he said quietly.

"Tag, why were you sent away?" Lucia blurted out.

His expression closed. "Pontius said I could learn more at his friend's school in Rome."

They both knew that was only part of it. The silence between them grew thick again. Lucia plucked at the hem of her dress. Finally, she cleared her throat and said, "I'd better get back. Maybe Father and Vitulus will have drunk enough wine not to notice how long I've been gone."

"And if they do notice?" he asked.

She looked down at her dress. "I'll . . . I'll say that one of the household slaves got injured, and that I got dirty helping the young healer fix him up."

"No, don't say that," he said. "He'll know I was . . . busy."

"Right. I'll say I was helping Metrodona. Come on, Minos," she called as she crawled out.

"*Domina* —" he blurted.

She looked back in. "Out here, call me Lucia."

"*Luciaaa*," he said, as if recalling how it felt to say her name as easily as he once had. "I am . . . It is good to see you again."

She beamed at him. "It is good to see you too, Tag," she replied. "Welcome home."

CHAPTER FOUR

TAG

The next morning, Tag rested his chin on his hands as his father swabbed his back with fresh honey. He knew the treatment was necessary to keep the swelling and fevers away, but that did little to lessen the pain of actually having every welt pressed on with the sticky stuff.

Almost worse than the physical pain, though, was waiting for "the lecture" from his father — the one where Damocles told his only son that it was *his* job not to incite the master. Yet his father hadn't said a word when he'd first washed his lashes with vinegar the night before, and he wasn't saying anything now. The silence was unnerving.

"*Apa*, are you feeling all right?" Tag asked.

Damocles grunted, dismissing the question as if he was already tired of it.

Tag closed his eyes. What was happening to his father? Damocles's changed appearance still took him aback — the parchment skin, wispy white hair, and permanently stooped shoulders. Where had the vigorous man he remembered gone? How could his father have aged so much in just three years?

He wondered, for the millionth time, where he and his father would be if greedy Romans hadn't caused his family's downfall.

Tag's great-great-grandfather had been a highly respected haruspex, an Etruscan priest and healer of the Pompeian old guard. After the Romans invaded, a newly installed magistrate plundered the Pompeian "colony's" wealth like a greedy child. When Tag's ancestor threatened to complain to the Senate in Rome, the magistrate had him executed on a trumped-up charge of treason. Then he took the family's property and sold the rest of them into slavery.

True, Tag's family had it better than most, in that they'd been put into the service of healing rather than the mines, but he still burned with the indignity of the dishonor to his family. His late mother had never let him forget that his blood was of noble Etruscan heritage. "When you were born, the prophetess Lasa came to me in a dream," she often said. "She held you to her breast and said you would free yourself from Roman chains — that you would lead your family into freedom. It is your destiny to be free, you see, to reclaim your sacred heritage."

"But how, *Ati*?" he had always asked. "How will I become free?"

"Shhhh," she would whisper. "Your *apa* does not like it when I talk of these things. The gods will reveal your path when you are ready."

Well, he'd been ready for a long time, and no gods had emerged. So he'd taken to figuring out a way for himself. In Rome, the fighters he'd treated encouraged him to train as a gladiator, and as his skills grew, winning his freedom in the arena seemed like a viable option. But the training ended with his summons back to Pompeii. Somehow, he needed to convince Pontius to let him fight with the others.

"Ow!" Tag grunted when his father patted the last lash with honey — a little too heartily, he thought.

"At least we didn't have to cauterize these," Damocles said.

Tag sat up and rolled his shoulders.

"This is all your mother's fault," the old man continued. "I must talk to her again about how she needs to stop encouraging your pride. It will only get you killed one day. Do you think she's back from the market yet?"

He turned away, carrying the bowl of honey and the linen rags out of the room. Tag stared openmouthed after him. His mother had been dead for almost a decade.

With a troubled heart, he went to the small shrine of the healing god Asclepius in the corner of the medical room. The smoke-smudged ledge was crowded with flowers, herbs, and a small statue of the bearded god, leaning against a staff on which a fat snake wound itself.

A small crystal rock caught his eye. Lucia had found it in the woods years ago, he remembered, and with large, shining eyes, she had begged him to offer it to Asclepius for help when her mother went into labor. Clearly, the god had rejected the sacrifice — in double measure, considering the loss of the baby.

Tag removed the crystal and asked the god for forgiveness in case he was insulted at their oversight in leaving it there. It was his father's duty to purify the shrine every year on the healer's day. Had Damocles not performed the ritual at *all* while he'd been gone?

Reaching into a dirt-stained plant-collection bag, he pulled out a fresh sprig of verbena, appreciating the plant's clean, citrusy smell. He then lit singed wood chips with a small oil lamp in the shape of a man's hand. When the fire sparked, he sprinkled a tiny amount of myrrh to release the scent that appealed to the god.

Riffling through a box of small terra-cotta body parts, Tag wondered what votive to use for his father since he didn't know exactly what was wrong with him. He recalled that Damocles sometimes rubbed his face when confused, so he picked a clay head and placed it beside the smoking bowl.

Guide me, O god, in healing my father, Damocles. I beseech thee to extend your hand and balance the humors that are confusing his thinking and disordering his speech. Show us —

A little boy flew into the room, skidding to a stop at the sight of Tag. The child put his hands on his hips. "Where's the healer?"

"Why, is someone hurt?"

"No," the boy said, still looking suspicious. "Are you stealing the *medicus*'s magic herbs?"

Tag blinked. "No, I am the *medicus*'s son. Back from Rome to help him." Quickly, he finished his prayer and turned to the child. "Why are you looking for my father?"

The barefoot little boy shrugged. "The cook told me to get out of her kitchen. When I asked her what I should do, she told me to go bother the *medicus*. So here I am."

Tag wondered if the grimy little slave child was a recent purchase of Titurius's. Then it came to him. "Hold on. Are you *Castor*?"

The boy's eyes grew wide. "How did you know?"

"Father made me assist the midwife when you were born! You were probably about three when I left. Do you remember me?"

Castor shook his head.

Tag wondered when young children started remembering. Could there be a connection between that and when the elderly *stopped* remembering? If only he could find out what that might be, so that he could help his father.

"Can I mix some medicines with you?" Castor asked.

"No, absolutely not."

"Why? Your father lets me!"

Tag ran his hands over his curls. Damocles should never let a child this young near the medicines.

The little boy grinned and puffed up his chest. "Sometimes he thinks I'm his son! Is your name Tages? Because that's what he calls me sometimes."

Tag closed his eyes for a moment as fear for his father ran through his bones. What was happening to him? More important, how could he keep him safe from the master? He needed to distract this child so he could think. Tag pointed to a bundle of fabric in a fraying basket. "Why don't you help me by rolling up those linen bandage strips?"

Castor squatted like a little monkey and began pawing through the basket. Tag reached for the agrimony root, henbane, and madder leaves he needed for a muscle salve. He sat at the mixing table and began measuring out the ingredients.

"I helped *Domina* tie up her dog yesterday," Castor said. "It got free when the earthquake shook the ground."

"I bet she was grateful for your help."

"Yes. I like it when Lady Lucia smiles at me."

Me too. Tag had been thinking about the way she'd looked at him when she'd said, "Welcome home." Such a simple sentiment, but her smile had been like the sun unexpectedly breaking through a heavy gray sky.

"I'm bored," Castor groused after rolling three strips. Tag couldn't complain — it was two and a half more than he thought the boy would do. Castor picked up a long wooden spoon and held it out like a sword. "I'm going to be a gladiator when I grow up!" he announced, scowling furiously at an imaginary opponent.

"No, you don't want to do that," Tag said as he scraped lard into a clay bowl.

"Yes, I do! And I'll fight so well, the emperor himself will crown me the best gladiator in the world!"

Tag wondered if his desire to fight for his freedom sounded as silly to Pontius as this little boy's dream sounded to him. After sprinkling in the herbs, he began blending the mixture with a thick wooden spoon. "Well, you'd better learn to keep your arm closer in. You're exposing your whole chest to your opponent."

The boy looked down at his grimy tunic. "I am?"

"And you need a shield."

Castor rushed over to a pile of wax writing tablets on the side table. "Can I use one of these?"

"No. Leave those alone. Those are our fighter records."

"Fighter what?"

"Before every man begins training, we have to know his health, illness, and injury history. It helps us healers take better care of them."

"Can you make a record of me? Since I'm going to be a fighter?"

"Sure. The blank tablets are on the floor."

Castor scrambled under the wooden table and picked up a tablet. He held it out to Tag. Still stirring his mixture, Tag pointed with his head to the jar with styluses. "Grab one."

When Castor shoved the tablet and stylus at him, Tag set the ointment aside and scribbled on the wax. "Here," he said, showing Castor.

"What is this?" he asked.

"Repeat after me," Tag instructed, pointing to each letter. The boy imitated him: "*Kappa . . . Alpha . . . Sigma . . . Tau . . . Omega . . . Rho.*"

"That's your name in Greek," Tag finished.

Castor looked up at him, wide-eyed. "Greek?"

"Healers have to know how to read Greek. Did you know that?"

Castor shook his head.

"See if you can copy that first letter on the wax," Tag said. "And maybe after a while, you'll be able to read your name like an educated *medicus*."

The boy grinned up at him as if the very idea was magical. He dropped to the floor, cradling the tablet between his stick-thin legs, and began cutting lines into the wax.

"Now," Tag murmured to himself. "Where was I?" And he set back to work.

CHAPTER FIVE

———❦———

Lucia

(Three and a Half Weeks Before)

Lucia appeared late to her father's *tablinum*. He showed his displeasure by refusing to look up when his man announced her. She could not bring herself to care. It wasn't that she liked angering her father; she just never seemed to please him. So why bother trying?

It hadn't always been that way. She remembered spending countless hours on his lap as he told stories about famous gladiators while she combed through the dark hairs on his forearm. He'd changed after her older brother, Lucius Titurius Bassus, had been killed years ago. She wished she could conjure up her brother's image, but he was nothing more than a vague memory of a stocky young man in gleaming armor, smelling of leather as he kissed her head on his way out of their lives. He died as a soldier somewhere in the hinterlands of Germania.

Once, she'd asked her father why he'd let him go; as paterfamilias, he could have forbidden his eldest and only surviving son from joining the army. But her father had said Bassus convinced him that making connections in the military would be good for the school. Contacts with Roman officers, he was sure, would bring prestige to the family and even possibly new sponsors. Prestige and money — Father's endless obsessions.

She stood, hands clasped, and waited. Her father's small study always smelled of lampblack and metal, as if the coins exchanged in that room left an odor behind. Had it smelled differently when her mother had been alive? Would her perfume have lingered in this room?

Gods, she missed her. It was hard to believe that it had only been three years since she had died of a broken heart after she lost their last baby in childbirth. Her once beautiful mother had given birth eight times, and Lucia was the sole survivor. She knew this was her father's greatest disappointment: It should have been her brother who lived, not her.

Finally, he raised his head, leaned back, and inspected her. "It would not kill you to put some effort into your appearance," he said.

"Yes, Father." She was wearing her dingy gray *tunica*, and, to her nurse's horror, she hadn't allowed her to rebraid and repin her hair.

He sighed. "You should thank the gods that you take after your mother and not me," he said. "You should not dishonor them by ignoring the gift of your beauty. Soon you will be a married woman, and you will need to be presentable to your husband and his people at all times."

His people? You mean the six grandchildren he already has?

Lucia kept her eyes on the desk between them. Even though her father had put the wood stylus down firmly, she noticed it suddenly made several revolutions toward his wine goblet. What had caused that? There was no wind in the room. Was this yet another type of tremor, invisible to them somehow, but strong enough to make small objects move as if of their own accord?

"Did you hear me?" His stern voice broke through her thoughts.

"Yes. I mean, no, Father."

"I *said* that your betrothed is anxious to proceed with the wedding, but because of the tremors, he insists the ceremony take place in Rome. We will have to leave before the Meditrinalia to prepare. That's in just three weeks."

Her mouth dried up like that disappearing spring in the woods. Miss the wine-tasting festival in Pompeii? How could they? It also meant missing the Fontinalia, the day garlands were placed on all the fountains and wellsprings in the city. These were her favorite festivals. She didn't want to celebrate them in big, dirty, miserable Rome!

"Father, *please* don't make me marry him," she begged. "I don't want to move to Rome! I love Pompeii. This is my home. This is where my friends live, where *Mater* is buried —"

He brushed his palm over his face as if he were weary. "It's not as if you are going to Britannia, child! I will come and visit you often. Especially once the colossal amphitheater opens."

She willed herself not to cry, her throat growing tight with the effort.

"You will see, daughter," he said kindly. "Once you have a child, it will all be worth it."

"Unless I am cursed like Mother," she mumbled.

"What did you say?" he asked sharply.

"Nothing, Father."

"Good. Then, you are dismissed —"

"Wait, there is something I wanted to ask," she said. The sight of Tag's back right after he'd been whipped had haunted her for some days now. She took a deep breath, hoping her practiced speech would come out effortlessly. "I am concerned about the rough treatment of some of the slaves in the household. And I thought —"

He began to laugh. She snapped her mouth shut as heat spread up her neck.

"Are you *practicing* running a household on *me*?" he asked. "Now?"

She swallowed. "No, I . . . I just thought —" she began.

He put a hand up to stop her. "I *appreciate* you trying to help with the household, daughter, but you must understand that for most slaves, physical punishment is the only language they understand. Also, you must remember that the paterfamilias makes the decision about how property is managed, as he makes the decisions in all matters. When you move into Vitulus's household, you will see that *Vitulus* ultimately decides how to manage his household slaves, not a softhearted girl like you. Understand?"

Lucia looked down. She wanted to remind him that Mother had often discussed those matters with him. Had he forgotten? Or perhaps it had made him angry, and he didn't want her following her mother's example. Either way, she had not expected her opinion to be so thoroughly disregarded. She wanted to argue, but no words came.

"Now, is there anything else, daughter?"

"No. I mean, yes." She cleared her throat. "May I borrow one of your scrolls — the third book of Pliny's *Histories*?"

He blew air out of his cheeks. "Why? I have already told you, part of your problem is that you read too much. I am convinced that it has corrupted your female mind."

"I wish only to read what the admiral says about prodigies of the earth in Campania," she explained. "I have noticed some strange activity around Vesuvius, and —"

He put up a hand irritably. "Fine. I should warn you, though, that your future husband is of stern Roman stock and does not hold with women reading and studying. This may be your last chance to read the old boy's works."

Gods, that can't be true, can it? Well, even if it were, she would find some way to continue studying, no matter what the old man said. When she found the scroll she was seeking, Lucia pulled it out by its tag and shoved it under her arm. "Thank you, Father."

He grunted without looking up.

Later that day, Lucia sat on her haunches, pulling weeds in the garden. She would much prefer to be out in the woods with Minos, but she'd missed her chance: Metrodona was awake and watching her from the stone bench.

With a sigh, she broke off a sprig of rosemary and sniffed, relishing the sharp tang of it. Why were the gods ignoring her pleas for help in getting out of the marriage? she wondered. Had she not served them well enough?

A thought stopped her hand as she moved to prune a potted quince tree. Maybe the gods *were* angry with her. Maybe they wanted her to pay them more attention. Well, she could do that.

Brushing her hands off and scooping up a quince and another sprig of rosemary, Lucia marched toward the kitchen hearth and the lararium, the household shrine. Garlands of pine, rosemary, and thyme hung over the mini-pediment within the small arched niche built into the stucco wall. A painted green snake — bringer of peace and prosperity — coiled underneath the shelf of offerings.

Two bronze statuettes of the dancing *lares*, the household gods, grinned up at her. Behind them on the wall was the painted image of the *genius* of the family — the essential spirit of the household — showing her father's ancestor in a toga, his head covered in the act of worship. Perhaps if she could reach the *genius*, she might get more help from the rest of the gods who were painted around the shrine. The stern face of the patriarch, however, did not look accommodating. She could almost hear the admonition — *Accept your fate. We know what is good for you.*

She turned her focus instead on the painted gods — Apollo, Diana, Minerva, Fortuna, and even Hercules, the patron god of gladiators. For the first time, she realized Venus was not represented among them. Was that the problem? Was Venus punishing her for this oversight by forcing her to marry an old and bitter man? She quickly scrounged up foods she hoped the goddess would appreciate: tiny blushing apples, dried pomegranate seeds, and bright wild berries — all shades of red, the goddess's favorite color.

After placing the new offerings on the shrine, Lucia bowed her head, only to realize she did not know what to ask of Venus. She wasn't looking for love. Perhaps that was another reason the goddess was angry.

Venus was forced to marry the vile, misshapen Vulcan. She of all the gods would want to help Lucia avoid a similar fate, wouldn't she? So Lucia asked for guidance in finding a plan to evade the marriage altogether. To sweeten the offering, she promised the goddess yearly sacrifices of the purest white lambs if only she did not have to marry Vitulus.

After a few minutes, she sensed someone watching her, so she lifted her head and opened her eyes.

"Tages," she said in surprise. "What are you doing here?"

A flush crawled up Tag's neck, and he looked away. "I . . . I was going to make my own offering, but I did not want to interrupt you."

She tilted her head at him. "The lashes on your back . . . they are not causing you fevers, are they?"

He shook his head, the corner of one side of his mouth tweaking up. Was that how he smiled now? Barely a movement? Her memory flashed back to the long-ago day when he had found a strange sanctuary in the woods, how his childish face had beamed with pride when he'd brought her to it.

". . . *Domina?*"

"I am sorry. What?"

"I asked if you were praying for something health-related, in — in case I could help you in some way."

"But don't you have your own shrine in the healing rooms?"

He held out a small terra-cotta foot. "Your father's stallion stepped on the stable boy's foot and crushed the bones. I have done what I can, but I thought an appeal to the household gods might help as well."

"Oh, yes. Good." She stepped aside to give him room.

He placed the clay foot on the shrine and murmured prayers. They stood side by side.

"So how fare things for you?" he eventually asked in a quiet tone.

"Fine," she whispered back, surprised at the bubble of warmth that grew in her chest at speaking with him again. "How has it been for you back in the House of Titurius?"

Something flashed across his face, but just as quickly disappeared. "It goes well, thank you," he said.

In the silence that followed, her skin tingled at his nearness. Earlier, she'd had dozens of questions she wanted to ask him about Rome, but suddenly she couldn't remember a single one.

"Well, I must go," Tag said after a time. He didn't move, though, and quickly added, "But . . . you never said if you needed me to appeal to the god of healing for you."

"Oh, no . . . unless the god of healing can help me find a way of getting out of my impending marriage."

"Unfortunately, no. But perhaps I can ask the old gods of the city — my Etruscan gods — to help you, if you would like."

"I would like that very much," Lucia said, surprised and touched. "And I presume they will listen to you since your name means *prophet* in your language, right?" she added, smiling up at him.

He smiled back. "You remembered."

"How could I forget? You reminded me every chance you got!"

Tag's face flushed slightly again and she couldn't tell whether it was from embarrassment or pleasure. "Have you been able to get out to our wooded cave at all?" she asked.

"Not as much as I would like." He cleared his throat. "When do you usually make it out there?"

"After the midday meal when Metrodona naps. But sometimes later. It all depends on when I can sneak away."

He nodded, looking at the fire. Should she have been more

specific? She was about to ask him when he went, but the cook pushed her way between them on the way to the hearth.

"'Scuse me, 'scuse me, *Domina*," she said, carrying a heavy cauldron. "I need to get in here to begin the stew."

Tag gave Lucia a quick smile, murmured, "*Domina*," and disappeared around the corner before she could say another word.

CHAPTER SIX

TAG

Lucius Titurius was yelling for Pontius in the training yard as Tag checked the splint on a fighter's arm. He tensed at the sound of the master's voice and peered into the sand pit.

A small hand grabbed his — Castor. "What's happening?" the little boy whispered.

"Don't know. Shhhhhhh."

Pontius turned from supervising the gladiators as they lifted and threw immense logs over a wooden target. He marched toward Titurius. Studying the person standing beside the master, Tag noticed the rich cut of the man's clothes and the golden rings on both hands. A young nobleman, Tag figured, here to rent a few fighters for entertainment at a banquet.

Titurius talked briefly with his head trainer, bowed obsequiously to his guest, and left them standing together. The young man did not return Titurius's farewell. Tag suppressed a smirk at the insult to his master.

"Tag, come here," Pontius yelled, and he jumped in surprise.

"Go back to the medical room," Tag instructed Castor as he headed toward the overseer.

"This is Quintus Rutilius," Pontius announced as Tag

approached. "He is joining the *ludus* for a couple of months of training. *Dominus* wants him to get a medical examination and have him prepared to join us out here tomorrow morning."

The man's thick, wide citizen ring featured a crest that marked him as a patrician of the highest order. Tag had heard of rich patricians and free citizens joining a school for gladiatorial training and even fighting in the arena, but he'd never actually *seen* it happen. Not at their school, anyway. Tag couldn't train to fight for his freedom, yet this man could saunter in and playact at fighting just to have stories to share with his drinking buddies later. The very idea of a man willingly giving up his freedom for sport sickened him. Yet Tag forced his face to bear the impassive expression of the compliant slave.

Well, the young patrician likely wouldn't last long. "Follow me, please," Tag said to him. But Quintus did not move. "Follow me to the medical room," Tag repeated, a little louder.

The man turned his attention to him, his eyes widening. "Oh, excuse me. Were you talking to me, slave? Address me as *Dominus* in the future."

Red heat spread through Tag's chest, and he fought the desire to twist the young man's curled head into the sand like Archimedes's screw. His attitude must have aggravated Pontius too, because the giant Samnite stepped up inches from Quintus's face and stabbed a fat finger into his chest.

"Listen here, ye privileged pansy," he hissed. "Nobody out here calls ye *Dominus*, got it? That's what ye call *me*. Now, I don't know why ye came here or what game yer playin', but there are no guarantees that you'll make it out alive. Yer under my control now, and if ye make me mad, it may slip my mind to ask my men to go easy on yer pampered backside. Are we clear?"

Quintus hesitated just long enough to skirt the edge of politeness. "Yes . . . *Dominus*," he said.

"Tag, take this piece of trash outta my sight," Pontius ordered him, turning back to the sand.

"Follow me," Tag said again as he walked away, not bothering to look back. Inside the medical room, Castor ran under the table for an empty record tablet when Tag nodded at him.

"I must ask you to strip," Tag said to the young nobleman.

"But we've only just met," Quintus replied, quirking one eyebrow and crossing his arms.

"For the medical examination," Tag said coolly, taking the wax tablet and stylus from Castor.

The patrician untied his filigreed, embroidered belt and began shrugging out of his tunic. Tag noticed how carefully he protected his oiled curls as he pulled the tunic over his head. Gods, the other gladiators were going to eat him alive.

"Castor, go help my father, please."

Clearly intimidated by the rich man, the boy nodded and careened out of the room.

"Wait! Don't run —" Tag began, but stopped at the sound of cascading, clanging metal. He winced.

An equipment slave cursed loudly in a mix of guttural Latin and Greek over what Tag guessed was a spilled basket of shields. "Watch where you're going, you stupid little sot," the man roared after Castor.

Tag shook his head, then tossed Quintus a *subligaculum* — a canvas loincloth — and a wide leather belt. Quintus let them fall at his feet.

"You cannot be serious," he said. "I will not wear another man's sweat-stained undergarments!"

"Then you can train naked," Tag said nonchalantly. "Some of the Celt warriors insist on doing so when they first come. It usually doesn't go well for them. I've learned there are some surgeries I really don't like to perform."

Quintus blanched, then stepped into the *subligaculum*. Tag suppressed a smirk. He could feel the patrician examining him from head to toe as he opened the wax tablet.

"So," the man said. "You are a medical slave. Interesting. By the young-Apollo looks of you, I would have had you pegged as the lanista's *personal* slave. . . ."

Tag narrowed his eyes. "I am a trained healer. That is my sole purpose."

"What a waste."

Tag ignored his baiting and began. "All new fighters to the *ludus* — free or slave — must answer the following medical questions." He sped through them as quickly as possible in order to get the man out of his room.

Have you ever had a broken bone? If so, where?

A cough that caused labored breathing?

Have you had the falling-down sickness?

Quintus answered all his questions with an attitude of superior boredom. The scabs on Tag's lashes itched with irritation, and he rolled his shoulders to ease the tension during the interview.

"Let me smell your breath," Tag said. The man's breath had a slight metallic undertone, indicating that the patrician's blood was too hot — a sure marker that his humors were out of balance. Excess yellow bile likely accounted for his odiousness. Tag carved his observations into the wax with the stylus.

"Now let me look at your nails." He was looking for yellowing or ridges, but Quintus's nails were buffed and manicured beyond anything he'd ever seen. Tag swallowed his revulsion, trying to imagine having so much free time — not to mention money — that he could own another human whose sole purpose was to massage and buff his fingertips.

"Why are you here at this *ludus*?" he asked, pretending it was one of the questions on the list.

"To irritate my father, mostly," Quintus said, shrugging. "I am, of course, the fifth son, determinedly *not* following in the footsteps of my overachieving brothers. My father bleats that he's tired of my gambling, drinking, and whoring. So he gave me a choice — serve as a butt wiper to his friends' officers at a military outpost in Britannia, or come here to dry out and toughen up for a few months."

"So you came here? Kissing some officer's backside would've been a lot easier."

Quintus smirked. "I am not going out on any military post unless *I* am the officer in charge. My father should have known this. In truth, I believe he never thought I'd choose this hellhole. Which is, of course, why I did. I live to enrage him."

"Well, you have a talent for enraging others too. You should watch yourself around the gladiators," Tag warned. "Have you been told which barracks you will be sleeping in?"

Quintus laughed. "Barracks? No. I'm staying in the big house with your master."

"But haven't you signed your freedom over to the school?" Doing so meant the patrician would have to live like the rest of the fighting slaves.

Quintus scoffed. "My father has made special arrangements with your master to accommodate me. Besides, your master wouldn't dare insult a patrician like me by making me sleep with you filthy brutes."

Tag shook his head. His throat would be cut by sunset.

The young man seemed to read his expression. "Oh, I'm not worried. In addition to the significant amount of money my father has given your owner to cover this little adventure, I've managed to slip him even more gold to make sure I come out of this with nary a scratch. I'm sure the overseer slave —"

"Pontius is not a slave — he's a freedman."

"I'm sure the former slave will receive his instructions about this. I think your master is hoping to get a wealthy sponsor out of this little arrangement. Which he just might, if I come out of this as handsomely noble as I went in." He touched his hair again.

Tag stared at him in disbelief.

Quintus picked up a small square of metal and gazed at his reflection. "Speaking of pretty faces, I understand the lanista's daughter is quite a little beauty. I imagine every gladiator here fancies himself half in love with her."

"She is betrothed," Tag pointed out.

Quintus shrugged. "Yes, but she isn't married *yet*." He smiled wickedly. "Oh, wouldn't my father love that."

"Love what?"

"If I suddenly claimed that I'd fallen for the daughter of a 'Butcher of Men.' The scandal would serve him right."

"I do not recommend such a game," Tag said. "It is well known that if any gladiator so much as looks at the girl, he will be whipped to within an inch of his life."

"Ah, but I'm not a gladiator, am I?" Quintus said, walking

around the small room, sniffing at the small clay bowls full of dried healing herbs.

Tag clenched his teeth. "I believe we are done here."

"Excellent. Can I go get my sword now?"

"You do not get a sword. We train with wooden weapons. You know this. Everyone knows this."

"But I want a real sword! What's the fun of this if I don't get to play with a real sword?"

"Go out to Pontius and tell him you're ready for your 'real sword.' He'll take care of you."

"Splendid!" Quintus sauntered out of the room, giving Tag a smile of amused condescension.

Again, Tag had to take multiple breaths to beat back the urge to twist Quintus into sausage links. How dare he talk about Lucia like that! Were people truly just playthings to the very rich?

With an irritated sigh, he began the report for Pontius and the master on the new "trainee."

CHAPTER SEVEN

Lucia

The next time I visit Cornelia, Lucia thought as a rivulet of sweat snaked down her back, *I absolutely* must *leave earlier in the day*. Like clay in baking ovens, the paving stones in Pompeii's streets absorbed the sun's heat and threw it back in people's faces. But while the weather normally cooled off in September, it still felt like high summer — almost as if the ground itself was generating heat. *Just one more thing to add to my list of strange happenings in Pompeii.*

"Would you like a drink, *Domina*?" asked the barefoot little slave boy scampering after her and her attendant, holding a skin filled with watered wine.

"I am not thirsty yet, Castor," she said.

"Well, when you do get thirsty, I will be right here!"

She smiled at the child, who grinned up at her with pride. How old was he — five? Six? The wineskin was almost the size of his head. The poor little slave was the only child in the household. She'd had Tages to play with when she was that young, but Castor had no one. If any of her mother's babies had survived, she was sure Castor would be running through the woods with them, just as she used to with Tag.

Occasionally, she watched Tag from the balcony as he made his rounds of the gladiators, fascinated by the changes time had wrought. The funny, mischievous little boy she remembered had disappeared, though sometimes she caught glimpses of him when he laughed at some joke a gladiator threw his way. Still, for the most part he seemed to be always scowling. Which — remembering the whip marks on his back — she supposed made sense. She hoped she would run into him in their hideout again sometime soon.

At Cornelia's villa, Lucia left her slaves outside the kitchens to rest and headed toward the private baths. Her friend had done well for herself in marriage: Her husband was only ten years older and was sweetly devoted to her. Lucia would not be fighting her father's plan for marriage so tirelessly if he could find someone like Antyllus for her.

When Lucia entered the baths, she saw Cornelia already seated in the water. "What, you couldn't wait for me?" she teased.

"No, I couldn't," Cornelia answered, her arms waving under-water like pale fins. A young female bath slave scurried over to help Lucia with her clothes. "I trusted you'd understand."

Lucia took a deep breath of the warm, moist, scented air. Another young female slave rushed to her side, carrying a tray with an array of tiny, glinting blue, clear, and green glass flasks. "Saffron oil today, *Domina*?" the girl asked. "Or perhaps essence of rose?"

Lucia pointed to her favorite — yellow citron oil gleaming in a clear vial. While the slave oiled her body in preparation for scraping with the strigil, she watched Cornelia in the bath. Gods, pregnancy suited her! She looked so happy, even with her belly poking through the water like an island emerging from the sea.

"Stop staring at my monstrous belly," Cornelia complained with fake petulance.

"It's not monstrous, it's beautiful!"

"Then why are you doing everything in your power to avoid getting into my condition?" Cornelia laughed. "You are sixteen, not six."

"If you met my betrothed, you would understand."

Cornelia rolled her eyes. When Lucia had been properly scraped, she descended into the water. "Oh, it is not as cool as it looks," she mumbled.

"I know. I'd much prefer it if we could move into the frigidarium, but Antyllus wants me to avoid extreme temperatures, even though the midwife says it wouldn't be a problem."

"And you don't dare disobey your lord and master," Lucia said with a sly grin.

Cornelia splashed her. "That's right, I don't. Because he makes me swoon."

Lucia laughed. "*Swoon?* That's a new one."

Her friend sighed. "Just you wait. One day, you will fall in love —"

"Or lust."

"— and you will see. It's not that I have to do what he tells me, it's that I *want* to."

"Oh, Venus protect me," Lucia muttered.

Cornelia snorted. "She's the last one to ask. You'd best turn to Diana if you're determined to stay a virgin your whole life."

"I don't want to be a virgin my whole life. I just don't want to marry a man who needs a cane to get around! Or whose nose-hairs are bushier than his eyebrows!"

Cornelia laughed. "Oh, do stop about the poor man's nose-hairs. He can't help it!"

"Yes, he can! Plus, he probably hasn't smiled in decades. I bet if he *tried* to smile, pieces of his skin would flake off like old frescoes in an earthquake." She shivered. "At least your husband is kind and gentle and handsome. Did I mention how noble and wonderful he is?" ·

"Yes, you did, but I don't mind hearing it again. I am very fortunate," Cornelia said, touching her thumb to her forefinger and pressing the hand between her breasts for protection against the evil eye. "May the gods keep us so." Cornelia's eyes widened. "Oh!" Her hand flew to her belly. "Come here and feel this!"

Lucia swam closer as Cornelia retreated to the top step of the pool. Her belly rested on her thighs like an egg in a nest. She looked so insanely hopeful and happy, so young and beautiful, Lucia found that she could not stare into her friend's face without her throat constricting.

She dived under the water and emerged at eye level with her friend's belly. Cornelia leaned back, murmuring something to the bath slave, and Lucia saw her friend's stomach ripple — it actually *moved* — as the child shifted positions, like a small creature undulating under the skin of the sea. Had that been an elbow? Or a foot? It took Lucia's breath away.

Cornelia saw her expression of wonder and grinned, rubbing her belly.

"The . . . the child moved! I *saw* it!" Lucia exclaimed. At what point did infants in the womb begin doing that? she wondered.

47

Was it truly independent, or did the mother's mood or thoughts drive the movement? Did little chicks flutter and kick inside eggs too? What *animated* life like that? Lucia wished she had her wax tablet to write down her questions.

Cornelia smiled. "Hecate is bringing us chilled wine," she said. "And now tell me what you need — you said you had a favor to ask."

Lucia lifted herself out of the water and sat at the edge of the pool next to her friend. "Oh, no, you don't." Cornelia laughed as she playfully pushed her back into the water. "I do not need to see your ridiculously tiny and beautiful body next to mine. Forget it."

Lucia shook her head, but stayed in the water anyway. "Well, I was wondering if you could arrange a meal with Pliny."

Cornelia's mouth dropped open. "The admiral? Why?"

"Well, as Antyllus's patron, it would not be so odd to have him visit, would it? And if I just 'happened' to be here, I could discuss my natural observations with him —"

"Oh, not this again!"

"Something strange is afoot in Pompeii," insisted Lucia. "And I think Pliny would have an idea about what it may all mean. I have been formulating some theories that he might find interesting."

Cornelia rubbed at the spot between her eyebrows. "Lucia, if you tried to share any of your 'theories' with the admiral, he would look at you as if you were a monkey that suddenly started reciting the *Iliad*!"

"Cornelia, that is not true. The upper classes educate women. I bet his sister Plinia joins him in conversation all the time. I don't think he will find it that odd."

Her friend scooped water with her palms and dribbled it over her belly. "I don't think I can do it, Lucia. I really don't."

"It's just that . . ." Lucia paused and took a breath. "I leave for Rome soon. My wedding is the day after Meditrinalia! It's only weeks away. While you're enjoying the tasting of the first wines, I'll be facing the worst day of my life. I may never have another opportunity to meet the admiral."

Cornelia's expression sobered. "It's definite, then. You will move to Rome. For good?"

Lucia nodded. "Yes, you knew that."

"I . . . I just had not thought about it actually occurring."

"In truth, I don't know what upsets me more — marrying a man older than my grandfather would have been, or moving away from Pompeii. I won't be able to see you anytime I want. I won't be here when the baby comes. . . ."

"Gods," Cornelia said, her eyes growing wide. "I don't want you to move away."

"Well, you know *I* don't."

"We should be working on a plan to break this betrothal rather than planning a dinner with the admiral," Cornelia cried.

"Trust me, I've tried everything. I even attempted to get our healer to tell Father that I was barren, but Damocles refused to do it. There's no way around the marriage. But if I met Pliny, it would be like a dream come true — a memory I can cheer myself with when I am lonely in Rome."

Cornelia sighed. "I will talk to Antyllus."

Lucia grabbed her friend's hand. "Thank you, Cornelia. You are wonderful."

"No promises. But, you know, if we are able to arrange it, you must look . . . well, more polished in his presence."

"Will you help me?"

Cornelia's face lit up. She'd forever been trying to get Lucia to wear her hair in the more elegant and modern upswept styles, rather than in a plain braided knot at her nape and to dress in the fashionable colors and fabrics that could show off a woman's body without seeming vulgar or obvious. "Of course!"

"But only if you can get the dinner with Pliny, yes?"

Cornelia splashed her.

Lucia's leather sandals echoed through the hall as she walked to the triclinium. Who had her father invited to dine with them this time? Flames from the wall sconces flickered against the fading red-and-black frescoes on the walls of the small dining room.

"Ah, daughter, come meet our guest," Lucius Titurius said from his dining couch. "Quintus will be staying here with us for a few months."

The young man stood to greet her. "Ah, what a lovely vision of rustic beauty!" he said, bowing his head slightly.

Rustic? Was that an insult or a compliment?

"I am Quintus Rutilius Bucco," the man continued, his dark eyes shining. He was slender, with thick brows over a straight nose, and his carefully curled hair smelled of expensive lotus oil. His thin lips stretched into a haughty smile. "My father owns the largest villa in Herculaneum."

"Oh." What was she supposed to say to *that*? She smiled. "Welcome to our home. May I ask what brings you to Pompeii?"

"The opportunity to train like the brutes your father owns," he said pleasantly. "One must be open to all kinds of experiences, I say!"

"So you are *training* here?" she asked, wrinkling her brow.

Her father sat up and shot her a look. "We have a special arrangement for our guest. He will be staying in the main house with us and training with our gladiators as he sees fit."

Lucia stared at her father, trying to see if he was joking. She'd never heard of such a thing. Free citizens who wanted to train with gladiators had to sell themselves to the *ludus* and agree to be treated like slaves. She puzzled over this as Quintus resumed his position on the dining couch of honor. She caught him staring at her legs before she could cover them completely as she propped herself on the lowest-status couch.

Quintus reached for his wine goblet — her father's best silver one again. A large emerald on the man's forefinger caught the lamplight. The golden ring that marked him as a Roman citizen of the highest rank was so wide and thick, Lucia wondered how he could even raise his hand. Well, his wealth, at least, explained the unorthodox arrangement.

Why hadn't her father tried to betroth her to someone like him? At least he was young and healthy. Yet something told her a patrician like Quintus would probably require her father to pay *him* great sums for the privilege of marrying a man of his station. The elderly Vitulus's interest in her, she knew, was such that he had not only waived the requirement of a dowry from her father, but had also agreed to pour money into the school afterward. Lucia swallowed her disgust at the whole arrangement.

"Your father tells me you are betrothed to Vicious Vitulus," Quintus said to her. "Congratulations, I suppose."

Lucia almost choked on her wine. Carefully, she put down her goblet and cleared her throat. "You suppose? Why do you call him Vicious Vitulus?"

"Oh, that is his nickname in Rome. Did you not know?"

Lucia looked at her father, who was conveniently avoiding her eyes by contemplating a fat green olive.

"Oh, do not look so alarmed, my dear," the man said. "He is a viciously clever politician. I'm sure that is all to which it refers."

Quintus began asking her father about their house champion — a Germanic fighter named Sigdag. Lucia tried to drink her wine, but her throat felt tight. She had to get out of this betrothal. But how? If only her mother were still alive. Her mother would fight this arrangement. She knew she would.

Her ears perked up when the men's conversation turned to the recent rumblings in the earth.

"Yes, we've had tremors in Herculaneum as well," Quintus said. "The superstitious slaves are making our lives miserable."

"How is that?" Lucia asked.

"We actually had some try to run away after the last set of tremors," he said, waving a roasted quail leg with disdain. "So, of course, we were forced to brand them when they were dragged back."

Lucia suppressed a shudder. She'd recently seen a branded slave — a Celt with red hair and pale, sunburned skin. The letters *FUG*, for *fugitivus*, had been burned on his forehead, the skin still an angry, puckered pink. He'd also worn a wooden plaque that said, *If found, return to the Villa Hortensia*, tied with rope around his neck.

"Not only that," continued the guest, "but our neighbor's eel *piscina* has been compromised; it overflows with rotting carcasses. Something in the water is killing them. When the wind is right, the smell is horrendous, but what can we do? The owners are traveling and their slave staff keeps dwindling away, so it's a right mess."

"We've had some odd events here in Pompeii as well," Lucia chimed in. "Recently, I came upon a spring that completely disappeared. I did not know that was even possible."

"*You* came upon a spring? Out there? By yourself?" Quintus asked, pointing with his chin to the city walls.

Lucia swallowed. "Oh, no, I mean, one of the slaves told me about it. And . . . and my nurse heard about a goat herder on the mountain who lost a goat when the ground opened beneath the animal, and then closed up again."

"The tremors are also making the gladiators very nervous," her father added. "They claim the giants under the mountain are restless and want to burst forth in a battle to destroy the world."

Quintus laughed. "Oh, of course those brutes would see perfectly natural events as some form of physical battle."

"How do you know they are perfectly natural events?" Lucia asked, popping a honeyed mushroom into her mouth. "Added up, it all seems terribly *unnatural* to me. I have been looking through Pliny's *Histories* to see if there is any record of —"

"Lucia . . ." her father interrupted.

Quintus took another sip of wine. "Oh, it's fine, Lucius," he said. "I find it charming that a girl growing up amidst such barbarity is educated at all."

Again, insult or compliment?

"What did you think of the production of *Phaedra* at the theater last month?" Quintus asked Lucius.

It took Lucia a moment to realize how smoothly her comments

about Pliny had been dismissed. But her father only stared blankly at Quintus.

The young patrician laughed again. "Oh, I am sorry, I forgot to whom I was speaking. What did you think of Nuceria's champion being felled by the falling sickness? Rumor has it that a curse was put on his *ludus* —"

"There should be a law banning curses!" her father interrupted, his face reddening.

"Yes, but then what would the ignorant poor do for entertainment?" Quintus quipped, taking another swig.

Lucia nibbled on a piece of celery covered in olive spread, swallowing a sigh. How long before she could slip away without causing offense? Clearly, her father was bending over backward to accommodate the rich young man, but she didn't have to be a part of it, did she? When the arrogant patrician began lecturing her father on the proper way he should manage his gladiator slaves — and worse, when her burly father *allowed* it — she knew she had reached her limit. She "accidentally" knocked over her clay cup of wine and yelped. A slave came running.

"Oh, no, I've gotten wine on my dress," she said with mock concern. "I must rinse it before it stains. May I be excused, Father?"

"Of course, of course," Lucius Titurius said, not even glancing in her direction.

"It was a pleasure meeting you, sir," she said to Quintus as she scuttled out of the room.

"The pleasure was all mine," he called after her.

CHAPTER EIGHT

TAG

(Three Weeks Before)

Healer!" yelled Pontius from the training yard. Tag rushed out of the room, almost colliding with his father. Pontius was moving toward them, holding a dazed-looking Quintus, who was bleeding copiously from the nose.

"What happened?" Tag and his father asked at the same time.

The overseer addressed Damocles. "I think he broke it."

"I'll handle it," Damocles said. "Bring him into the treatment room."

"No," Quintus said. "I want the younger *medicus* to treat me."

Tag groaned inwardly. "I am mixing medicines," he said, hoping that would get him out of treatment duty. He'd much rather his father dealt with the annoying patrician.

Pontius nodded. "Go with the senior healer."

Quintus crossed his arms and locked his knees. "I am not going with him. I said I want the younger healer to treat me."

"I don't have time for this," growled the overseer. "Tag, take this idiot and let your father finish the potion mixing."

They could not contradict the command. Tag told his father quickly what he was mixing, and they traded rooms. It was clear by the set of his father's jaw that Damocles was angry too. How could one rich *asinus* irritate so many people at one time?

Taking Pontius's lead, Tag grabbed Quintus by the upper arm and guided the slightly unsteady young man into a treatment room. He could hear Pontius yelling at the other fighters as he reentered the sandpit.

He inspected Quintus. Blood coated the man's upper lip and chin. His nose was already swelling. "Who hit you?"

"No one."

Tag raised his eyebrows at him as he prepared a vinegar wash in a terra-cotta bowl. "So how —"

"My own shield."

"I don't understand. . . ."

Quintus mimicked holding up a shield. "Training exercise. We were supposed to run full speed into the barrels with our shields up, but I wasn't holding mine high enough, so when I crashed into the barrel, my nose had an intimate encounter with the metal edge of the shield."

"Ouch." Tag shuddered in sympathy. He began washing the injured area with a sea sponge soaked in the vinegar. Quintus closed his eyes and tried not to wince.

Tag looked for the source of the blood. There was a cut under the nose, but the bigger issue was its crookedness. *Clearly broken.* He pressed around the bridge and Quintus hissed in pain. "I'm going to have to push this back into position," he said.

"Is it going to hurt?"

"Yes."

Quintus groaned.

"The alternative is to leave it, but it will heal crooked. Some gladiators prefer this because it makes them look more dangerous."

There was a gleam in Quintus's dilated eyes. "Oh, my father would love that," he muttered.

"But you are not a gladiator," Tag reminded him. "And your noble patrician profile would be ruined. To get it back in place, I need to make the adjustment now before the swelling makes it more difficult. Here, bite this." He gave Quintus a roll of leather indented with teeth marks to put in his mouth. Then Tag dipped his pointer finger into the vinegar wash and slowly inserted it into the right nostril until he could feel the protrusion. Quintus panted through the pain. "On the count of three," Tag instructed. "One . . . two . . ."

He pushed hard from both the inside and outside of the nose until it snapped back into place. Quintus howled.

". . . three," Tag said, removing his finger. He rinsed his hand in the vinegar and mopped up a new flow of blood. Eyes still squeezed shut, the patrician spit out the leather bit. "The worst is over," Tag said.

"Anybody ever teach you to count, boy?" Quintus asked, squinting up at him. "Also, why didn't you give me some poppy tea or wine *before* you cracked my face?"

Tag paused. "Our gladiators never get such accommodations." Giving the man something to ease the pain hadn't occurred to him. Gladiator slaves were expected to learn to withstand greater and greater levels of discomfort, so Tag had been instructed never to offer relief unless he was performing surgery of some kind. And even then, he was to use only enough to keep the patient from interfering with the treatment.

"Well, I'm not a real gladiator."

Tag tightened his mouth to keep from saying anything sarcastic, and turned to Castor, whom he had heard sneak up behind them. The boy held up his own small finger and stuck it up a nostril, pretending he was snapping his own nose back into place.

"Be careful you don't damage anything," Tag teased him quietly. "My fingers are too big for your nose if you break it by accident." The boy whipped out his finger and hid it behind his back.

"Castor will escort you to your rooms in the big house," he told Quintus.

"No, you must take me."

"I have other work to do."

"*You* are to escort me," he commanded.

Tag swallowed a sigh. "Yes, *Dominus*," he mumbled, assembling his face into an impassive mask.

Quintus leaned heavily on him as they ambled toward the house, and Tag barely controlled the impulse to shove him off and call him a weak-kneed *mundus excrementi*. He'd sent many a fighter right back into the training pit after snapping a nose back in place. It was all he could do to keep his tongue.

When they entered the atrium and spotted Lucia reading in the shade, Quintus acted even more debilitated, forcing Tag to not just hold him by the upper arm, but to put his arm around his back to steady him. Knowing the reason for Quintus's added dramatics left him wanting to break the patrician's nose all over again.

"What has happened?" Lucia cried, rushing over.

"I took on one of your burlier brutes," Quintus said. "The beast broke my nose."

Tag's jaw dropped as he stared at the patrician.

"Oh, my," Lucia said. "Does it hurt much? Can I get you anything — some wine, perhaps?"

"I am taking him back to his room to rest," Tag said, trying to pull the man away from Lucia.

But Quintus turned back to her. "Oh, wine would be divine right now! Do you know that your healer didn't offer me any pain medicine?"

Lucia looked at him wide-eyed, as if to ask, *Is that true?*

"Wine, willow bark, and poppy tea are expensive," Tag said coolly. "The master wants his gladiators to be able to withstand pain."

"I will have some strong wine sent to your room," Lucia said.

Quintus put on a pitifully pained expression and said, "No, no. Let me rest here in the shade with you. Help me to the bench." Lucia went to Quintus's other side, and he put his arm around her shoulder, shifting his weight toward her. Tag fought not to roll his eyes. They eased Quintus down where Lucia had been sitting.

"I will leave you now," Tag said. He turned and walked rapidly away.

"Wait! Healer!" Lucia called. He stopped as she caught up to him. "I need to know what to do if he should . . ." She looked at Quintus. ". . . if he should grow dizzy or ill."

Tag turned toward her. "He will not grow dizzy or ill except to gain sympathy from you," he said quietly, watching Quintus puff up with her concern for him. Suddenly full of energy, the patrician began gesturing to a servant about what refreshments and other comforts he required.

"I know that," she said softly as they continued walking farther away. "I just wanted to say hello. . . . It's been several days since you told me about the stable boy's foot."

She looked up at him, and his heart began to pound. Had she always had golden lights in her eyes? How could he not have noticed that before? "The boy's foot is healing as well as can be expected."

"Good," she said. "I'm glad."

"Hey, what are you discussing over there?" Quintus called. "I'm in great discomfort here!"

Lucia turned. "I'm just instructing him on how you must receive pain treatment in the future."

Quintus smiled and then winced at the pain it caused in his nose. Tag noted with disgust that as soon as Lucia turned her back to him, the patrician began combing his fingers through his hair to fix the oiled curls that he had sweated out of order.

"You really do not like him, do you?" Lucia laughed at Tag's expression.

"He's a spoiled baby. Plus, he brags that he is going to seduce you."

"What?"

"Yes. Ever since he learned that the men are strictly forbidden from even looking at you, he's been telling the other fighters that not only does he share the house with you, but soon you will share his bed too."

"Ugh!"

"I thought I should warn you."

"Thanks for letting me know." She sighed with irritation. "Well, I'd better get back to being a good host." She turned to leave, but Tag stopped her.

"Wait, *Domina*," he said, looking anxiously over at Quintus and lowering his voice even further. "I . . . er, was planning to head out to the woods later this afternoon." He cleared his throat, flushing slightly. "Just in case you might be planning to . . . um . . ."

"What a coincidence," she said, her eyes shining. "I was going to head out there later too, right after Metrodona leaves for the market."

She gave him a wide smile, turned on her heel, and glided back across the courtyard to tend to the patrician.

Tag forced himself not to grin as he returned to the medical rooms.

CHAPTER NINE

―∾―

Lucia

B ut much to Lucia's chagrin, Metrodona insisted Lucia go with her to the market that afternoon.

"Why do you want *me* to go with you?" She had planned to see Tag in the woods. She'd *told* him she was going to their hideout!

"The Egyptian is expecting you. He is going to read your face and your palm. It's important to know your future before the wedding!"

No amount of pleading or complaining could dissuade her nurse, and when Metrodona began asking what she'd planned instead, Lucia had no other choice but to relent.

They set off, ambling in the shade of the multistoried *insulae* that towered over the well-worn stone road. Lucia slowed her pace in time with her nurse's sluggish, rolling gait.

"You know, you could have bought your freedom ten times over if you hadn't spent so much on these charlatan fortune-tellers like the Egyptian," Lucia said.

"Bah, what would I do with freedom?" Metrodona huffed. "I am too old to start taking care of myself. Besides, who will watch your babies except for me — me, who wiped your bottom from the day you came into the world screaming?"

"I'm not having babies any time soon," Lucia snapped.

Metrodona cackled. "You will be married shortly. If you are as fertile as your mama, you will be knee-deep in 'em before you know it."

Lucia didn't want to be as fertile as her mother, not if it meant her babies died at birth or in her womb. She briefly took her nurse's arm to help her navigate the large stones that got them across the street without having to step into the excess water from overflowing fountains. When Lucia realized she'd gotten too far ahead of Metrodona, she slowed again and began idly reading the graffiti scratched onto *insulae* walls. "Secundus defecated here," she read, wrinkling her nose and checking the bottom of her shoes. *Gods.* Most were just as crude, but one stopped her cold: "Learn this: While I am alive, you, hateful death, are coming."

She shook off a shiver. Why would someone scratch such a morose thought on a street wall? Scanning for something more uplifting, she lighted on "Figulus loves Idaia." Much better.

The market announced itself with a cacophony of noises — coppersmiths hammering on gleaming pots, leather workers punching holes into harnesses with iron mallets, wine sellers hawking their latest vintage, butchers extolling the sweetness of their ewe meat. They walked past a poultry farmer hawking the newest craze — parrots strung up by their strange little feet, looking like bunches of feathered fruit. "Only for the best banquets in Pompeii!" he called out. Behind the man with the parrots, a boy yelped as his teaching master caned him in front of the other students attending the open-air school.

They found Metrodona's Egyptian sitting on a low wooden stool in the shade of the colonnade near the flower stalls. Lucia leaned against a dusty red column as she examined the old man, who had leathery skin scored by the sun into deep ravines around his mouth and forehead, under a turbaned head. The man held out a dirty palm and Metrodona slipped some coins into it. In a blink, the coins were gone and the man turned to stare at Lucia. Metrodona waved her closer.

"What am I supposed to do?" Lucia asked through the side of her mouth, afraid to look away from the old man's strangely piercing stare.

"Nothing," Metrodona said. "He is reading you."

The man signaled, and Metrodona grabbed Lucia's right hand and held the palm out for him to inspect. His brow furrowed and Lucia fought the impulse to snatch her hand away. But then he grinned, showing three brown teeth hanging from inflamed gums like tiny figs about to drop from their branch. He began chattering with Metrodona in heavily accented Latin. Lucia caught the words *love* and *a great passion* and decided she'd heard enough. The very idea of "passion" with her doddering betrothed made her shiver.

"I'm going to go look at the incense," she said, bending toward Metrodona's ear. Her nurse nodded and waved her away as she continued her lively conversation with the old Egyptian.

Dozens of terra-cotta bowls filled with tiny hills of brightly colored powders — yellow, red, blue, brown, purple — crowded the incense seller's cart. Garlands of myrtle and rosemary hung from wooden beams, mixing with the sweet and tangy smells of the riot of offerings.

"Ah, I have something special for a pretty young girl like you," said a fat old woman with wiry gray hair. She drew out a small leather pouch and opened it, stroking the worn brown leather as if it were a lover's face. "Venus the goddess of love favors my special mix of rose and narcissus," she said in a low tone, as if sharing a secret. "It will draw the true love of the one you seek."

"I need . . . do you have something for . . . making sure a marriage *doesn't* happen?" Lucia asked.

"Hmmmmm. Sometimes the goddess of love is insulted by unions that should not be so. To attract her attention to it, use powder of lilies in her sacred fire." The woman quickly drew out another pouch. "These have been dried under moonlight. The goddess will notice this special blend and grant you your wish. I am certain of it."

"How much?" Lucia asked, and the haggling began. When they finally settled, the woman handed Lucia her portion wrapped in a carefully folded piece of old papyrus.

"Purchasing something special?" a familiar voice asked from behind her. She turned, her heart skipping a beat.

"Tag! What are you doing here?"

He held up several small cloth bags pungent with the smells of earth and dried bitter herbs. "Pontius made me come today to pick up some things for him," he said. "And I needed to refill some of our herb stores."

"Metrodona insisted I come today too. Funny, isn't it?"

He nodded, his eyes crinkling.

"Healer! Healer!" came a high little voice. Castor ran up to Tag and pulled on his tunic. "Can we go see the monkey now, *pleeeeease?*"

"You're here too?" Lucia asked the boy, laughing.

"I go where the healer goes, because I am going to be a healer when I grow up," he said.

"Wait," Tag said, pretending confusion. "I thought you said you were going to be a gladiator."

The boy scowled up at him. "I am going to be both!" He turned to Lucia. "I am the healer's appistant."

"A-what?"

"Assistant. I am helping with everything."

"Helping create a mess, more like it," Tag said. Something about the way he ruffled the slave boy's hair made her heart contract.

"The monkey! Please, can we see the monkey now?" Castor begged.

"I want to see it too," Lucia said, following as the boy pulled Tag to the small gray-and-black monkey leashed to the fruit and nut seller's stall. Castor dropped to his haunches before the creature, grinning from ear to ear.

"Little monkey, meet little monkey," Tag said, looking down at the boy. "You know, Castor, the resemblance between you two is downright troubling."

But the boy didn't hear the teasing, so entranced was he by the small creature that looked into his eyes with a defeated, soulful gaze.

"I let you feed the monkey if you buy from me," the seller said.

Castor shot up and bounced on his bare toes. "Oh, please please please please buy something! I want to feed him!"

"Let us see," Tag said, then turned to the grocer. "Show me your best Persian walnuts."

After Tag purchased a wrapped bundle of nuts and Castor had excitedly handed the monkey his treat — a piece of cucumber, which the creature took with tiny, delicate hands — they walked slowly away. Lucia asked, "Walnuts? Doesn't the cook buy those?"

"Yes. But these are not to eat — they are medicinal."

She looked up questioningly at him.

"They are for my father," he explained. "I have read that ground walnut powder mixed with bone ash may help with his mental confusion. That and the occasional bleeding should help, I hope." He paused. "Which reminds me, my supply of leeches is getting low."

"Ugh. I'd rather be cut and bled than have leeches used on me."

"I will remember that."

They promenaded around the market, occasionally stealing glances at each other as they chatted about the household. Sometimes they bumped shoulders or brushed arms. Lucia felt as if all her awareness and sensation were gravitating toward Tag like iron to a magnet rock. She wondered how the weight of it didn't make her tip over into him. Why was she reacting this way? This was *Tag*.

"Well, do you?"

His question startled her. She blinked. "Do I what?"

"Want some bread? I'm hungry."

"Oh, sure." She hadn't even noticed that they'd stopped in front of a baker's cart. They exchanged a few coins with the baker and ripped into the crusty, scored round loaf with relish. Castor stuffed so much into his mouth at once it looked like he'd shoved a small *trigon* ball in his cheek.

After finishing his bread, Castor ran toward a clutch of dirty, ragged chickens pecking at seeds near the vegetable carts. A great squawking of outrage ensued, and not just from the chickens. The sellers cursed at the boy to go away.

"Gods, he never slows down," muttered Tag.

"It is very sweet that you have taken him under your wing," Lucia said.

"He is a smart boy," he said. "What a waste it would be if no one ever bothered to train his mind."

His eyes were the color of dark, rich honey. She looked away quickly, her cheeks warming. "Yes, of course."

"In fact," he continued, "he seems to pick up Greek naturally. Much faster than you ever did."

She stopped in her tracks. "That is not true! I learned it so fast, Father didn't even *know* I was joining you in your lessons."

"I am teasing, Lucia," he said, smiling down at her.

"Oh. Yes." His smile was devastating. Apparently, she wasn't the only one who found it so. Some of the other young women in the market were looking at Tag the same way she was — and some of the men too. Yet the moment someone attempted to talk to him — even if just to ask which baker had the best bread that day — his scowl returned. The expression was his shield, she realized, and it pained her to think how much he needed one.

Castor bounced through the forum and toward the Temple of Venus. They slowly followed.

"So, how fares Quintus?" he asked. "Or maybe I should ask, 'How much sympathy has he been milking for his nose?'"

She chuckled. "Half the time, I can't tell whether it's all an act or if he really is as insufferable as he comes across. Do you know how he introduced himself to me the first time I met him? He said, 'My father owns the largest villa in Herculaneum.' I wanted to say, 'How nice for you — my father owns the smelliest gladiators in Pompeii.' Really, it's a wonder to me that no gladiator has pummeled him to death yet."

"Give it time," he said.

They walked in silence, dodging the people moving to and from Venus's temple and altar. Wooden scaffolds climbed up the sides of the temple as builders scraped and pounded the walls, which always seemed under some sort of renovation. As they neared the outdoor altar, Lucia pulled out her powder of lilies. "Excuse me a moment," she said to Tag without looking at him.

She sprinkled the fragrant powder over the dancing orange flames. The powder made a crackling sound, releasing a burst of sweetness mixed with apple-wood smoke. Closing her eyes, she murmured her prayer to the goddess of love:

Save me, O goddess, from a terrible union
One that would be an insult to your ways of love
and I shall sacrifice a white lamb for you every year
and spread word of your kindness and magnificence to all in Pompeii.

Tag leaned against a red-painted column in the colonnade, waiting for her. After she rejoined him, they trailed Castor to the edge of the complex, where the child began jumping from rock to rock.

"Have you ever been to the secret temple?" Tag asked.

"What secret temple?"

Castor ran back, staring up at him with large, round eyes. "There is a secret temple? Where?" he squeaked.

Tag pointed to a depression in the rocks. "Down there. To Mephistis," he said. "The goddess of poisonous vapors."

The little boy looked at Lucia. "Can we go, please? Please?"

Lucia shrugged. "Sure."

Tag led them to a section of scrubs and rocks at the edge of the old quarter, where they climbed down an embankment.

"I've never heard of Mephistis," Lucia said.

"She is a Samnite goddess. The Romans built the temple to

69

Venus over her ancient shrine when they conquered Pompeii," Tag said, holding his hand out to help her down the moss-covered rocks. "A great many old-timers are convinced Mephistis will not take the insult lying down. They await her punishment."

He released her hand to lift Castor and "fly" him down, the boy whooping with glee. She curled her fingers around the lingering warmth of his touch.

"They've been waiting a long time, then," she said, forcing her attention back to his words. "Sulla took Pompeii many generations ago."

"The gods work in their own time," he said. "Many believe she will exact her punishment on the Romans in her own way. My father told me about this shrine, and one day I'll tell my son."

The rocks and brush around them buffered the sounds of the marketplace and temple complex, the calls and voices sounding more like the murmurs of waves sliding on sand. Tag pushed aside a large myrtle bush to reveal blackened, pitted stone steps leading down into a crevice. They took the steps in silence. Lucia sensed the sacredness of the space — the power of it. Castor must have too, because he stopped chattering.

Deep within the rocks stood a small tholos, a circular columned shrine. In the middle stood a well-worn altar covered in flowers, palm leaves, and sprigs of rosemary.

"People are still honoring your goddess," she noted, looking around for other worshippers. The place was empty.

"Mainly the old-guard families, like I said." Tag drew a walnut and some herbs from his linen bags and placed them on the altar with a bowed head. Feeling like she needed to give something to the goddess too, Lucia added the remainder of her lily powder.

"Why is her altar here?" asked Castor. "Among the rocks?"

"Because she has the power to breathe her poison out through them," Tag explained. "Some say she lives deep in the earth, and when she is angered, she rises up, brings her lips to the underside of the ground where we stand, and exhales her poison to consume her enemies. And so she must be appeased."

"I wonder why I never knew about this shrine," Lucia said.

Tag shrugged. "Because she is Samnite, perhaps. And because you are Roman."

"Gods, I hope she doesn't hold that against me," she said with a smile.

After they climbed up from the secret rock grove, Castor begged, "Can we go to the wharf now? You said we would go to the wharf!"

"Not yet," Tag answered. Turning to Lucia, he asked, "Why don't we take another turn around the market?"

He doesn't want to leave me either, she thought. A thrill of pleasure filled her chest. They circled the stalls again, commenting on which seller had the tastiest *garum* and which herbalists picked their plants according to the cycles of the moon. Castor followed a band of raggedy, barefoot boys giving chase to pigs snuffling in piles of rotting vegetables strewn around the carts.

"What do you go to the wharf for?" Lucia asked Tag.

"You do not want to know."

She grinned up at him. "Oh, now I *have* to know."

He sighed. "Cat dung. For treating ulcers of the skin, a paste of dung mixed with powdered mustard and oil has been shown to be quite effective."

She stopped and looked at him incredulously. "You are joking, aren't you?"

"No," he laughed. "It's a proven remedy."

"So then why the wharf?"

"The cats who feed solely on fish scraps, I have learned from experience, provide the most effective . . . er, samples. So I go after the droppings of the cats who live on the wharf and around the boats."

She made a face.

"It's medicine," he said, shrugging. Then, with a mischievous grin, he added, "But thankfully, Castor likes to collect the samples for me."

"How wonderful to have your own little slave to do the dirty work for you," she teased.

He stopped cold, his scowl returning. "I don't *own* Castor," he said, his mouth a thin line. "You do. And I would give whatever I had to keep that little boy from growing up a slave like me."

She felt her cheeks warm. "Oh, I am sorry, Tag. Of course I know that. Sometimes I forget that you are not . . ."

"Like you. *Free*."

"I meant no insult," she said. "Truly." As children, teasing him about being a slave was the only thing that seemed to break him — so she'd quit doing it. Along the way, she had stopped thinking of him as a slave altogether. And now she'd brought their lovely time together to a grinding halt with her big mouth.

Tag resumed walking. "Castor, come on," he called. "Time to go to the wharf."

The boy whooped with joy and ran, weaving in and out of the pockets of people toward the marina gate outside the temple complex. "Good-bye, *Domina*!" Castor shouted over his shoulder to Lucia as he scampered away.

Without another word, Tag followed the boy.

"Wait," she said.

He faced her, his expression blank. "Yes, *Domina*?"

Gods, how she hated when he used that title with her. "I . . . I wanted to thank you for taking me to see the sanctuary of Mephistis."

"You are welcome," he said, coldly formal.

She opened her mouth to say something — anything — to regain the warmth they had enjoyed just moments before, but no words came. He looked behind her. "It appears your nurse is looking for you. May Mercury watch over you on your journey home," he added. Then he turned and set off after Castor.

CHAPTER TEN

TAG

Tag neared the wooded hideout and spied Minos. That meant Lucia was inside. *Good.* He picked up his pace.

He'd felt bad about the way he'd reacted to her comment about Castor being "his" slave the day before. Sure, it had been a thoughtless remark, but maybe she really did forget about his status when they were together. He certainly forgot about *hers.* Also, she had *apologized* to him, an act of kindness from a slave owner that still had the power to stun him.

"It's me, Tag," he called at the hideout's opening as he scratched Minos, who grinned and panted up at him. "May I come in?"

"Sure," she replied. He noticed her putting a scroll into a cloth bag as he crawled inside.

"What are you writing?" he asked.

"Nothing. I'm rereading some of Pliny's scrolls." He settled himself across from her. When he looked up, she was staring at him with a worried expression. "Tag, I wanted to apologize for what I said —"

"No, you don't need to," he interrupted. "I know you meant no insult. I should have seen that."

"Oh," she said. "I was worried you were still angry."

He looked away and shook his head, smiling.

"What?" she asked.

"I've just never even imagined that there existed a slave owner who could be worried about how a slave *feels*."

"I am not your owner."

"True. But you are still *Domina*."

"Again, out here, I am Lucia, your childhood friend."

"All right." He nodded. "Why are you rereading Pliny?"

"Because I'm hoping that I might meet him soon," she said, her eyes shining. "My friend Cornelia is trying to arrange it."

"*Admiral Pliny?* Why? How?"

"Pliny is her husband's patron. I figured this might be my last chance to meet the man before I'm shipped off to Rome."

"Can I go with you?" he asked, only half joking. He had often used Pliny's *Natural Histories* to check remedies and plants. "Perhaps he knows something about the nature of aging and memory that's not in his scrolls — something that could help my father." He sighed. "I need to start shielding him from the master somehow."

"Why does he have to be shielded from my father?" she asked, her brows knitting.

"Because your father is liable to put him out on the street when he realizes *my* father might make a medical mistake with one of his precious fighters."

Her mouth dropped open. "My father would *never* do that!"

"Of course he would."

"I wouldn't let him!"

"But soon you'll be gone."

She looked out toward the hideout's opening. "Well, I will . . . I will make sure he doesn't! I'll extract a promise."

75

Tag didn't bother responding. Did she really think she could have any impact on her father when it came to how he managed his human property?

Lucia stiffened. "Did you feel that?"

"I didn't feel anything. Did the earth shake again?"

"No, this is different. See, this is the kind of thing I want to discuss with Pliny. I think the earth is trying to tell us something —"

"That another big earthquake is coming?"

"No, I think it's something else. It seems to me the land is undergoing some kind of — *transformation*."

The earth vibrated ever so slightly, and this time he did feel it. She scuttled out of their hideout. "Come, let me show you something," she called.

He didn't move, and she popped her head back in, twigs pulling strands of black silk from her braid to float around her face. "Come with me. You will enjoy this."

With a sigh, Tag crawled out of the enclosure after her. Even when they were little, her intensity for whatever captivated her — usually some creature or plant in the woods — was always stronger than whatever resistance he could offer up. Besides, he was curious now.

It took him a few minutes to wonder if this hadn't been a very bad idea, especially when he noticed that she'd grabbed the bottom of her long *tunica* and tucked the ends into her belt so that she could walk more freely. He could tell it was an unconscious act, a necessary maneuver if she was going to walk through the woods without ripping her dress to pieces.

But watching her smooth legs move confidently through the brush was a reminder that they were no longer children. These were the shapely, beautiful legs of a young woman. Which, of course, led to him noticing the sway of her hips, and when she turned to say something — which he didn't catch — the fullness of her breasts. Had she always been this lovely? Or had she just blossomed into a beauty in the last three years?

He forced his gaze back to the bottoms of her feet, but that felt terrible as well, because it reminded him of his status as a slave. So he compromised and stared at the loose curls that had come undone from her pinned-up braid as they swung back and forth down her back.

"Look," she whispered, stopping suddenly.

He almost ran into her. "What am I looking at?"

"The web," she whispered as she pointed again.

A huge spiderweb spanned the length between a rotten log and the roots of an oleander bush. "That is one immense web! What kind of spider is it?" he whispered back. Then, "Why are we whispering?"

She ignored him. "I don't know what kind of spider it is, but that's not what's important. Be still and watch."

Nothing was happening with the web, but he quickly became aware that their arms were almost touching. He looked down at her hand and at the soft skin on the underside of her wrist. Did her skin feel as silky as it looked? Gods, why was he thinking this way?

"There!" she said. "Did you see it?"

He glanced back to the web. "See what?"

"By Diana, you haven't changed a bit! See how the web is *vibrating*?"

"No, I don't. . . . Oh, yes. I see it." She was right. The iridescent threads trembled delicately. "It's the wind. So what?"

She turned to him. "Do you *feel* any wind? It's another strangely hot and airless day. There is no wind."

The golden lights in her eyes made him think of sunlight glinting off bronze.

"My point is," she continued, "that the earth is constantly trembling. It's not at a level where we can detect it, but I think many animals sense it."

"The gladiators all say that Vulcan is angry and that the giants are stirring."

"Yes, I know. And Metrodona says her seer in the market has visions of all the statues in Pompeii falling to the ground in positions of agony."

He smiled ruefully. "That is strange and unnerving."

Her face changed.

"What?"

"I like it when you do that," she said softly.

"Do what — say something is strange?"

"No, smile. You're always scowling these days."

"Oh. Thanks for reminding me." He stopped smiling and exaggerated a scowl.

She laughed. They gazed at each other for a long moment.

"I missed you when you were in Rome," she said.

He'd thought of her often too, but only as the young friend he explored the woods with, as his fellow wood-cave builder. He would not have been able to conjure the creature that stood before him, this beautiful girl who left him with a strange hollow feeling in his chest. The hollowness grew when he looked into her eyes, so he forced himself to look away — his gaze lighting on her neck, at the way the fabric of her dress clung to her curves, at her mouth. He didn't know where to look, but he didn't want to stop looking either.

"Tag," she called softly.

Gods, the way she said his name . . . Her voice vibrated within him, deep and low. Ever so slightly, she tilted her face up to his. Was she going to . . . ? The warm scent of her body made him dizzy. He felt her soft breath against his mouth.

He suppressed a groan and took a step back. This could not be happening. She was the *master's daughter*. He could be put to death — crucified — for touching her. "We cannot," he managed to get out. She stared up at him, her mouth still partly open, and she looked so beautiful, so inviting, this time he did groan.

"Why not?" she asked.

"Because . . ." Breathing suddenly seemed very difficult. He swallowed. "Because I am a slave."

"I don't care."

"Because it is wrong."

She blinked. "Why?"

He had no answer. He couldn't think. His lungs seemed incapable of taking in air.

"Lucia . . ."

"Just once, before I'm married, I want to know what it is like to kiss someone I *want* to kiss," she said. "Just once, *I* want to make my own choice about it."

For her it would be a kiss she stole from a slave on a whim; she'd just said as much. But for him . . . for him, he knew suddenly, one taste would be torture, to know that she would be forever out of reach afterward.

Another sickening realization tightened his chest. Did *he* have a choice?

He took another step away. "Are you going to order me to obey? Take away my choice too?"

Her eyes widened. "Gods, no, Tag. I just thought . . . I only wanted to know what it would feel like. I thought maybe you might want . . ." She put a hand to her throat as her face flushed. "I'm sorry. Oh, Diana, this is so embarrassing."

"Don't be embarrassed."

She shook her head. Her eyes began to fill. "I . . . I need to go," she said, turning away.

He reached out and grabbed her wrist. "Wait. I'm sorry. I *do* want to —" What was he doing? He should let her go. But now that he was touching her . . .

She stared up at him as he moved closer. He released her wrist and cupped her cheek, his thumb caressing soft, flushed skin. He paused to drink in her scent, her warmth, the way her breath hitched when he bent toward her. Yes, this was a very bad idea, but as he lowered his mouth onto hers, his fears melted away. Everything disappeared, in fact — the woods with its strangely vibrating spiderwebs, his status as slave, even the knowledge that he could be killed for touching her.

There was only Lucia.

CHAPTER ELEVEN

―∽∼―

Lucia

She hadn't planned on kissing him. It had seemed, in the moment, like a way to show defiance, a way to take control. Her first kiss would *not* be from the old man her father had chosen for her, but from a beautiful boy *she* selected.

But when he touched her — when they kissed — all thought disappeared, leaving only sensation — warm, wet, soft, tingling all the way down her spine. He'd blotted out the sun as he leaned over her, and then he blotted everything else out too.

He pulled away. She stared dumbfounded at his full mouth. *Why had he stopped?* She angled her mouth up to his again, but he stepped back. *"Domina,"* he said, his voice low and husky.

"Don't call me that," she breathed.

"What are we doing?"

She blinked. "If you don't know, then we must be doing it wrong."

The side of his mouth quirked, and he shook his head slightly as if trying to clear it. Gods, he was so beautiful — a young flushed Apollo, god of light and beauty, with untamed curls, whose lips tasted like wine and honey. She wanted to press her face against his neck and drink him in — his scent of woods, herbs, and smoke.

"Your father would crucify me. . . ."

"He never has to know."

He drew in a ragged breath as she pressed herself against him, her mouth soft on his throat. His arms wrapped around her and he pulled her even tighter, breathing her in too.

Minos barked in sudden outrage, and they jumped away from each other. But the dog was turned away from them, hair up, tail stiff. Lucia recognized the bark — he was warning someone off.

"I need to get back . . . in case Metrodona is wondering where I am," she whispered. "In case she sent someone looking for me."

He nodded, swallowed. "I'll stay out here to draw whoever it is away if they keep coming in this direction."

She turned, then hesitated, not wanting to leave. "Will you . . . get in trouble if you are discovered?"

He shook his head. "I'll say I was . . ." Looking around, he plucked a leaf and scooped the spider onto it. Then with one quick swipe, he destroyed the large web and rolled it together to form a small mass of threads. "I'll say I was collecting spider-webs. We never have enough to deal with all the cuts we see."

She remembered reading in Pliny that cobwebs moistened with oil and vinegar were useful in treating cranial fractures. Was it true? There was no time to ask.

"Go," he mouthed.

She gave him a quick peck on his beautiful mouth and sprinted toward the opening in the wall.

The next morning, Lucia sat in the shade of Cornelia's sumptuous gardens. Trees rustled in the breeze as water tinkled from the clamshell-shaped fountain beside them.

She stared at the glimmering drops of water, thinking over and over again, *I kissed him. I kissed Tag!* Remembering the feel of him — reliving every moment — left her constantly wondering when she could touch him again.

"Lucia, where are you?" Cornelia called in a singsong trill.

Lucia flushed. "I'm sorry, what did you say?"

"I asked if you really do not want children," Cornelia repeated as they sorted through the pile of baby clothes between them on the marble bench. Antyllus's mother had passed them on, and there was enough there to clothe an army of babies. Cornelia held up one stained but soft baby wrap. "Oh! Antyllus must have worn this!" She pressed it to her bosom.

Lucia smiled at her friend. "That is adorable. And yes, I do want children eventually. But not with Vitulus."

Cornelia made a sympathetic noise. "Still, once you have a child, it will all be worth it."

"That's what everyone keeps saying," Lucia muttered.

"Flavia is our age and already on her second child," Cornelia pointed out. "You should see how sweet her baby is. She seems very happy."

Lucia considered sharing her fears about her mother's experiences with stillbirths. What if the shades that cursed her mother in the birthing chamber now followed *her*? But she didn't want to remind Cornelia about the dangers she faced, so she shrugged instead. "I have a question for you," she said, rubbing her palm over a soft blanket decorated with faded threads of ocean waves and wide-eyed fish.

"Hmmm?"

"What is the difference between physical attraction and . . . between lust and something . . . else?"

Cornelia dropped the baby tunic she'd been holding and gaped at her friend. "What?" She laughed. "Are you in love with someone? Goddess, who with?"

"I'm not in love with anyone," Lucia said. Obsessed, however, was another matter. Either way, she would never tell her friend it was Tag. As children, Cornelia had often joined her and Tag in games in the woods when her parents visited. She couldn't very well say she was longing for a slave, could she? "And that's what I'm trying to figure out — how do you know when it's just . . . you know, physical attraction rather than something deeper?"

Cornelia gestured for her servants to leave the room. When they were alone, she leaned forward. "Tell me everything. You're not actually . . . I mean, you are still a virgin, yes?"

Lucia's face flushed as she nodded. "All we've done is kiss."

"He must be an amazing kisser."

Lucia slapped her friend's shoulder with the baby blanket. "It's just that I find myself thinking about him all the time. I am constantly trying to figure out how to be alone with him again."

Cornelia grinned. "You little *lasciva*, you!" Then her eyes widened. "It's not a gladiator, is it? Ugh, those men are such brutes. Though one can't deny some of them are quite attractive — in a feral kind of way. But really, you would never stoop so low!"

"He is not a gladiator."

"Good."

"How did you know you loved Antyllus?"

Cornelia sighed and rubbed the sides of her belly. "Well, my heart raced every time I was near him. I dreamt about him, about his touch. I longed for his company and missed him terribly when I didn't see him."

"How is that different than . . . than, you know, lust?" Lucia persisted.

Cornelia giggled. "I don't know! I've only ever loved Antyllus. But my guess is that it's probably just lust, because you barely know him."

"No —" she began, then stopped herself. She *did* know Tag. They had their shared childhood and their wooded retreat. He wasn't a stranger to her.

"Even if you feel like you know him," cautioned Cornelia, reading her expression, "you are betrothed to be married. You cannot take the risk of pursuing anything more with this man. You know that, right?"

Lucia nodded miserably.

Cornelia put a hand over hers. "But I understand how anyone would be better than old man Vitulus," she continued. "Is this man of yours someone of means? Perhaps he can speak with your father about changing your betrothal —"

Lucia laughed bitterly. "No. He is not a man of means. Vitulus's wealth is what Father is after." With a moan, she added, "And I only have a matter of weeks."

Cornelia huffed. "I've said this before, but I still don't see why your father couldn't find a rich man here in Pompeii. Why does he have to marry you to someone who lives all the way in Rome? I wish Antyllus had a brother so that we could live like sisters."

They both stared at the pile of soft baby clothing.

"You're really not going to tell me who your amazing kisser is? I'd tell you."

"You don't know him," Lucia repeated. "And it's best I don't mention his name."

"I'll get it out of you eventually," Cornelia said, returning to sorting. After a few moments of silence, she added, "Is it that patrician who is staying with you?"

Lucia shook her head emphatically.

"Still, he is an option, is he not? You told me yourself that he brags about his family's wealth. Perhaps you can try to get *him* to fall in love with you."

"Quintus? I wouldn't have any idea how to get a man to fall in love with me."

"Just flirt."

Lucia gave her a disbelieving look. "That may come naturally to you, but not to me. Besides, I think the arrangement Father has brokered with Vitulus makes it highly unlikely that anyone else could compete."

Cornelia's eyes glittered with mischief. "Still, you should try. He's got to be better than old Vitulus. Then you would be free of him and you could stay here in Pompeii —"

"He lives in Herculaneum."

"Close enough. Our children would grow up together. Oh, please consider it!"

Lucia shook her head. "Cornelia, are you not listening? A man of his patrician status would never marry someone like me."

"Not necessarily. It happens more and more these days. And since he is the fifth son, maybe his family won't care whom he marries."

"Oh, thanks a lot!"

"You know what I mean. But I think it's true. The family probably doesn't have that much riding on his alliances. You may have a chance."

"But that sounds so cold and calculating."

"It's not any more calculating or cold than what your father is doing."

Lucia didn't know what to say to that. They continued going through the clothes in silence.

"Any word from Pliny?" Lucia asked after a while. "I would still love to talk to the man."

Cornelia shook her head. "It doesn't look good."

"Why?"

She shrugged, not meeting Lucia's eyes. "Antyllus is not very encouraging."

"Oh, please push him! We are running out of time."

"All right, I will try again." She put down the blanket she was holding. "I wonder if Antyllus knows your patrician."

"He is not *my* patrician."

"Well, I'm hoping soon he will be. What is his name again?"

"Quintus Rutilius," Lucia said. "Cornelia, I don't like that look in your eyes."

"What look? I'm just going to ask my husband if he knows him. You should not underestimate the power of connections, my dear. Antyllus may be able to help here."

"I'd rather he helped with the Plinys, please."

"Either way, you know you have to stop seeing the amazing kisser. You can't risk a scandal. Now, what you do *after* you're married is up to you."

"Cornelia!"

"I'm just being realistic. But really, I think you need to stop seeing him and start working on Quintus."

Stop seeing Tag? She'd only *just* kissed him. The very idea of never doing so again left her feeling hollow.

Cornelia must have read her thoughts because she leaned

toward Lucia and said, "Your only focus must be on finding an alternative to marrying Vitulus and staying in Pompeii near me. This is your *home*."

Lucia's shoulders slumped. Cornelia reached over and squeezed her hand. "Have faith. It will all work out in the end," she said. "We will be together forever in Pompeii. I just know it."

CHAPTER TWELVE

TAG

Tag realized he'd lost count yet again of the dried coriander seeds and, with an irritated huff, swept the piles together to start over. All day, he'd been trying to bring his attention to heel, without much success. His mind constantly turned to thoughts of being out in the woods with Lucia, of the feel of her body pressed against his, of the honey taste of her mouth, of the warm softness of her skin.

"Healer." Someone tugged on his tunic. "Healer. Healer. Healer."

"What?"

"Look!" Castor pointed outside, where Tag could see men running toward the sandpit.

"Is somebody injured?" he asked.

"I don't know, but I hear yelling," the boy said.

Tag rushed outside with his surgical box under his arm. He'd learned early from his father that having scalpels and clamps on hand could mean the difference between life and death if a gladiator was bleeding heavily.

"Where's Pontius?" he asked as he caught up to a gladiator running toward the increasingly large knot of men.

"Dunno. Saw him leave with Titurius a while ago," the man said.

Tag wondered whom Pontius had left in charge. He hoped it was someone the men respected, because whatever was brewing didn't look good. A knot of sweating, nearly naked gladiators encircled a pair of fighters. Taunts, insults, and laughter roiled around the men. Two gladiators fighting outside the sparring ring was likely to end in serious injury or even death, enraging the master. Tag decided the best way to calm the situation was to play dumb.

"The *medicus* is here!" he called out, pushing through the knot of men. "Tell me who is injured. Make way. Make way for the healer." If violence had a smell, he thought, this was it — an almost visible miasma of male sweat, aggression, fear, and blood.

To his surprise, he found Quintus in the center, being taunted by a red-faced, stocky fighter from Iberia named Hamilcar. Tag looked around for the overseer in charge. His stomach knotted to see Pontius's second laughing along with the rest of the men.

"Who is injured?" Tag repeated, pretending he still did not understand what was happening.

"The better question is who is about to get *more* injured," the Iberian growled in heavily accented Latin. He pushed his finger into Quintus's chest. "And this pasty little flower here is about to get a taste of what *real* gladiators do."

Blood trickled down the side of Quintus's head. His eyes were wide with panic. Tag locked gazes with the overseer in charge, silently appealing for the man to step in and stop Hamilcar. But the man only grinned at him, showing brown teeth.

"This man is under Titurius's special protection," Tag tried.

Some of the men laughed. "So?" Hamilcar taunted. "The master is not here. And if I break his jaw, this little worm won't be able to speak my name."

Tag moved in closer to the two men. "Look, you don't want to —" he began.

Hamilcar seized Quintus's wrist and, with lightning speed, twisted two fingers as if he was intending to break them. Quintus hissed, trying to lean into the direction of the twist to take the edge off the pain. "And if he tries to identify me," Hamilcar said, "I will break *all* his fingers."

Again, Tag looked toward the overseer in charge. The man crossed his arms.

"Come on, healer boy," one of the men called out. "You know he deserves this."

"Oh, I agree, he deserves it," Tag replied. "And I'd be the first in line to crack him in the head a time or two . . ."

Some of the men chuckled.

"But," he added, louder, "I've already had one whipping recently, and I'm not interested in another one. And even if this *mundus excrementi* does not identify you, Hamilcar, we will *all* get whipped for not stopping you. Am I right, Titus?" He stared at the man in charge, who had stopped smiling.

Everyone knew it was true. Some of the men began muttering and moving their feet. "He ain't worth another whipping," someone called out.

"The boy is right," said a deep voice from behind them. Tag turned. The men had broken the circle for their *primus palus*, the house champion, the long-haired German Sigdag. "Let that weasel go, Hamilcar. We all know you could kill him with one blow. Where is the honor in that?"

More mumbling as men began moving away.

"Come, let us spar, Hamilcar," Sigdag continued. "Fight a real man and not a little girl."

Choruses of "Yes, yes, let's see that" increased as Hamilcar turned his attention to the big German. Tag grabbed Quintus's arm and steered him rapidly across the sand toward the treatment room.

Once inside the dark room, Quintus began to shake.

"Sit," Tag commanded, pointing to a squat three-legged stool. Quintus just stared at it. Tag took him by the arm again, led him to it, and pushed him down by the shoulders. The sounds of laughter and wooden swords thumping against one another drifted into the room.

Tag poured Quintus a cup of medicinal wine, barely cutting it with water. "Here," he said, thrusting it into the man's face. "Drink."

Quintus drained it in one gulp.

"What in Pluto's name happened out there?" Tag asked.

"I only asked him if he felt shamed about being a fighting slave when he carried the noble name of Hannibal's father." Tag closed his eyes, momentarily awed by the man's sheer stupidity. "Where is your injury?"

Quintus pointed to a cut on the edge of his hairline. Tag mopped it up with a vinegar solution, then applied a thin coating of honey and goose fat as gently as he could on the gash. Once the cut was cleaned, he swabbed at the blood on Quintus's neck and chest, checking for abrasions the fool may not have realized he'd gotten. He could feel the patrician staring at him as he worked.

"That was . . . that was very brave of you to help me," Quintus said.

Tag nodded, guessing that was as close as the blue blood was ever going to get to actually thanking him for saving him from the mob of infuriated gladiators.

"I wish I could have you by my side for protection whenever I'm around those animals," he added.

Tag did not respond as he checked the bones of Quintus's fingers and hands.

When he was done, he noticed the patrician still watching him. "With all due respect," Tag said, "I suggest you keep your mouth shut around the others."

As he began to turn away, Quintus grabbed his wrist. "Were you telling the truth? Would you have wanted to beat me too?" He suddenly looked very young.

Tag knew he should lie, as all good slaves must to survive — to tell him, *"Of course not, I was just trying to gain the men's trust"* — but, for some reason, he just couldn't. He held his tongue.

Quintus released his wrist, his cheeks flushing. "One day I will find a way to make you see me differently." He stood and stalked out of the room.

"Tages!" Pontius called the next day as he stepped into the medical room, stooping under the lintel.

"Someone hurt?" Tag asked, jumping up.

Pontius waved him back down when Castor jumped in front of Tag as if defending him, waving a pretend shield and sword. "Beware! I will slay you like a sausage!"

Pontius grinned at the child and said, "Terrible stance, boy. Go get me some fresh honey water from the kitchen and maybe later I'll show you how to do it right."

Castor flew out of the room, grinning. When the child was gone, Pontius turned to Tag. "Remember when ye asked if ye could train to be a gladiator?"

Tag froze. "Yes . . ."

"Well, *Dominus* is allowing it."

"What? How?" He grinned. Were the gods finally seeing fit to give him the chance to win his freedom?

"There is, however, one catch," the overseer said.

Tag's smile disappeared. "And what would that be?"

"I need ye to train alongside Quintus. He is a disaster. The master wants him to feel like he is getting a gladiatorial experience, but I can barely keep the men from tearing him to pieces every time he opens his mouth."

Tag stared at him. "You cannot be serious!"

Pontius sighed. "I can't let Quintus train or spar with anyone else. Him always lording himself over everyone . . . Everyone wants to slit his throat before they even step into the sandpit. And since the master has made 'special arrangements' with the man, I need to pair him with somebody who won't kill him."

"Wonderful. I am pleased to hear how much confidence you have in my fighting instincts."

"Yer fighting ways are probably just fine. I'm sure ye could kill him without much effort. But yer a healer. So I know I can count on you *not* to kill 'im."

"In other words, you're asking me to babysit him."

"Yep. And by the way, it was his idea."

"Quintus's?" Tag asked incredulously.

Pontius nodded.

Tag groaned. "But I despise the man."

"Welcome to the brotherhood. But now pay attention." The overseer leaned in and lowered his voice. "This is yer opening. Show some skill and I just might be able to convince *Dominus* to let ye continue when that perfumed pig leaves."

Tag nodded.

"But yer first priority is to make sure that Quintus doesn't get himself killed by some hothead who won't stand for his insults — which I've heard ye already have some experience with. The rest we'll see about. So anytime yer not needed to treat anyone, you'll be out with the rest of us *brutes*, as he calls us."

"Thank you, Pontius."

A grin emerged from the Samnite's mass of black beard. "We'll see if yer still grateful after I put ye through yer paces."

CHAPTER THIRTEEN

Lucia

(Two and a Half Weeks Before)

Lucia looked out the opening of her wooded cave. Was Tag coming? He'd hinted he was going to get out there that afternoon.

But what if he couldn't get away? Waiting inside the enclosure felt too constricting. She needed to be *doing* something, whether he came or not. So she reached under the old blanket for her leather bag, pulled out a wax tablet, and crawled outside. At least she could review her notes and maybe jot down some other observations while she waited.

The cracks in the earth, the disappearing spring, the tremors slight enough to vibrate only spiderwebs — there had to be a pattern. It had to *mean* something. But what? Were the phenomena localized to Pompeii? Or were strange things happening over all of the Bay of Neapolis? What about the sea — had fishermen reported any strange events? What about all those eels dying in their sea pools in Herculaneum that Quintus had mentioned?

An image of Cornelia's unborn babe moving under the surface of her skin came into Lucia's mind. Her friend had complained that sometimes the baby's movements were so frequent or intense, they made her jump in pain or woke her from a sound sleep.

What if . . . what if something similar was happening in Pompeii? What if the gods were preparing to push new life into the world like Cornelia's babe, and these rumblings and tumblings were part of it? But what would the earth be giving "birth" to? Had anyone ever witnessed such a thing? Who could say how mountain ranges or great rivers like the Sarnus were born? Perhaps a new mountain range was readying to burst through the earth, connecting Mount Vesuvius to the Apennines. Or small springs were drying up in one place, gathering strength to burst forth into another river across the valley.

The thought of Cornelia and the earth's stirrings reminded her of the danger of childbirth in general. She said a silent prayer to Juno, Vesta, and Diana on Cornelia's behalf. *May you watch over her and her baby; may they both survive.*

Gods, what she would give to speak with Pliny about her observations and theories. It would be such a shame to not meet the great man at least once before she was exiled to Rome. And despite what Cornelia thought, once he realized just how well-read Lucia was in his own works, she knew he wouldn't mock her. He might even be impressed. She would have to ask Cornelia again about her progress in setting something up.

Tag's shadow fell over her. She jumped up in surprise.

"Sorry. I didn't mean to startle you. I made as much noise as Hannibal's trumpeting elephants, but I guess you were lost in your writings."

"I am developing a theory," she said, snapping the wax tablet closed.

He blinked and tilted his head slightly.

"Never mind," she said. "I wanted to show you something." She hadn't intended to go into the woods with him again, but suddenly she could not look him in the eye, and walking at least gave them something to do. If she were honest with herself, she'd admit she invited him out there just for the opportunity to kiss him again. But what if he didn't want to kiss her? Would she feel forced to obey her if she tried? Gods, the first time she'd kissed him had been a thoughtless impulse. Why couldn't the second time be as easy?

"Where are we going, Lucia?" he asked as they started walking.

"You'll see. I hear you are training with Quintus now. Is that true?"

"Yes. Mostly my job is to keep him from getting killed," Tag said with disdain.

"Why do you dislike him so much?" she asked.

"You mean besides the obvious? Besides the fact that he is a self-important, narcissistic prig who casually gives up his freedom to play at sword fighting, when I would give my life to be free of slavery and of your father?"

She stopped. "You hate my father that much?"

He ran a hand through his curls. "Do you want me to answer that honestly?"

"But all your needs are met, aren't they? You're educated, clothed, you don't suffer from hunger, you have a roof over your head, the respect of the other slaves —"

His eyes grew wide. "Are you suggesting that I should be *happy* to be a slave? That I should count my blessings rather than fight for the freedom that was stolen dishonorably from my family? Just because I am fed and watered and sometimes whipped like a dog — like Minos?"

She looked away. "No, that is not what I meant. I'm sorry, I just . . ." Gods, why did she keep saying the wrong thing?

"Why are we here, Lucia?" He sounded exasperated.

Heat flooded her cheeks. "I . . . uh, well, found something that I thought you would like." She turned and walked on, hoping he would follow.

"Oh, look. There it is," she cried with relief after an excruciatingly long and silent walk. The remainder of a tiny circular temple — three columns dusted with green mold and crumbling with decay — surrounded a vine-covered altar in a clearing before them. High in the branches of a huge cypress tree hung corroded bronze bells that tinkled with the breeze.

"You found this place years ago when we were playing in the woods," Lucia said, recalling his grin of satisfaction when he'd shown it to her. "It has an old well too," she added, pointing to a circular brick structure in the ground in front of the altar. "Do you remember it?"

Tag looked around. "Yes. Vaguely." He threw a large rock in the empty well. They heard a muffled thud but no splash. "Must have dried up long ago."

She pushed a piece of hair off her forehead. "It reminded me of the altar to Mephistis you showed me. . . ."

He nodded in agreement.

"Perhaps it was abandoned after the big earthquake, which would explain why it's in such terrible condition."

"Makes sense," Tag said.

Gods, why was she so nervous? He was a slave*!* "I will . . . I'll leave her an offering," she said. "Just in case." She headed for a patch of marigolds and picked an armful. She placed some on the altar and began dropping the rest one by one into the well, watching as they tumbled head over stem into the blackness.

"Don't throw all of them in. I should take some back," Tag said, sitting with his back against a tree. "I can make a paste for bruises from them."

Lucia nodded and gathered more flowers. She laid them at his feet and he began separating the petals. A small flash in the sunlight caught her eye. She walked over to the well and brushed aside a pile of ivy and overgrowth. Looking up to see if Tag was watching — he wasn't — she plucked at the metal object. It was embedded in the dirt, so she dug her fingernails in to pull it out.

It was a corroded piece of lead with a rusty nail hanging from it. "Huh." She brought it over to him. "Look at what I found."

Tag looked up at the thing she held in her hands. His eyes widened and he scrambled to his feet. "Where did you get that?"

She pointed. "It was half-buried by the well. Why, what is it?" He was looking at the object in a funny way.

"Tag, do you know what this is?"

"You shouldn't touch that."

"Why?"

"It's a curse tablet."

She looked down at it. "How do you know?" She brushed the dirt away and turned it over. If she held it in the light a certain way, she could see letters scratched onto the surface. Curious, she tried to read them. A lot of the writing was rubbed away, but she caught the sense of it. Haltingly, she read aloud what she could decipher:

" . . . *may he be consumed by flames and choked by poison vapors. May Mephistis steal his breath, rot his lungs from the inside.*"

She looked up. "By the gods, somebody was *very* angry at this person, wasn't he?"

Color had drained from Tag's face. "Was there a nail attached?" he asked.

She nodded but then realized it was gone — it must have fallen out.

"Put that away where you found it," Tag said. "Curse tablets are dangerous, destructive magic."

"I'm sure the person who made this is long gone — and maybe his victim too. Doesn't that mean the curse has lost its power?" she asked, quickly returning the tablet, throwing dirt over it, and backing away.

"I hope so," Tag said, still agitated. He turned toward her. "Why did you ask me out here, Lucia?"

What could she say? She rubbed the dirt off her hands, unable to look at him. It wasn't as if she could just say that she wanted to see him alone because she couldn't stop thinking about kissing him, could she? How could she admit that she wanted to know if she would always respond like that to a kiss, or whether it was just *him* that caused her to feel that way? Secretly, she'd hoped he would sweep her up in his arms and kiss her the moment he saw her in private. But instead, stupidly, she'd sent them on a hike.

When she didn't answer, he sighed and said, "Well, I should probably be heading back."

She didn't want him to leave yet. "Tag, you know I've never seen you as a slave, yes?" she asked, leaning forward.

He blinked. "That is . . . nice. But I am one."

She flushed. "No, that's not what I'm trying to say."

He raised his eyebrows, waiting. She snatched at leaves from a nearby bush in irritation — at herself, at him. "I am not free either. Like you, I don't have any say in what happens in my life —"

He laughed. "Are you comparing your situation to *slavery*? Your limitations are *nothing* like being a slave."

"But they are close. I am being purchased, essentially, simply because some rich old man has decided he's bored. I have no say in this *transaction* with Vitulus. No say about who will 'own' me, where I will live, whether I want children — anything, really. I'm going to be used like a shiny new amphora and then tossed away."

He rubbed his face in irritation. "Fine. You are not free. But you are not anything like a slave."

"Well, no matter what I say or do, I can't get out of marrying Vitulus, so I might as well be one," she said.

He shook his head. "Poor little rich girl," he mumbled.

Her throat constricted and her eyes stung hot. This was *not* how she'd wanted this to go. "I am *not* a poor little rich girl," she shot back, frustration turning into anger. "I am being sold and used, and I don't like it."

"But you are still free," he insisted. She opened her mouth to argue, but he put his hands up. "Look, I don't have the *luxury* of having a philosophical discussion about the nature of freedom. As a slave, it means only one thing to me — no longer being owned by another human being." He turned away. "And now I need to get back."

"Wait." She swiped at her eyes.

He sighed. "Lucia. Did you really bring me out here so that you could lecture me on how you marrying a rich man is like me being a slave?"

"No. I brought you out here because . . . because I wanted to kiss you again," she mumbled, looking at her feet.

He took in a breath. When she peeked up at him, she saw that his eyes were wide and his mouth was open in surprise. Focusing on his lips made her blush, so she looked down again.

She felt him move in closer. Her breath hitched. A sudden thought made her blood run cold. Maybe he hadn't enjoyed kissing her as much as she'd enjoyed kissing him. Maybe there was a slave girl he loved, and he was only obeying his *domina*, like all slaves must.

She snuck another look at him. He didn't look disgusted or forced. He looked . . . *hungry.*

Tag put his hand to her cheek, his thumb lightly brushing across her bottom lip. She could not get enough air into her lungs. He made a small strangled sound and leaned down to put his mouth on hers.

CHAPTER FOURTEEN

TAG

Quintus came to the medical room on his way to the training yard and paused in the doorway. "Are you ready?" he asked Tag.

"Yes, let me just put these herbs away," he said. When the jars were secured, he untied his belt, pulled his tunic over his head, and reached for the wide gladiator belt he'd left on a hook.

"You know, you look more suited to posing for statue carvers than being a healer or a fighter," the patrician said. "Except for those lashes on your back. What a shame to mark a body such as yours."

Tag ignored him. Quintus always seemed to be goading him in some way, almost as if he was seeing how far he could push him to react so that he could have Tag punished for being disrespectful. Well, he would not fall for any of it. "Let's go," he said after buckling the belt.

"Wait," Quintus said, stepping into the room. He pulled something from behind his back. "I have something for you." He held a leather-bound box out to Tag.

Tag blinked. "I don't understand."

Quintus flushed. "It's a gift. For what you did the other day. You know, for saving me from Hamilcar."

Tag bit back the response that came to his lips — that he hadn't done it to save *him*, but to avoid getting whipped again. Not to mention to avoid having to treat Hamilcar and multiple gladiators who would've been lashed for hurting the master's special guest. "A gift is not necessary, *Dominus*," he said.

Quintus shoved the box toward him. "Open it."

Tag took it from him and rubbed his hands over the smooth leather. He'd never owned anything so fine. Creaking the box open, he gasped at what was inside: an array of the finest surgical equipment he'd ever seen. Light from the oil lamp gleamed on bronze scalpels, forceps, bone levers, scissors, probes, needles, clamps, and bone cutters. There were even two small cups for collecting blood during bloodlettings. He touched a particularly fine scalpel. "I cannot accept this," he whispered.

Quintus was grinning like Castor coming upon the small monkey in the marketplace. "Of course you can. I thought this might please you. And it pleases me that you are pleased. But you must know that I also offer this gift not just because you saved me," he continued, "but because I'm determined to prove to you that I am actually not the odious person you seem to think I am."

Tag ran his fingers alongside the shining metal instruments, barely hearing him. He suddenly wished someone was injured or hurt so that he could test these fine instruments on real flesh.

Someone shouted their names from outside, and Tag jumped.

"We have to get out there," Quintus said.

"Thank you for such a fine and generous gift, *Dominus*," Tag said, closing the box and placing it on top of his warped wooden one. He walked out of the room toward the training area. It took him a moment to realize Quintus had not followed him. He looked back and saw the patrician staring at the floor while rubbing the back of his neck. *What a strange little man.*

Titus, the second overseer, glared at them when Quintus caught up. It was clear he hated working with the beginners. "Nice of you to join us, ladies." Turning to the rest of the men in his group, he roared, "Before we begin, let us repeat the oath all gladiators must take."

"We kill with honor; we die with dignity," Tag and the men grumbled. Dying with dignity, Tag knew, was even more important than killing with honor. A gladiator who begged to be spared shamed his school.

Titus pointed to a basket of wooden swords. "Grab your *rudis* and face your *palus,*" he barked, gesturing to the man-sized wooden stakes upon which they would practice their sword strokes. "Let's start with an easy warm-up. Undercuts and overcuts, high and low, two hundred fifty times with each hand. Start with the right. Opposite leg out. Remember to switch your front leg when you change hands."

Tag was always surprised at how heavy the *rudis* was. The training swords were weighted with a strip of metal on the inside, which helped fighters gain strength quickly.

Quintus, as expected, took the heavily nicked pole next to Tag. "I bet I'll finish before you," he said.

I bet you won't.

"Let's go," Titus yelled, looking at him and Quintus. "Undercuts and overcuts, high and low. I want to see your form."

Tag attacked his *palus* with a fury. The gods had seen fit to give him this chance to prove himself, and he would take it for all he was worth. He quickly found his rhythm, ignoring the pain of the scabbed-over lashes that stretched and tore as he swung. It had been weeks since he'd trained in Rome, and it felt like he was starting over now, but he knew his body would adjust quickly.

The *thump-thump* of wood on wood echoed in the training yard. He paused to switch the *rudis* to his left hand, surreptitiously trying to catch his breath.

"No breaks!" roared Titus. "Go!" Then to Quintus, "Speed it up, princess. Everyone else has already switched hands."

As Tag swung, he couldn't help but glance over at the patrician, whose face was red with exertion. Sweat poured off the still-oiled curls pasted to his forehead. Tag almost felt sorry for him. He really had no business here.

When everyone had finished with the *palus*, the overseer sent them to the end of the yard, where thick, sanded logs waited for them. Tag groaned silently as Titus explained that they had to pick up a log and run with it across the sandpit and back.

As Titus instructed them on squatting correctly ("Use your hips and thighs, not your backs. That's where your strength is."), Tag glanced at Quintus, who had his face turned upward. He followed his gaze and caught his breath. Lucia stood on the viewing balcony, leaning on the wooden barrier that extended over the training yard. In the afternoon light with her hair shining, she looked like a nymph rising from the sea.

He must have made a sound, because Quintus turned to him with a curious expression. "I believe that the pretty lady is looking for someone," Quintus said, watching Tag very carefully. "And it could only be me."

They both looked up again, but she was gone. Tag forced himself to shrug as if he didn't care.

CHAPTER FIFTEEN

～⁓～

Lucia

S o, have you stopped seeing your amazing kisser like you promised?" Cornelia asked as they toured the rooms she and Antyllus were having painted with new frescoes. The three men working on the wall in the triclinium bowed to the lady of the house without interrupting their rhythm. One worker spread plaster with a wide trowel while another used a thick brush to paint large swathes of the wall a brilliant red. A third painter used a detail brush to add white architectural touches to a nearly completed section. The room reeked of the chalky, earthy smell of wet plaster and male sweat.

"Tell me again about the scenes you are having painted here," Lucia said, ignoring the question. She wasn't about to tell her they snuck kisses in the woods at every opportunity.

Cornelia smirked and gave her a sidelong look. "Well, there is my answer. Let's see, on this side, Ixion is being tied to a giant, fiery wheel. On that one, Prometheus will be bringing fire to mankind, and on that one, Sisyphus prepares to move the boulder up a hill."

"Oh, it's going to be so lovely," Lucia said distractedly.

Cornelia laughed. "*Lovely* isn't what we're going after. We want new and *interesting*."

"Yes, of course," Lucia said, wondering what Cornelia thought of the fading, cracked frescoes in her house. Her father never saw the need to invest in anything except new fighters.

They left the triclinium and headed for the *peristylium* garden. Cornelia, with both hands rubbing her belly, said, "You know, even Antyllus thinks Quintus would be a better match for you than Vitulus. Are you at least *trying* to entice the man?"

Lucia sighed. How could she think about anyone but Tag? Her desire to be near him, her ardor for kissing him — for touching him — had only increased with every contact. But it wasn't just that. They complemented each other. When they went for walks, she showed him unusual fauna or flora, and he pointed out the medicinal uses of what she had thought were just weeds. Sometimes, she even helped him collect rare herbs and plants — in between kisses, of course. With Tag, the woods had become more magical than they had ever been.

She swallowed, thinking about seeing Tag the day before in the training yard. The image had been seared into her mind — his body, bathed in sweat and gleaming in the sun, with a sword in one hand. He'd looked like a bronze statue of a young god come to life. She could barely think of anything else.

"I hope the painters finish soon so I can show the frescoes off at a small dinner party I am hosting in a few days," Cornelia said. "Which, of course, you are invited to."

"Hmmm, mmmm," Lucia said noncommittally.

"Well, I think you will want to come, because a special guest is attending."

Lucia took a couple of steps before she registered what Cornelia said. She stopped and grabbed her friend's arm. "Pliny? Pliny is coming?"

Cornelia looked down at the floor and away. "Well, I — The special guest is a surprise. But you must come. Do you promise to come?"

"Of course!" Lucia squeaked. "When? Oh, I need to gather my notes. Did you notice the tremors we had last night? I've heard some of the grape harvesters on the mountain are saying that the vines are dying from the inside out, which they've never seen before. And . . . and that on the wharf, they're saying that the fishing is almost nonexistent around the bay. It's as if all the fish have left the area! Can you imagine? Oh, I need to write all this down and fine-tune my theory for him —"

"Lucia . . ." Cornelia began, a frozen smile on her face.

Lucia hugged her friend. "Oh, you are so wonderful. Thank you."

Cornelia opened her mouth, then closed it. "The dinner is the evening after next. Come in the morning to dress and to prepare with me. We will make a day of it, yes?"

"Yes, yes! But, oh, I can't be still now. I must go home and get my notes in order. I can't believe this is really happening!" She kissed her friend's cheek. "You don't mind if I go now, do you?"

Cornelia shook her head.

Lucia grinned, squeezed her friend's hand, and dashed toward the front of the house, calling for her attendant.

After reviewing her notes, Lucia could not sit still. Was she really, finally going to meet her hero? She decided perhaps some fresh air might help her relax.

She had planned to stroll by the *impluvium*, the rain pool, until she spotted Quintus sitting on a stone bench in the atrium, reading beside a giant potted fig tree. Lucia stepped behind a column before he could catch sight of her. Despite Cornelia's insistence that she should flirt with the man, she just couldn't bring herself to —

"Are you spying on me, lovely Lucia? And here I thought you were trying to avoid me."

She stepped away from the column, her face flaming. "I . . . I wasn't spying," she said.

"Your shyness is adorable," he said. "Come sit with me."

She swallowed a sigh of irritation and took a seat opposite him. "What are you reading?"

"Strabo."

She blinked. Her father didn't have any of the great geographer's scrolls, though she had pleaded mightily for some of them over the years. "You brought your own copy?"

He nodded. "Yes, I have all of his *Geographica*. I must have some educated reading at hand, or I will go mad in this hellhole."

She marveled at his ability to leave her speechless. How was she supposed to respond to someone who called her home and her father's livelihood a "hellhole"?

He cleared his throat. "Here Strabo talks about a visit to a region in Phrygia where there is a huge swath of land with no trees. It's filled instead with the vines that produce Catacecaumenite wine."

"Is that a good wine?" she asked.

He laughed. "It is one of the finest indeed, but really only enjoyed by those with refined tastes. I imagine you've never had it. Perhaps I'll introduce it to you someday. I could have it sent over from the villa. Although one taste of that, and you'll have a hard time going back to the swill you're used to."

She shook her head. "No, really. It isn't necessary —"

He snapped his fingers at a passing servant. "All this talk of wine has made me thirsty," he said, barking at the slave, "Bring us wine and food."

"Yes, *Dominus*," the old woman said, which made Lucia bristle. Quintus was not *dominus* of *this* house. But she bit her tongue.

"This is interesting," he continued, reading aloud: "The surface of the plains is covered with ashes, and the mountainous and rocky country is black . . . Some conjecture that this resulted from thunderbolts and from fiery subterranean outbursts, and they do not hesitate to lay there the scene of the mythical story of Typhon."

She sat forward. "Really? You just said that they grow fine wines there, yet he makes it sound as if the whole area is a scene of devastation."

"That's right, black rock and ashes — except for the grape arbors. He also says," Quintus paused, scanning the scroll, "that the blackness of the lands was probably created by 'an earthborn fire.'"

"What does that mean?"

"I think he might be referring to mountains that spew fire, like Mount Aetna in Sicily. He conjectures that long after those fires are spent, the black dirt makes for excellent vine growing."

"Huh." She looked out toward Vesuvius looming over them. The mountain was as green and lush as ever, with fall touches of gold and orange. Vineyards dotted the landscape up and down the mountain's flanks. "I wonder if Vesuvius once spewed fire."

"Not likely. Look how lush the land is. It says clearly that in Phrygia the land is empty and black except for the vines."

"Does Strabo talk about any region that experienced constant tremors like ours?"

"Not that I'm aware of. But I have to say I am getting tired of all the slaves and old women wailing about omens and portents. Pompeii has always been shaking. People have frightened themselves so much, many are packing up and returning to Rome."

"But you have to admit, it's shaking more often than usual. And there have been strange happenings in the grazing fields and around the springs —"

"Yes, yes," he said, cutting her off. "My father also wants to return to Rome early in case another big earthquake hits."

"Return to Rome? I thought you lived in Herculaneum."

Quintus frowned as he lifted the terra-cotta cup of wine the kitchen woman had brought. "Our villa in Herculaneum is only our country home, dear," he said. He passed her a cup. "Now, drink, drink."

She sipped the well-watered wine. He lived in Rome. So Cornelia's plan wouldn't work, even if she *could* bring herself to flirt with Quintus.

"Why do you look so disappointed?"

"Oh, no reason."

He leaned forward, grinning. "You're going to miss me when I return to Rome, aren't you? Well, that pleases me more than it should."

Gods. She made herself look down so he wouldn't see that the only thing she was going to miss was the possibility of getting out of her betrothal with Vitulus.

He reached over and lifted her chin. "How sweet you are. You're blushing!" He leaned in for a kiss, but she turned her cheek to him.

"I . . . I'm sorry," she stammered, moving back. "It's just that Father —"

"Yes, yes. Your father would kill me if he caught me touching you or any of the household slaves. I got the lecture about that. I keep forgetting how provincial everyone in Pompeii is. In Rome, everyone is much freer with their affections."

"Even betrothed women?"

"*Especially* betrothed women," he said. "And especially young women like you, who are being bartered off to old men who don't deserve them."

"I really should go," she said, starting to rise. "My nurse will be looking for me."

He put a hand on hers to still her. "Your nurse? You are about to be married. You should not have to listen to old nursemaids."

She bit her lip as impulses warred within her. Cornelia's voice inside her head admonished her to *"Stay and flirt. It could mean getting out of marriage to Vitulus."* But all she wanted to do was run, preferably into the woods. And into Tag's arms.

Besides, she reminded herself, he lived in Rome, so there was no point, right? Before she could make up her mind about what to do, Quintus surprised her by leaning forward and gently pressing his mouth to hers. She froze for a moment and then pulled away, her cheeks flaming.

"I . . . cannot . . ." She stood.

He chuckled. "What a sweet little piece of untouched fruit you are."

Gods! "I'm sorry, I must go," she managed to get out before she dashed from the atrium.

Just before she turned the corner, she heard him exhale and mutter, "Yes. Very, very sweet."

CHAPTER SIXTEEN

TAG

Tag spied Quintus moving toward the armory for that after-noon's training session. The patrician dragged his feet, which was unlike him. Tag wondered if his lack of energy was due to fear because they were finally having to kit out and fight. Or if he was ill . . .

Don't do it. Don't ask. But the healer in him couldn't ignore it. "Are you feeling unwell?" he asked as Quintus approached.

The young man shook his head. "No, not unwell. Disappointed perhaps."

Tag said nothing. If he was not ill, it wasn't any of his business.

"Don't you want to know what has disappointed me?" Quintus asked.

No, not particularly.

"Somebody I have fallen for seems to be avoiding me," he said. "And I find that distressing."

Tag's heartbeat pulsed in his ears. What was he saying? Had Quintus's game of pursuing Lucia to aggravate his father resulted in him actually falling for her? Gods! The idea of the odious nobleman touching her made him want to shudder. He became aware that Quintus was watching him very carefully and made his face slave-blank again. "Well, um, since the young *domina* is betrothed," he said, "it's probably for the best that she is avoiding you."

"Interesting how you immediately think of lovely Lucia," Quintus said. "She comes up often in your thoughts, doesn't she?"

Tag groaned inwardly. *Why was he watching him so intently?* "No, no . . . it is just that she is the only young lady in the household, so I assumed . . ."

Quintus sighed. "Tell me. If you had fallen for someone who did not think very highly of you, would you give up, or would you keep trying to get this person to see you differently?"

Gods. Why did he talk in riddles? He cleared his throat. "If it were impossible, I would give up."

The nobleman's eyebrows rose. "Really? And what if there was an outside chance that this person could be persuaded to soften toward you?"

"Well then, um. I guess I would keep on trying." *No. No, leave her alone!*

Quintus slapped him on the back, rubbing it for a moment in brotherly affection. "Perhaps you are right. I shall keep on trying. Thank you."

He moved away with more energy than he'd had before, and Tag shook his head. What had he just done? Had he just convinced the loathsome patrician to redouble his effort to seduce Lucia? He would have to warn her to be even more careful around him.

Inside the armory, one of the freedmen gestured Tag over and pointed to a pile of equipment. "Pontius wants you as the *secutor* and Quintus as the *retiarius* —" he began.

"Absolutely not!" Quintus cried, stopping abruptly. "I will not be the fisherman! He cannot make me fight as the most inferior and undignified of all the gladiators. That is an insult!"

The freedman smirked with disdain. "In sparring, *Dominus* begins with the level he thinks you are most capable of handling."

"He's making me fight with a net and a trident to humiliate me," Quintus said, crossing his arms.

"Exactly," said the freedman.

Tag almost felt sorry for Quintus. No one ever wanted to be the fisherman. The trident was unwieldy as a weapon, and the net cumbersome. If you missed your "catch," you were essentially done for. At the same time, Tag felt a surge of pride in himself. Pontius thought him capable of sparring as a *secutor*, one of the more popular gladiator types.

"Come, let's get our weapons," he urged. "We don't have a choice anyway."

Quintus's color was high. "Well, I am not a slave, so I *always* have a choice!" He stormed out — to find Pontius, Tag presumed.

Not too long after, he came back, face still flushed, teeth set, but compliant. By Hercules, Tag would've given anything to hear how Pontius had handled the spoiled patrician.

The slave in charge of outfitting Quintus handed him his rope net. Quintus looked surprised at its heft.

"It's the lead weights," Tag explained. "So the net stays down when you throw it."

Quintus scowled at him. "I know it has weights," he said.

"Let him put your arm into the shoulder guard before you try throwing it," Tag said. "You need to have a feel for how the *galerus* affects your range of movement."

Quintus grunted and held his arm out for the weapons slave. Meanwhile, another slave continued tying Tag's *manica* on his right arm, the heavy linen padding secured with what seemed like dozens of leather ties. While the slave moved on to Tag's left leg, Quintus went out into the sand to practice throwing the net and wielding the trident. A few of the gladiators made rude comments at him, laughing and whistling. Tag followed him into the pit.

A slave approached with the *secutor*'s heavy rectangular shield. Tag rubbed his palms with sand for a better hold on the leather-covered shield handle.

The slave handed him his helmet. Tag took a deep breath and examined the headpiece. The heaviness of it surprised him. Only two round fish-eye holes were cut into the thick metal, and there were no nose or mouth openings. The top was curved so that no angle would catch the net. It was going to get scorching fast.

"Quintus, you ready?" he called. He did not want to put on that heavy head-bowl until the last possible moment.

His sparring partner raised his arm, and Tag adjusted the felt cap that would cushion the top of the helmet. Slowly, he lowered the thick metal over his face. Everything went black, the stink of old sweat and metal almost overwhelming. Even when he got the eyeholes adjusted, he could barely see. He needed to make this fight a fast one.

One of the freedmen, acting as referee, signaled them to move into position, then held a wooden stick between them until he was satisfied that they were both ready. Tag leaned forward on his left leg, the greave biting into his ankle, preparing to attack. When the stick went up, Tag thrust forward, using his shield to push Quintus back.

In the stifling helmet, Tag's sight was so limited, he couldn't see his opponent's face, let alone read his expression. So he focused on Quintus's hands — was he trying to throw the net? Where was the trident? The *retiarius* also came equipped with a dagger in his belt, he reminded himself.

Quintus kept moving backward, which only made Tag move forward more aggressively. Quintus thrust with the trident, but Tag easily blocked it. He lunged forward and smacked the patrician backward again with the heavy rectangular shield. His right arm tightened as he thrust with his weighted wooden sword. Quintus barely stopped it with the trident, stumbling back.

Tag's labored breathing reverberated inside the helmet. It was like being underwater. As Quintus raised the net to throw it over him, Tag slammed him with his sword. He could feel the clang of Quintus's shoulder guard all the way up his arm. Quintus dropped the net.

He wished he could see the patrician's face. It helped immensely in a fight to know whether your opponent was tiring or panicking. But like a half-blind bull, all Tag could do was keep attacking. He stumbled and almost fell over the net, but caught himself at the last moment. Quintus poked the trident at him, but he swatted it away with his sword.

Watch for the other hand, he reminded himself. Once the *retiarius* threw the net, his left hand was free to pull the dagger. When he thrust his own *gladius*, the *retiarius* could attempt a sideswipe to the ribs on his unprotected side. But Quintus had not pulled out the dagger, instead taking the heavy trident with both hands.

Stupid move. Tag lunged forward and attacked with an overhead swing. Quintus again barely blocked it. As Tag readjusted, he thought he could hear yelling and whistling from the other gladiators. He swung his sword again, but this time Quintus dropped the trident and ran.

This was what made the *retiarius* such an object of derision, Tag thought. No Roman should ever run. Tag gave chase, but because of the helmet, he had to turn his whole body to see where Quintus was going. Was he trying to get behind him?

The shield grew heavier and heavier. Even over his labored breathing, he could hear the other men laughing at Quintus. The referee should have stopped the fight by now. Indeed, Pontius should have stepped in the moment Quintus dropped the trident, then demonstrated what the patrician should have done instead.

And then Tag understood. This was all a big show to put Quintus in his place. Again, he almost felt sorry for the rich fool. He caught sight of him at last across the pit. Quintus was trying to leave the space, but groups of gladiators kept pushing him back in.

Tag wanted this over with too. He ran at Quintus and feinted a lunge left, thrusting with his shield. Quintus jerked backward, lost his balance, and went down hard on his back. Tag instantly swung the wooden sword at his neck, stopping at the last moment. If it had been a real sword, he would have drawn blood. Through the thick metal, he could hear the other gladiators calling — *Kill! Kill! Kill!* — as if they were really in an arena.

Finally, he felt the referee's stick slap him on the shoulder to end the fight. Tag immediately dropped his shield and *gladius*, using both hands to remove the heavy helmet. A wall of noise met him as the other fighters jeered at Quintus and cheered him.

"Patrician pansy!" "The healer boy can fight!" "Wooden or not, I woulda sunk that gladius into his neck!"

Tag sucked in big gulps of air as someone took the helmet from him. He put one hand up in the signal of victory. He extended the same arm down to help Quintus up, but the patrician only glared at him.

"No hard feelings. It's all part of the training," Tag said, keeping his arm out.

Quintus took it but, in the same instant, swung one of his legs against Tag's ankles. He fell hard on his back in the sand, the wind leaving his lungs with a grunt. Vaguely, he was aware of the other gladiators making sounds of disgust and moving toward them.

"You need to keep in mind, boy," Quintus said, suddenly straddling him and pinning his shoulders. "I get what I want. You remember that, Tages. In the end, I always get what I want."

In a blink, Quintus was pulled off of his chest by several gladiators outraged at his conduct. Pontius was instantly in the thick of the tussle, using his whip handle and roar to get the other trainees to release Quintus. When he finally succeeded, he shook the patrician and yelled, "Get out of my pit. You dishonor this *ludus*. And don't come back today, do you hear me? I am tired of saving your idiotic *asinus*!"

He gave Quintus a little shove and Quintus staggered off, giving Tag one last inscrutable look over his shoulder.

CHAPTER SEVENTEEN

※

Lucia

(Two Weeks Before)

O
h, stop being such a baby," Cornelia said when Lucia
flinched.

"She is *sewing* my hair with a needle! It hurts when the
needle scrapes my scalp."

Cornelia tutted while a slave oiled and massaged her swollen
feet. "She is not 'sewing' your hair. And it's not a needle — the
tip is rounded! How else can she weave that lovely ribbon through
all that hair?"

"All that hair" was right. Somehow, Cornelia's *ornatrix* had created the illusion that Lucia had three times the volume of her
usual hair. It had been wound and twisted and curled and now
sewed with ribbons into tiers of what was supposed to be the latest elegant look out of Rome.

Lucia sighed and looked around Cornelia's dressing space,
which seemed to her more like a torture chamber than a lady's
room. A fire crackled in a wide-bowled stand where Cornelia's
hairdresser heated the irons that had curled her hair. The room
reeked of hot metal, singed hair, and sweet almond oil. Long and

thin tweezers, files, buffers, and brushes for kohl and rouges littered the ivory-topped table.

"I'm not sure I'll be able to hold my head up if she weaves anything else into it," she grumbled.

"Oh, stop it," Cornelia said. "You look lovely."

"Why isn't your hair as fancy?"

"You're the focus today," Cornelia said without meeting her gaze.

Today was the day of the great dinner with Pliny. Lucia had come over within the first *hora* of the morning, and Cornelia immediately set her hair and makeup sorceresses to work on her. She could tell Cornelia's *ornatrix* was annoyed by Lucia's impatience and ingratitude because she tugged hard at her scalp every time she moved her head slightly out of position.

"Can I at least have a scroll to read?" she asked Cornelia as the hairdresser pushed her head forward. "I'm bored."

"No. Your head will be at the wrong angle, and besides, I don't want any of Antyllus's scrolls to get singed by accident."

"Oh, but singeing *me* is not a worry."

"Why are you being so difficult?" Cornelia asked.

"Nerves," Lucia said. "Do you realize I will be married within two weeks? TWO weeks! And very soon I will be meeting the great Pliny himself!" She fanned her face. "I just hope I can string a coherent sentence together and not make a fool of myself."

Her friend did not meet her eyes. "You'll be fine." Cornelia stood, a three-part process that involved thrusting her belly out, leveraging her weight on the counter with one hand, and then pushing off with a grunt. "I'm off to the *latrina* — *again* — and will be preparing in my anteroom after that. Come see me in there when Clio has finished dressing you," she instructed Lucia, then waddled out of the room.

Lucia wasn't used to having someone fuss over her as she dressed, but she had to admit, Cornelia had very fine tastes. The lavender dress she had picked out from her pre-pregnancy collection felt like silk — and who knows, maybe it was. The jewelry was sumptuous too — a golden snakelet on her wrist and pearls dangling from her ears. She was fingering the earrings as she walked into Cornelia's room.

Cornelia looked up at her and smiled. "Oh, Lucia, you look beautiful."

"Thank you, but I feel like an overdecorated honey cake. I still don't understand why I had to dress up like this. I think Pliny will take me more seriously if I'm dressed soberly."

"About Pliny . . ." Cornelia said, nervously adjusting the draping of her elegant *stola*.

Lucia looked at her friend. "Oh, please don't tell me he has canceled!"

"You know, I only said I had a surprise guest for you. I never said it was Pliny."

Lucia's mouth dropped open. "What are you saying? He's not coming? He never *was* coming?"

"The special guest I have for you is not Pliny," Cornelia admitted. "Instead it is someone who I think will be more valuable to you."

"I don't understand!" Lucia's throat constricted. How could Cornelia do this to her? She'd been so excited. Meeting Pliny was going to be a dream come true! "Who could possibly compete with Pliny? Cornelia, please explain what is happening."

At that moment, they heard male voices being ushered through the atrium toward the triclinium. One of Cornelia's slaves entered the room. "The guest has arrived," she announced. "The master has instructed that you join him now."

"See, Antyllus is waiting for us. Come, I will explain on the way."

Lucia felt heat spreading up her chest. "No, explain *now*."

Cornelia waved the slave away with a *tell him we are coming* command. Then she looked at Lucia. "Maybe I should have said something earlier. I was just afraid that you wouldn't come if I told you."

"Cornelia . . ." she said through gritted teeth.

"It's just that you were being either too shy or too stubborn to pay serious attention to the opportunity. So I decided to help it along."

Lucia leaned forward. "I. Still. Don't. Understand."

"Quintus Rutilius is our special guest," she said. "He is an excellent contact for Antyllus. And . . . and if we can arrange something between you two, your father will see that Quintus clearly is a better marriage choice for you than Vitulus."

Lucia gaped at her friend. Cornelia took her hand. "Don't you see? He lives in Herculaneum. At least I wouldn't lose you to Rome."

"His *villa*, his father's 'country house,' is in Herculaneum. The rest of the year, he lives in Rome," Lucia said. "So there is no point."

"Even so, part of the year you'd live close by. And once you have babies, you could convince him to live in Herculaneum year-round. See? We would not be separated. Our children would grow up together, just as we always dreamt."

Lucia's disappointment was so profound, she could barely make sense of what her friend was saying. She sat down dully on an ornate bronze stool. "But . . . but why lead me to believe it was Pliny?"

"I didn't mean to!" Cornelia said. "I was just afraid that if I told you who was really coming, you would have refused to join us."

Lucia stared up at her. She was right on that point. "So he is here, now."

"Yes. He told Antyllus that he thinks you're charming but that you seem to be always avoiding him. So I just thought —"

"That throwing us together like this would lead to romance and a betrothal," Lucia said, scowling. "This is so outrageous, so unlikely, I do not even know what to say."

Cornelia's face was flushed. "Well, at least I'm *trying* to help you get out of marrying the old man — which is more than what *you* are doing!"

Lucia stood, halfway tempted to rip the ribbons out of her hair, turn around, and go home.

Cornelia's eyes filled. "I'm sorry, Lucia. I . . . I could have — should have — handled this better. But don't you see? I don't want to lose you to a terrible old man and to Rome forever. I know you cannot defy your father, but don't you think this is at least worth a try?"

The impossibility of the situation made her bones feel like they were filling up with molten bronze. She had willfully refused to think about Vitulus or try to do anything about her upcoming marriage, choosing, instead, to focus on Tag. But perhaps her friend was right. She did not care for Quintus, but he was certainly better than old man Vitulus, wasn't he?

Sighing deeply, Lucia nodded. She was still angry at Cornelia for tricking her like this, but she also knew her friend had guessed correctly — she probably wouldn't have come for a dinner if she knew Quintus, her own *houseguest*, for Minerva's sake, was going to be there.

Cornelia smiled. "Come, then, my friend," she said, linking arms with Lucia. "Let us have a fine meal. The food will be good and you can still share your theories with all of us while, hopefully, dazzling Quintus Rutilius."

CHAPTER EIGHTEEN

TAG

Tag stood stiffly beside a red column outside a glittering triclinium where he had been told to wait. Quintus had insisted he accompany him to a fancy dinner party. He had argued against it — what if someone needed medical treatment at the school? — but Quintus had gone to Titurius, so there he was, a trained *medicus* escorting one spoiled rich man to another rich man's party. He gritted his teeth at the indignity.

He turned to the sound of approaching footsteps and lost his breath at the sight of a very pregnant woman arm in arm with . . . *Lucia?*

He blinked, trying to make sense of the image. Her dress clung to her breasts and hips. She looked older, more elegant, and even more enticing with her hair piled up. She stopped at the sight of him too. "Tag? What are you doing here?"

"Tages, from your household?" Cornelia said. "It is good to see you."

"Thank you, *Domina*," he said, inclining his head at Cornelia. "May Juno and Diana continue to bless you with health for you and the baby."

"What are you doing here?" Lucia asked again.

He tried to keep his face impassive. "Quintus commanded I attend him tonight." He wanted to ask the same question of her, but he didn't want to appear overly familiar in front of her friend.

Cornelia released Lucia and said, "Let me go in and greet our guest. Take a moment out here and make a grand entrance, Lucia. You are going to dazzle him." She waddled into the torch-lit room.

"There is no Pliny," Lucia said despondently, in a low voice. "There never was. This was all designed to get me and Quintus together!"

"What?" Tag nearly hissed.

"It's Cornelia's plan for getting me out of marrying Vitulus. I'm half tempted to leave and go home. I was so looking forward to meeting Pliny!"

"I will accompany you home if you so desire —" he began. He did not want her going in there. Not after what Quintus had said about redoubling his efforts to win her affection. He clenched his fists to keep his hands at his sides.

"Luciaaaa," trilled Cornelia. "Come in, come in!"

"Too late," she murmured. Straightening her spine, she gave Tag one last desperate look and entered the room.

Tag heard the oohs and aahs, heard Quintus's voice praising her "more polished" appearance, and wanted to run. Now Lucia's friend was trying to arrange something between her and Quintus? But why? Why had Quintus insisted he accompany him? Did he suspect about him and Lucia? A deep sense of unease spread through his middle.

"Boy!" an elegantly dressed slave snapped at him.

Tag raised his eyebrows. Clearly, this richly dressed triclinium slave thought himself superior to Tag.

"Your master wants you to pour his wine," the slave said. "Go. Now."

"He is not my master," he mumbled.

The man flicked his eyes up and down over him. "Whatever you say, pretty boy." He hustled off toward the kitchens.

Tag closed his eyes. Quintus, it seemed, was determined to humiliate him. And all in front of Lucia. Another slave scurried by and whisper-yelled, "Your master awaits!"

Reluctantly, Tag entered the room, looking for Quintus. He had been placed at the couch of honor with Lucia stretched out next to him. He gritted his teeth at the sight of their forced intimacy and walked over to stand behind the patrician.

Quintus's eyes crinkled at the sight of him, and it took everything Tag had to not turn around, walk right out of the room, and keep on walking until he got home. He was laughing at him. The patrician *asinus* was laughing at him! He wouldn't look at Lucia; he did not want to see his humiliation reflected in her eyes. When they were alone, he could forget his status as slave and knew she did too — but *this* . . .

Quintus held up an exquisitely carved silver goblet. With a set jaw, Tag took it. "I know not what to do," he said softly, bending toward Quintus's ear. His insides bubbled with mortification. "As a slave, I know only of *lora*," he added. *Lora* was the thin, bitter brew made from the dregs of grape skins and stalks. How could he possibly know what rich people drank?

"Ah," Quintus said, turning his hot breath to Tag's ear. "We are starting off with *mulsum*." He waved his hand in the direction of a large, bronze, wide-bellied container with three lion-paw legs on a table manned by a slave. "Bring my cup to that slave and he will pour you the hot wine. Then mix in some honey from the flask next to it. You can never add too much honey in my view."

With ears aflame, Tag went to the wine server, who ladled the warm gleaming liquid into the goblet. Tag added a glop of honey and mixed it with a bronze spoon. Stiffly, he walked back and handed the cup to the patrician. Quintus took a sip and smacked his lips. "Falernian wine and Attic honey! This *mulsum* is fit to be served by Ganymede in Olympus!"

Cornelia tittered. Tag swallowed his indignation. *I am not a cuphearer like Ganymede, but a highly skilled surgeon and healer,* he wanted to shout. He just needed to get through this without making a scene, if possible. But sneaking a look at Lucia — seeing her stretched out comfortably in her bare feet, swathed in shimmering fabric — reminded him once again of just how far apart their worlds were. His spirits sank even lower.

A line of slaves bearing trays of food entered the room. Cornelia beamed. "To begin, we have milk-fed snails," she said, pointing to the first plate, "some wonderful cheeses soaked in wine and *garum*, and my personal favorite, squash with minced lamb brains. But leave room for the sow udders later! Now, please — eat. Eat!"

Cornelia's husband — what was his name, Antyllus? — seemed bored and irritated. He downed a cup of wine and indicated with a head jerk that his slave should fill it again. His attendant swooped in, refilled it, then dabbed at the corners of the rich man's mouth with a silk napkin. Tag willed himself not to roll his eyes. If Quintus expected him to wipe his mouth for him, he had another thing coming.

Cornelia turned to Quintus. "So, please tell us how a man of your stature ended up training at a gladiatorial school?" she asked.

"I did not sign myself up," Quintus began, smiling. "You can thank my father for that."

"I am curious why you ended up at the Titurius School and not at the better one near the amphitheater," Antyllus added, wrinkling his nose as if the Titurius name itself came with a stink. "There must be a story behind that."

Tag looked at Lucia. She had stiffened at the insult to her father's name.

Quintus chuckled. "My father purposely picked the lowest-ranked school in Pompeii," he said. "This was all a gambit to humiliate me, to throw me in with the worst beasts of the lot. But I outsmarted him. A bit of gold dangled in front of the owner's face, and I am shielded from the vermin and treated like a prince."

"Gentlemen, you are aware you are speaking of my *father*," Lucia said, sitting up. Two spots of red flared on her cheeks.

Quintus chuckled and rubbed her arm. "Oh, such loyalty to family. I am impressed, Lucia."

Tag wanted to swat his hand away.

"We apologize," Cornelia said, giving her husband a sidelong glance. "No insult meant, truly, my dear. But yes, Quintus, Lucia is very loyal. However, her shyness can be quite debilitating, you know," she added with a mischievous sparkle in her eye. "It especially shows itself when she likes someone."

"Cornelia," Lucia warned. "Stop —"

"Oh?" Quintus said, leaning forward. "I had feared that lovely Lucia had taken a dislike to me. She always seems to avoid me."

"Oh, no," Cornelia said. "You are all she talks about!"

Tag swallowed. This couldn't be true, could it? He calmed when he noticed Lucia staring daggers at her friend. Quintus leaned up a little higher on his left arm and grinned. "Really? And what does she say about me?"

"Why, how fine you look when you train as a gladiator," she said.

"Cornelia!" Lucia squeaked.

"You said it yourself, darling. 'Not many men of such high status could carry off the *subligaculum*.' I hear you fill out yours quite well. But, sir, you had better move fast — her wedding to that loathsome Vitulus is in just two weeks. You do not want to miss your chance now, do you?"

Tag was stunned at Cornelia's bluntness. Lucia groaned and dropped her face into her hands.

"No, I do not — Oh, now look what you've done. She is going to run away from me again," Quintus said. "Every time I try to steal a kiss, she runs."

Every time?

"Oh, no, she won't run now," Cornelia said. "I won't let her."

Tag clenched his fists. Quintus turned to glance at him, and Tag wondered again if he suspected him and Lucia. Luckily, his blank slave expression held steady.

Lucia cleared her throat. "You know, there was a terrible misunderstanding. I thought Pliny would be joining us, and so I came prepared to discuss my theories on the strange happenings in Pompeii."

Antyllus almost spit out his wine. "You actually thought that you were qualified to tell the great man *your* theories?"

Lucia stared at her host in dismay during the silence that followed. "I am sorry, but I do not understand your meaning," she finally managed.

Antyllus glanced at the hand his wife had placed on his arm. "What I meant to say is that I'm sure we would all be interested in hearing your theories, just as Pliny would," he said, as if he had been coached. Tag clenched his teeth at the condescension in his voice.

Lucia glanced at her friend, who smiled and nodded encouragingly at her. She paused, then told the group about the strange phenomena she had seen, many of which she'd already shared with Tag: the earth tremors, the springs that disappeared, the smell of sulfur, and the smoke-like white birds people claimed to have seen atop the mountain. "I had hoped to ask Pliny if he had seen any similar strangeness in Misenum."

"I think he would tell you that shaking in this part of the world is so ordinary as to be unworthy to discuss," Antyllus said.

Tag glanced at Quintus, whose brow was furrowed as he took another sip. His host's antagonism, it seemed, was bothering him too. Tag studied Cornelia's husband. He looked to be in about his late twenties, with long limbs, a strong nose, and hair styled with curls arranged forward on his forehead in the style of the emperor. With his fine tunic and large colorful rings, he almost rivaled Quintus in his ostentatious display of wealth.

"Aside from the shaking," Lucia continued, clearly determined to ignore his disrespect, "I have also noticed movement that is more subtle, more like vibrations. Look at your wine cup, sir, and you will see what I mean."

Everyone, including Tag, leaned forward to look into Antyllus's goblet, which he had placed on the small round table between the couches. And indeed it appeared the skin of the wine moved as if an invisible child was gently blowing on it. Yet Tag could feel no corresponding tremor or vibration. He thought of the spiderweb Lucia had shown him.

"Which only leaves me wondering what it could all mean," Lucia continued. "The animals seem to detect something as well. One of Father's horses kicked a hole through his stall recently, the roosters have been crowing at odd times, and do you know, I have even seen spiders in their webs —"

"Spiders!" Antyllus laughed. "Thank the gods Pliny is not here. Imagine how embarrassed we would all be for you in front of my patron if you talked about such inanities."

Tag forced himself to take a deep breath, swallowing the familiar rage of powerlessness, of being dismissed — but this time, on Lucia's behalf.

Lucia glared at her host. "Nevertheless, I think there is more to it," she said. "I have a theory."

"Do tell us," Cornelia jumped in before her husband could respond.

Lucia turned to her. "My apologies if my observations seem indelicate, my dear friend, but I have seen your unborn babe move and shift. It is an amazing sight. These movements of the earth, I believe, are similar in nature. The earth is twitching and rolling in preparation for some kind of event, perhaps a birth of some sort. . . ."

She trailed off at the sight of Antyllus and Quintus exchanging a look. Her cheeks warmed, but she plunged on. "Do we know how the gods create islands or new mountain ranges? What if all the phenomena we are witnessing is the divine process of a new mountain emerging, or a break in the earth for a new waterway? And if that is so, how do we protect ourselves and our cities?"

Antyllus gulped the rest of his wine and held the cup out to his slave again. "Perhaps your time would be better served on poetry, given your imagination," he said, waiting for his slave to blot his lips with the napkin. Turning to Quintus, he added, "Only the mind of a female would consider signs that have always existed as a precursor to a . . . a birth!" He sniggered. "Seems to me, someone's feeling a bit broody and wants to start having babies soon." He winked at Quintus.

Lucia swung her legs around and stood. She locked eyes with her friend. "I am sorry, Cornelia, but I must be leaving now. Thank you for the fine food."

Cornelia pushed herself to stand with a grunt. "Lucia, no, please don't leave," she said. "Antyllus is not himself tonight. He . . . he has been suffering from a terrible head pain. Please apologize, husband. My friend has misunderstood your attempts at humor."

To Tag's astonishment, Antyllus merely swirled and sipped his wine. A heavy, awkward silence filled the room as a slave brought Lucia's sandals to her and began helping her put them on.

"Lucia, stay," Quintus said, standing as well. "I find your theories charming."

Tag stepped forward. "I will escort you home, *Domina*," he said.

"No," Quintus said to Tag, unexpected iron in his voice. "You will stay here with *me*."

Tag blinked in surprise and confusion.

"Lucia, I don't want you to go," Cornelia said, her face splotched and her expression pleading.

"I must," Lucia said, and moved toward the door. Tag began following her out.

"Tages!" Quintus called. "You are to stay here with me."

Lucia turned to look at Tag, shaking her head almost imperceptibly, telling him to stay and not make a scene. She walked out of the room with her head held high. Tag gritted his teeth and returned to his position behind Quintus, watching as Cornelia waddled after Lucia.

Cornelia did not return. Tag was forced to pour drink after drink for the patrician he loathed, all the while seething at the insult to Lucia's dignity. When Quintus and his host — both heavy-eyed and drunk — fell asleep on their respective dining couches, Tag left for the compound. Quintus would have to find another slave to take him back to the school.

CHAPTER NINETEEN

Lucia

She could not sleep. How could she, knowing that her best friend's husband thought her both ridiculous and barely above contempt? Was it possible that he had always looked down on her and she had never noticed? She tried to remember the last time she had dined or socialized with both Cornelia and Antyllus. She could not recall even one occasion. He had always been "too busy" to join them. It had never occurred to her that that was by design.

Cornelia had never let on that her rich husband thought so little of her. Lucia's heart contracted at the idea of her friend trying to protect her from her husband's snobbishness. Still, she didn't understand why she'd had to. Cornelia and Lucia both belonged to the equites, and Antyllus had married Cornelia. Yet he treated Lucia as if she'd been an unwashed plebeian. Was it really all because of what her father did? She knew the noble classes looked down on gladiatorial school owners — calling them "Butchers of Men" — but did the disdain really go that deep?

If so, it certainly explained Quintus's endless, casual insults. And it proved that Cornelia's plan for her to go after Quintus was utter foolishness. A patrician of his stature would never marry a lanista's daughter.

Cornelia had clearly tried to coach her husband — she must have been worried that Antyllus might treat Lucia rudely. So why had she set her up for such humiliation? She had initially said that Pliny would treat her like a talking monkey. Was this her way of *showing* her that fact? But that was not like Cornelia. Cornelia was merely desperate for Lucia to stay near her in Pompeii, especially as her due date neared. Lucia wondered if Antyllus was dismissive of *Cornelia* as well — despite how often Cornelia warbled about his "wonderfulness" — and if that contributed to her determination to find a way to keep her close. Perhaps she needed Lucia more than she let on. . . .

When she could take her endless thoughts no longer, Lucia lit a small oil lamp, stepped over Metrodona snoring away on her straw-filled sleeping mat outside Lucia's *cubiculum*, and went in search of Minos. For years she had begged her father to let Minos sleep in her *cubiculum*, but no amount of pleading ever swayed him. "That's what poor people and farmers do," he always said. "And we are better than they are."

Well, apparently, not by much, according to Antyllus.

When Minos saw her, he whined with surprise and pleasure, tail thumping in circles.

"Shhhhh," Lucia whispered as she hugged his neck. "No noise." She untied him and signaled for him to follow. He trotted happily beside her as they headed into the woods.

Once outside the opening of the city wall, Lucia felt swallowed up by the blackness. She paused, wondering if maybe she shouldn't venture out. Minos seemed to sense her trepidation, for he stuck closer to her than normal as he led the way through the woods to her wooden enclosure.

Once in the clearing, she took a deep breath of pine-scented air. Maybe now she would sleep, even if only for a short while. She needed to be back in her bed well before dawn.

When she crawled inside, a dark form in the shadows shifted, and she froze.

"Who's there?" came a sleepy voice.

Her heart skipped a beat and her breath returned when she recognized the voice. "Tag? What are you doing here?"

"I was sleeping," he said, sitting up.

"But why come here? You should sleep in your own *cubiculum*!"

He rubbed his eyes and snorted. "There are no *cubicula* for slaves in this house," he said. "You know that. And this is better than sleeping on the floor of the herbal room."

Lucia stared at him. He didn't have a place to sleep? She remembered now seeing the kitchen slaves sleeping where they worked, the gardener slumbering in the shed. She'd never even noticed — or, more accurately, never paid attention. It seemed perfectly normal. But thinking about Tag not having the dignity of his own room made her ache with the familiar frustration of their different stations.

"It's still dark," he said, swallowing a yawn. "What are you doing here? Are you all right?"

"I couldn't sleep," she said.

"Right," he said, and she could see the events of the evening slowly come back to him. "Antyllus is an idiot, Lucia," he continued. "He may be your friend's husband, but he's a superior, rich, pompous idiot. You *have* to know that."

Her throat grew tight at how quickly he had come to her defense. She placed the lamp between them, sat, and pulled up her knees, draping her loose sleep *tunica* to cover her legs. He wore only a loincloth, and she found herself stealing glances at the planes of his smooth torso, the shadows pooling in the contours of his muscles, the unruly curls that gathered at the nape of his neck. In the small, flickering light, he looked like a sleepy young statue of Apollo, who just moments ago stepped down from his base for a quick nap. But unlike marble, his skin would be warm and soft with sleep.

She shook her head and looked away. "The worst part will be facing Cornelia," she said. "I don't know if I can look her in the eye again."

"You have no reason to be embarrassed. You did nothing wrong."

She wrapped her arms around her legs and put her chin on her knees. "I had no idea my best friend's husband thought so little of me. I also don't understand why it was so absurd that I might create my own theories and want to share them with a man like Pliny. And just because I used a birth metaphor doesn't mean it isn't valid. Something *is* happening in Pompeii, Tag. I know it. It could be a birth of nature that results in death. That is often a risk in childbirth, isn't it?"

"Yes, it is. Too often."

"So it is our duty to do what we can to prevent such deaths. But no — according to Antyllus, I am not capable of such thinking. Gods, Tag, all I have to look forward to is being forced to breed like a sow for a rich old man — who will likely look down on me like Antyllus — because my father needs the money. Why can't I be free to make my own choices?"

"I wish you could," Tag said.

"And . . . and then what if I'm like my mother?" she continued. "What if I cannot bear live children and then die of a broken heart like her?"

Tag blinked. "Broken heart?"

"Yes. *Mater* couldn't take the pain of her lost babies anymore."

"Lucia . . ."

She began to cry. "I miss her. I miss her so much. She would help me. She would stand up for me and not force me to marry a man who disgusts and frightens me like Father is doing. I know she would."

Tag cleared his throat and leaned forward, his brow deeply furrowed. "Lucia, your mother did not die of a broken heart," he said.

Something about his expression made her stomach contract with fear. What was he talking about?

"Tell me what you remember about that time," he urged her.

"When . . . when my mother went into labor, I was sent to Cornelia's house, where I was to stay until the baby came and Mother felt better."

"And . . ."

"And several days later, your *tata* came —"

"*My* father?" he asked. "Your father didn't even come for you after what happened?"

"No, he didn't. Your *tata* told me Father was too upset to fetch me. He — he told me the baby had died at birth, and that *Mater* had died of a broken heart because of it."

Tag put his head in his hands and shook it slowly.

"What?"

He raised his eyes and looked at her. "Nobody — your father or your nurse — ever told you the truth? What really happened?"

She shook her head.

"Did you know the sex of the baby?" he asked.

"A girl."

"The last several births were girls. Did you know that?"

She nodded slowly.

"The girls did not die at birth, Lucia."

Lucia stared at him, wide-eyed, a yawning pit of dread opening beneath her lungs.

"Your father . . ." He seemed to find it hard to get the words out. "He had the babies exposed. Because . . . because they were girls."

She shook her head. No. *No*. Her father could be harsh, but he would never do that. "You expect me to believe my father had his own babies thrown on the rubbish heap outside the city? Simply because they were *girls*?"

"It happens more than you think. And it *is* what happened," he said quietly.

Lucia shook her head. "That's not true. That's not possible! He never would have done that. *Mater* never would have *allowed* it!"

"Lucia. You know your mother had no say in the matter. After your brother died in Germania, your father became desperate to have more sons. When your mother only delivered girls, he commanded that they be left outside the city gates. With the last baby, your mother screamed and fought with your father, but he refused to relent."

Lucia covered her ears. "No. This cannot be true."

Tag gently removed her hands from her ears and clasped them in his. She wanted to lose herself in the warmth of his skin, to stop this conversation and pretend the whole day had been a bad dream.

"We all heard," he said. "I thought you knew. He claimed your mother had no right to complain, and that she deserved the punishment — that she brought it on herself for not giving him any more sons."

"I don't want to hear any more, Tag." Because somehow, she knew. Deep inside, she knew that what he was saying was true.

And she knew that what he was about to tell her was true too, and would change everything.

"Your mother killed herself," he said softly. "With poison. She told my father she couldn't keep giving birth only to watch your father kill her baby girls. So she put a stop to it."

"No. Please . . ."

"I'm sorry," he whispered, brushing the hair off her face.

Something broke inside her then. She felt the snap. Her mother had made the decision to leave, to abandon her to a father who had once adored her but now hated her for being a girl. "May . . . maybe that's what I should do. You could get me the herbs, the poison, yes?"

"No, don't say that. Please."

"But what's left for me? Marrying a man harsher than my own father? What will he make me do if I displease him? I couldn't bear having to surrender my babies, Tag, I couldn't!"

As she wept, he moved closer. He wrapped his arms around her and she curled into him like an animal seeking shelter in a storm.

There were two things she knew absolutely in that moment — he was telling the truth. And in Tag's arms was the only place she ever wanted to be.

CHAPTER TWENTY

TAG

When Lucia finally slept, he gently laid her down on her side and kissed her forehead. He knew he should leave. He could be killed for being alone with the master's daughter in such incriminating circumstances.

But he couldn't move. In all the years they'd known each other, he'd never seen Lucia so upset. Gods, why had he told her the truth?

At least he hadn't told her everything. He closed his eyes, remembering.

Three years ago, his father told him he was going to take a "special herbal tonic" to Lucia's mother, who had just had her newest baby taken from her.

Tag had wanted to be helpful to the kind, sad *domina*, so he grabbed the cup and rushed to her room. Damocles had called after him, but he outpaced his father.

When he entered, *Domina* sat up in her bed. "Your father prepared this?" she asked, her eyes looking haunted and her face pale and swollen from crying.

He nodded. Behind him he heard Pontius call out for Damocles. Someone had been hurt.

"Not now," his father had barked back, entering the room and staring at the mistress with the cup in her hand. "I can't —"

But a fighter was bleeding badly and Pontius insisted. Before he left, his father held *Domina*'s gaze with an expression Tag couldn't read. She nodded slightly and mouthed, "Thank you."

They watched Damocles disappear. Then, "You must do something for me," Lucia's mother said quietly, turning to Tag. "In place of your father."

He nodded, hoping that it wasn't anything related to the birth.

She reached into a small wooden chest beside the bed and pulled out a rectangular object covered in a baby blanket. He wondered if she had intended that blanket for the babe that *Dominus* had removed from the house. She handed him the wrapped bundle. "When I am gone, the true power of this will be sealed. Throw it into the sacred spring of Aegeria outside the city. Do you understand?"

He nodded again, although he didn't understand. When she was gone? Gone where? And why the spring pregnant women used to bless their unborn children? But there was something about the look in her eyes that kept him from asking any questions.

"Go," she said, suddenly smiling. "It will all be fine. My girls await their mother."

That made his heart beat a little faster. "*Domina*, what do you mean? Is everything —"

"Go now," she repeated, waving her free hand in a sweeping gesture.

He nodded and left. His last sight of Lucia's mother was her bringing the terra-cotta cup to her lips with two shaking hands.

Maybe he would have made it to the spring if he hadn't stopped in a dark corner of the compound to see what was inside the bundle. But curiosity overcame caution, and he unwrapped the blanket. Inside was a very thin lead tablet, partially rolled. An iron nail fell out of the fabric, clattering onto the pebbled ground at his feet.

His heart thudded in his ears. He looked around to make sure no one had spotted him. This was something he'd only ever heard about — a curse tablet. This was dangerous.

He unrolled the thin lead all the way. A beam of afternoon sun suddenly shone through a break in the terra-cotta shingles, lighting on the metal. It was as if Jupiter himself breathed on the tablet, heating it with his sacred power. Sweat broke out on Tag's brow as he read the scratchy words:

To the Goddesses Diana, Aegeria, Tawaret, and Proserpina,
I invoke you holy ones by your names to punish, crush, maim, and destroy Lucius Titurius for stealing the lives of your daughters; may his heart, liver, spleen, and stomach dissolve and may his holdings, wealth, and peace dissolve with them. Let him not prosper, let him not advance, let him not receive honors. May his death be caused immediately should he ever again take the life of another innocent of this household. Let it be so in your names.

Tag didn't know how long he stood there staring at the light-suffused metal. The strength of *Domina*'s pain and anger vibrated through the words. Dimly he became aware of people running and voices calling out. Someone wailed. He heard the master being summoned. And still Tag did not move.

As cries for the dead reverberated around the compound, slowly, thickly, understanding came. *Domina* had taken poison — poison that he had handed her. He heard a sound he never imagined hearing — the anguished sobs of the man who owned him. Tag thought of Lucia, grateful she wasn't around to witness this, and worried what would happen to her without her mother.

As the man's cries continued, Tag found himself unable to move. Was the power of the curse so strong that it held him captive simply because he'd read it? When a cloud covered the sun, the beam of light illuminating the tablet disappeared. He felt as if he could breathe again.

Domina had asked him to take this to the spring "in place of your father." Well then, he'd let Damocles do it — just as *Domina* intended. He picked up the iron nail, and after wrapping the tablet and the nail back up in the baby blanket, he retraced his steps into the compound.

Shouts came from the area outside the mistress's room, and he rushed toward the sound. He stopped at the sight of his father being held by two men as the master railed at him, his face red and tearstained.

"You did this! You did this!" Titurius roared.

"I brought her only a tonic to relieve the pain and the bleeding," his father replied calmly. "She lost a lot of blood. Her emotional agitation, I believe, set her humors out of balance and the potion caused —"

"You lie!" Titurius yelled and leapt at Damocles, pummeling him on his face and chest as the two men continued holding him up.

"No!" Tag cried, running forward. "Stop. Leave him alone!"

Titurius turned to him. His eyes widened at the sight of the baby blanket. Damocles shook his head at Tag, clearly telling him to stay quiet.

"What's in that bundle?" his master barked.

Fury crawled up Tag's throat at the sight of his father's battered face. He wanted to punish Titurius not just for hurting his elderly *apa*, but for every beating and whipping they'd both unfairly received over the years.

"*I* gave your wife the tonic," he said. "And she gave me this. These are her words." He let the blanket fall to the ground to reveal the curse tablet, holding the iron nail in his other hand. "She curses you for killing her daughters. And she told me that when she was gone, the power in this would be sealed. I felt the magic. The gods illuminated the tablet the moment she died. It glowed in my hands."

Titurius's face blanched. "Give that to me," he rasped. "I can have the curse undone."

"No," Tag said. It felt so good to refuse his master's command, he yelled it again. "*No!*"

Damocles groaned.

"There is one more way to seal the magic," Tag announced, holding up the nail. He wasn't sure this was true, but he'd heard other slaves whisper about strengthening a curse by piercing it with iron.

Titurius's eyes widened. "No!" He lunged at Tag just as Tag drove the nail as hard as he could into the metal.

Tag did not remember much of what had happened after that, as Titurius had almost beaten him to death. Pontius had pulled him off. "The master were going to kill ye," the overseer said later. "No doubt about it."

"So why didn't he?"

"Because the tablet said he would die right off if he killed anybody else in the household. Including you. It were simple — he didn't want to die."

"So why didn't he sell me, then?"

Pontius admitted that he had wanted to. "But a priest the master consulted told him ye had to stay part of the household to contain the magic."

Now doubt wormed through Tag's insides. Maybe he should have told Lucia about the curse tablet. She was as much a victim of the curse as her father, because the school had begun to fail after her mother's death, prompting Titurius to try to make a rich match for his daughter. But it seemed cruel to point out to her that one consequence of her mother's curse was that she was being married off to the highest bidder.

He sighed and stared at the flame from the boat-shaped little lamp she'd brought, following the flickering light as it danced over the contours of her body. Despite himself, he couldn't stop stealing looks at the way her *tunica* revealed the curves of her breasts and hips, or the way the fabric had hitched up her legs as she lay on her side. He longed to brush his fingertips along her warm, silky skin. . . .

He needed to stop torturing himself. But he drank her in with his eyes as if he were dying of thirst. As he followed the line of her neck up to her mouth, he sucked in a breath. Her eyes were open, and she was staring at him.

She opened her arms to him and everything inside him dropped. Gods, he needed to go. This was too dangerous. He needed to be the strong one, but how could he?

"Lucia," he whispered. "I should return to the —"

He stopped, mesmerized. She leaned up, her *tunica* sliding partway down her shoulder, exposing honey-smooth skin. The scent of her warm body surrounded him as she brought her lips to the base of his throat. He closed his eyes as she trailed soft kisses upward, his breath loud in his ears. When she pressed her mouth to his, he grabbed a fistful of her long, wavy hair and brought her hard against him.

After a time, he leaned up on one elbow, forcing himself from her. He could not catch his breath, and she was not making it any easier by running her hands up and down his body.

"I need to . . . I should go," he croaked.

"No, stay with me," she whispered.

He groaned. "We cannot, Lucia, you know that." The consequences were too great. He pulled away a little more and took another shuddering breath.

She sighed and closed her eyes. "I want to be with you," she whispered.

He swallowed. "We cannot take the risk," he said. "You know this."

"Let's run away, Tag. We'll disappear where no one will ever find us. We'll live free, together."

He touched his forehead to hers, surprised at the sudden lump in his throat. "There is nothing more in this life that I would want," he whispered.

"Let's dream together and make it come true," she said, snuggling into him.

And despite the ache in his body and soul, after a time he slept too, holding her close against him.

CHAPTER TWENTY-ONE

Lucia

She awoke in the dark, aware of Tag's deep, rhythmic breathing. The sky was still black, but she didn't know for how much longer. She'd better return to her *cubiculum*. Carefully, she extracted herself from beneath the arm he'd flung over her, and he rolled onto his back. How much younger he looked in sleep, more like the boy she remembered.

Her gaze traveled over his barely clothed body, and she fought the impulse to run her hands down the length of his lean, carved torso. But that would be cruel. He'd been right to stop them from going further, and it wouldn't be fair to wake him in such a manner. And yet her fingers itched to feel the smooth warmth of his chest and abdomen.

Her eyes pricked and grew hot as she stared at him, trying to imagine leaving him to marry Vitulus. How would she bear it? Maybe they really could run away together. Maybe it was possible. But inside, she knew she had no sense of what it would take to live outside the compound, no sense of how they could disappear so that he wouldn't be recaptured and punished as a runaway slave and her reputation ruined forever.

With a sigh, she gave him a soft kiss on the mouth. He muttered what sounded like her name as she pulled away. With one last longing look, she backed out of the enclosure and slapped her thigh for Minos, who stretched first his front, then his back paws at her feet.

"Home," she ordered. She grabbed his collar for guidance through the inky darkness.

Just as they neared the wall leading back to their compound, she released his collar. She expected him to race toward the house, but he froze, one paw up, as something rustled in the undergrowth. "Come on, boy," she whispered. "No time for hunting. We need to keep going." She moved ahead through the brush.

Then Minos, with a loud whine of excitement, launched himself through her legs at whatever creature he'd spotted. The force of his lunge sent her flying and she landed hard, rolling her ankle. "Gods, Minos!" But the dog was gone.

When Lucia tried to stand, she gasped, then cursed under her breath at the pain. Well, she had no other choice but to push through it. She had to get back before Metrodona discovered she hadn't slept in her bed. At the sound of her limping gait, Minos came crashing through the brush, smiling and wagging his tail.

"Bad boy," she said crossly. "Look what you've done." But the dog continued grinning. "Home," she repeated, sighing. Minos stayed nearby as she hobbled. The sky was turning purple.

Once in her own bed, she heard the first stirrings of slaves rising to their predawn work. *Thank you, Diana, for helping me return to my room undetected.* She prayed for sleep.

It did not come. She stared up at the low ceiling of her *cubiculum* in a daze. How could one day contain so many horrible events — learning the truth about her mother's suicide and her baby sisters' exposures; having her best friend's husband dismiss and belittle her in front of everyone; and now turning her ankle in the dark. . . .

The worst was thinking about her abandoned sisters. She knew exposure was practiced, but no one ever admitted to it. And now, her own father? Had his grief over his lost son so warped him that he would throw away daughters until he got the new boy he wanted? And poor *Mater* — used like a brood mare. Now that she recalled it, her mother did always seem pregnant, and always tired and worried too.

What about the babies? She covered her eyes against the image of her newborn sister, waving her little arms, all alone on a rubbish heap outside the city. Did wild animals get her? What about slave traders, who often searched for abandoned infants to rear for sale later? What if a brothel owner took her? That very moment, all of her little sisters could be enduring abuse worse than death across town or in some foreign hovel, simply because of what her father *wished*.

Gods, if she had known, could she have put a stop to it? Could she have joined forces with her mother to convince her father to accept what the gods had given them? Could she have found the means to recover the babes and pay someone to care for them until he softened?

Everybody had lied to her. Everybody. Even her mother. Tag was the only one who had told her the truth.

Someone was shaking her. "*Puella?* Lucia? Are you unwell?"

She opened her eyes. Metrodona. "Why? What's wrong?"

"Nothing," her old nurse said, the loose skin under her chin waggling. "I call for the healer next if you don't wake up this time. It is very late in the morning!"

"Oh." Lucia threw off her blanket and stood, forgetting about her ankle, then fell back on her bed with a cry of pain.

"What . . . what is this?" Metrodona asked with wide eyes, inspecting her swollen flesh. "When did you do this? You had no such injury when you went to sleep!"

Lucia stared dumbly down at her foot. Should she just say she fell when she used the *latrina* in the middle of the night? But then Metrodona would grill her about why she hadn't woken her. Without thinking, she blurted, "It must have happened while I slept."

"What do you mean?" Metrodona said. "That is impossible." The old woman's eyes widened. "Unless you were visited by a daemon! Have you angered a daemon?"

Lucia suppressed a smile and widened her eyes, glad she had accidentally hit on one of her nursemaid's endless superstitions. "I don't know," she said, adding a small quaver of fear to her voice. "It happened in a dream."

Metrodona came closer. "A dream? Tell me."

"I dreamt that Minos and I were running through the woods in the dark, and he saw a rat and darted through my legs to pounce on it. I fell hard," she said, screwing up her expression as if trying to recall a fading image.

"Where were you headed in your dream, child? And why were you hurrying? I must speak with the dream interpreter, and he will need to know this!"

"I was running through the woods back to . . . to my body," she said. "In the dream, I saw myself sleeping in my *cubiculum*, and I was rushing to join myself because something terrible was going to happen."

Metrodona put a knobby hand up to her mouth.

Lucia forced an expression of fear on her face. "Metrodona," she said quietly, "do you think it means something?"

"Of course it does! It is very rare for both worlds to combine like this." Her eyes lit up. "The rat! What color was it?"

"Gray. Maybe black," Lucia said. "The creature moved fast."

"Oh! Oh, my. I am sure the interpreter will have a lot to say about this!" She shifted her weight from foot to foot.

"If you want to head to the marketplace now to find him, you may," Lucia said. "I won't need you — I won't be going anywhere today."

"Yes, yes. But first let us get the *medicus* to look at your ankle. I will help you with your morning ablutions and then get the healer, yes?"

Lucia nodded, hoping it would be the younger one.

CHAPTER TWENTY-TWO

TAG

He got hit three times during the blocking exercise. By Quintus. The man who couldn't hit an ox if it was trussed up and stuffed and painted red. He *had* to focus.

Yet Lucia's comment about running away together had lodged in his mind like a splinter. He couldn't shake it. He'd thought about running away before, of course, but always dismissed it. Runaway slaves were branded and beaten to within an inch of their lives if they were caught. But the idea of running away *with* Lucia, of living a life *they* chose together, had grabbed him by the throat and wouldn't let go.

A house slave came to speak to Pontius. "Tag!" the overseer called. "Yer needed in the main house!"

Quintus looked at him and laughed. "*Eheu.* That is one guilty look. What'd you do, boy? Besides abandoning your post last night, anyway."

Frozen in fear, Tag said nothing.

Quintus stepped close. "I did not report to your master that you ran off from attending me last night," he said in a low voice, "if that is what you are worried about."

Tag blinked. "I did not run off. You fell asleep in your

host's home. I needed to be back here to attend to my duties as healer."

Quintus waved his hand. "Still, whatever it is, I will back you with Titurius if you need it."

Tag looked at the patrician, wondering at this sudden "solidarity."

"I am not as terrible as you think I am," Quintus continued. "Truly. You might be surprised."

"Tag!" yelled Pontius. "What are ye waitin' fer?"

"Er . . . thank you, *Dominus*," Tag said to Quintus and moved away. He dropped the wooden *gladius*, then grabbed his tunic and shrugged into it as he jogged after the house slave. His heart pounded with worry. If someone had told Titurius about the time he spent with his daughter, it would all be over. Seeing Lucia, training to win his freedom, everything.

He caught up with the house slave. "Where am I needed?" he asked.

"Women's quarters," he said. "The young *domina* has been hurt."

"Hurt? What do you mean?" Had her father found out and beaten her?

The man shrugged. "It's all I was told."

The house slave steered him into a small side garden where Damocles stood talking to Metrodona. Castor dug in the dirt at his feet. No Titurius. Tag released a breath.

"The younger healer is here," called the slave as he turned and left.

"Ah, finally," Damocles said. "I sent for you some time ago."

Castor ran to Tag, grinning, waving an imaginary sword. "Did you hurt someone today?"

"No, Castor," he said. Turning to his father, he asked, "What has happened?"

"Lucia turned her ankle," Damocles said, moving aside to reveal her sitting on a stone bench. She smiled shyly at him. His chest swelled with relief. He moved toward Lucia, but Damocles grabbed his son's arm and, with surprising strength, dragged him far enough out of earshot that they could speak in private.

"You *told* her about her mother?" he hissed under his breath. "Why would you do such a thing, son? The master made us all swear she was *never* to know what really happened!"

"She has a right to know," Tag whispered back.

"She has been demanding I tell her everything. She wants to know who gave her mother the poison —"

Tag blanched.

"She wants to know if all of the infants were really alive at birth. She wants to know who took the babies to the rubbish piles outside the gates! And all manner of things we can't know, like if the babies really died or if some slave trader picked them up. This is a horrible thing for a girl to have to consider right before she gets married! If *Dominus* finds out she knows, neither of us will survive."

If Dominus *finds out about a lot of things*, Tag thought, *none of them would survive.*

"What are you two discussing?" Metrodona called out. "My mistress is waiting!"

"Just poultices, Glykeria," Damocles called.

Tag blinked. Glykeria? Wasn't that Lucia's mother's attendant? The old woman had died soon after her mistress took her own life. How could his father be so lucid one moment and then make a mistake like that in the next?

They moved back to the women. "Tag will treat the ankle, Cassia," Damocles continued, calling Lucia by her mother's name. Tag and Lucia exchanged a look. "I have to get back to the cook's child, who is having trouble breathing." He turned and walked away.

Castor grabbed Tag's hand. "Can I stay with you instead of following your *apa*?" he asked. "I don't like it anymore when he thinks I am you."

Tag closed his eyes for a moment. "Yes, you can stay."

When he approached Lucia, she smiled up at him again, her cheeks flushing. Warmth washed over him, but there was something else too — a fierce wanting that ground and twisted his gut so hard he could barely breathe.

Castor, it seemed, was also mesmerized. "I like your lights," the child blurted.

Lucia blinked and looked at the boy. "What?"

"The ones in your eyes that dance when you smile," he said, flushing to the tips of his ears. "I want to marry you when I'm growed up."

Metrodona boxed the side of his head gently. "Stupid boy!" she huffed. "You are a slave. Ladies can't marry slaves. Now stop your nonsense and let the *medicus* check her ankle!"

"Right," Tag said, watching Lucia gently brush the hair off the little boy's forehead, the child wriggling in pleasure. "How did it happen?"

Metrodona rattled off the story Lucia had concocted, and he tried to act suitably impressed. But inside, he hated the idea of her making her way through the woods in the dark all alone. She should have woken him.

Lucia turned to her nurse. "Metrodona, go to the market to talk to the dream interpreter now. I am anxious to hear what he says." She nodded toward Tag and Castor. "The healers here will take care of me."

Castor pulled on Tag's hand, whispering with awe, "She called me a healer too."

Tag squeezed his hand. "May I see the injury?" he asked after Metrodona left, moving faster than he'd ever seen the old woman move before.

As Lucia extended her ankle, he bent on one knee and cradled her heel. It looked terrible, swollen and purple. Could it be broken?

"Were you able to — in this dream," he added for Castor's sake, "were you able to put any weight on it after the fall?"

She nodded. "It hurt, but I could still walk on it."

"Can you put any weight on it now?" he asked. She stood, but he could see her jaw clench in pain. He bade her sit again.

"How are we going to treat it?" Castor asked, looking up at him. Tag caught the "we" and exchanged a smile with Lucia.

"First we will need cool clay dug up near the cistern, for cooling the injury," he said. "Then we will need the leeches to bleed the injured area to further reduce the swelling —"

"No leeches!" Lucia cried. "Please!"

"Fine. I'll make some small cuts instead. We will also need linen bandages to wrap the foot for support," he added. "But let's start with the cool clay first," he said, turning to Castor. "Have the gardener dig some up near the cistern. Tell the cook to mix mustard powder into it, then bring it to me. After I bleed her, we will cover the ankle in the mixture. Do you understand?"

Castor nodded, gave Lucia a shy grin, and flew out of the small garden.

Tag watched him go, then turned to Lucia. Was he really alone with her? Inside her own *home*?

"I would have walked you back," he said under his breath, pretending to continue examining her foot.

"I didn't want to wake you."

He shifted positions, still keeping his head down as if working on her foot. "Lucia, why was Cornelia trying to arrange something between you and Quintus?"

She sighed irritably. "She thinks if I get Quintus interested in me, Father would break the betrothal to Vitulus and switch it to him."

"He has . . . Has he tried to kiss you?"

"Tag." She put a hand over his on her ankle, leaning forward as if inspecting the joint. "I have no inclination toward him at all," she whispered. "I only want you."

He released a breath he hadn't even realized he'd been holding. It was bad enough to know he would lose her to Rome, but to lose her to Quintus was unthinkable.

"I also wanted to thank you for last night," she added shyly.

He didn't know what she was thanking him for — for comforting her after the disaster at Cornelia's house, or for making sure they didn't do anything she would later regret? Probably both.

He wanted to tell her he was sorry that Cornelia's husband was such a fool and that she had to learn from him what really happened to her mother and her baby sisters. That if he could, he would take her away from this cursed home and protect her. That he would never expose a child she wanted to keep. But it all got clogged in his throat, because he could make *none* of that ever happen.

So instead, he caressed her injured foot and quietly answered, "You're welcome."

CHAPTER TWENTY-THREE

Lucia

"Daughter? May I come in?"

She looked up from her bed in surprise. Her father was here? To see her? "Yes, of course."

"What are you doing?" Lucius Titurius asked as he entered her small *cubiculum*.

She held up a needle and thread and the hem of one of her *tunicas*. "Just some mending." He did not need to know that she was fixing a *tunica* she'd torn in one of her many jaunts to the woods.

He nodded. "Good, good. But wouldn't you be more comfortable in the atrium?"

She pointed with her chin at her foot, which was propped up on several pillows on her sleeping couch. "Remember, I'm supposed to keep my ankle elevated."

He looked around her tiny room and cleared his throat several times. She tried to remember the last time he had come to visit her like this. She couldn't.

"I have been in communication with your betrothed," he began.

She groaned inwardly.

"He is aware you are frightened and uncertain, and he has given me his word that he will be kind and patient with you. He recommends that you begin sorting through your girlish things to select which toys you will sacrifice to Diana on the day of your wedding. We leave for Rome soon, as you know."

Lucia nodded. With a pang, she realized that the toy sacrifice was something that girls always did with their mothers.

He cleared his throat again and shifted his weight from foot to foot. "You know, your mother was terrified of marrying me too, when our union was arranged."

"She was?"

"I too was quite a bit older than she was —"

"Not forty-something years," she mumbled, but he went on as if he hadn't heard her.

"But we grew to love each other very much. Or, at least, I grew to love her greatly, and I think she returned the feeling."

How could he think that after taking her babies?

"I know it seems as if I am being cruel, but you must understand that I am trying to give you a safe and secure future, Lucia. I would not want any harm to come to you."

She kept her eyes on her fingers in her lap, thinking all the while that if she'd been born after her brother had died, he probably would have thrown her on the rubbish heap too.

"May I sit?" he asked after a long silence.

She nodded.

He sat at the edge of the bed and patted her injured foot. "Do you remember how we used to play Hercules and the *kerkopes*?" he asked, smiling. "You would come upon me when I napped and try to steal something."

Despite herself, she smiled. "Try? I always succeeded."

"Once you set off with your prize, I would wake up and roar like Hercules, and stomp through the house in search of you."

"I liked to hide under *Mater*'s blankets in her room," she added, recalling the sensation of being wrapped in her mother's fringed coverlets scented with rose oil.

"Yes, I always knew that's where you went, but I made a big show of upending furniture and being unable to find you. Finally, I'd jump on the bed to make you squeal, carrying you by the ankles just like Hercules carried the *kerkopes*."

They were both silent for a time.

"What happened to those days?" he asked quietly.

"They disappeared when Bassus died," she said flatly. *And when you started exposing my baby sisters. And when Mother killed herself to keep you from doing it again. And when you couldn't bear to look at me anymore because I was the one that survived and not your firstborn son.*

"I pray that you never have to experience the death of a beloved child," he murmured.

The outrageousness of *him* making such a comment after having her baby sisters *exposed* closed her throat, trapping her next breath. She flew into a paroxysm of coughing.

He waited until she caught her breath and stood. "I boxed up many of your mother's things and kept them for you. I'll have them brought here. I thought you might enjoy going through them and deciding which of her things you would like to take with you to your new home."

She realized he was waiting for a response, so she said, "Thank you, Father."

He sighed, kissed the top of her head, and left without saying anything else.

After staring stupidly at the wall for a time, Lucia put down her mending. Hearing her father out in the training yard, she decided to go to his empty *tablinum* to find something to read.

When she finally limped into the small room, she blew her cheeks out with disappointment. There was always a part of her that hoped a handful of new scrolls would magically be waiting on her father's desk every time she came in — even though her father had never been an avid reader. Her mother had, though. She'd especially loved Pliny, a love she had passed on to Lucia. Unfortunately, after she died, Lucia had been unable to convince her father to purchase any more of Pliny's books.

The thought of her mother and what really happened to her was like a punch to the chest. Yet, at the same time, her mother's weakness enraged her. Why hadn't she *made* her father see the error of his ways? If it had been her baby, *she* would have fought back. *She* would have marched out the city gates and *taken* her baby back from the rubbish heap, if that was what it required! Why had her mother given up?

The idea of facing such a bleak future made her want to scream. When she'd told Tag she wanted to run away with him, she hadn't meant it, really. What did she know about living on her own?

But standing in her father's cold study, she realized that *not* running away meant she'd turn into her mother, powerless and defeated. And that must *never* happen.

"Well, well," a voice said behind her, and she jumped. Quintus was leaning languidly against the dark blue door frame. "Once again, it seems that you are avoiding me. And yet your friend Cornelia claims you might have feelings for me. Which one is it, lovely Lucia?"

Gods. "I have not been avoiding you," she said, pointing to her wrapped ankle. "I injured it the other night and haven't been on it much."

He looked at her foot. "Yes, I've heard slaves whispering that you were cursed in your sleep."

An awkward silence descended, and Lucia pretended to scan the tags on her father's small collection of scrolls — as if she didn't have all the titles memorized.

"So, is it true?" Quintus asked.

Lucia looked at him. "Is what true?"

"What Cornelia said — about your feelings for me."

She quickly looked away. How was she supposed to answer that? "I . . . I . . ." She stared at the floor, trying to think. As if invisibly pushed by Cornelia, she sensed the only answer she could give needed to be a lie. "She was being truthful," she said in a trembling voice, not meeting his eyes.

"I am very glad to hear this," Quintus said.

Lucia cut a look at him and saw that he was grinning with a faraway look in his eyes.

"This might work after all," he muttered.

She blinked. "What might?"

He brought his attention back to her and pushed away from the door. "When I've figured out the details, I will let you know," he said. Then with a slight bow, he turned and left, leaving Lucia staring at his retreating back.

"Come, let us go into the garden," Metrodona said a few days later, leading her out of her room. "You are always happier outside."

Her ankle injury, to her frustration, had kept her housebound, which meant she couldn't sneak away to see Tag. He and Castor would check on her injury, giving them a few moments of contact — of shared smiles, surreptitious hand squeezes, and whispered words — but it wasn't the same. Fortunately, Tag's treatments had indeed reduced the swelling, and her ankle was healing nicely. But still, Metrodona insisted on treating her almost as an invalid. And when she complained, her nurse just shook her head and said, "We must be extra careful as your marriage date approaches! We cannot let any angry daemons curse your good fortune."

Lucia insisted they bring Minos along with them to the garden. Metrodona despised the dog, but without their regular outings to the woods, poor Minos stayed chained to his post at all times. Lucia hated how miserable that made him.

Metrodona settled herself into a cozy spot in the shade and promptly fell asleep. Lucia took the opportunity to hobble through the opening in the wall to the adjoining meadow. Minos ran around the area, nose to the ground, sniffing happily. After a time, Lucia moved to the shade of a plane tree. Minos flopped down beside her, panting.

"How is it that it is still so hot?" she said to the dog. By that point in early October, the weather usually cooled down. But lately, even the earth itself seemed to radiate heat, so it felt like they were pressed in on both sides. Even in the shade, she felt heavy, slow, and listless.

Minos dozed on his side, panting, tongue lolling on the dirt. Cicadas whirred and chirped in waves, like rounds in an endless lamentation. Her thoughts droned along with them as her eyes grew heavy: *Could Tag and I really run away? Do I have the strength to do it? But if I don't, I will turn into my* mater, *which mustn't happen. But* could *we run away? Do we have the strength? If we don't . . .*

Everything went silent and she was instantly alert. Bugs, she had noted, only stopped their infernal noise when they detected danger. Minos's head popped up and he closed his mouth, as if he didn't want the sounds of his own breathing to interfere with what he was trying to hear.

She knew a tremor must be coming. But what manner of danger was a tremor to the insects? When the shaking started, she put her palms on the earth and closed her eyes to experience the vibrations more keenly. The movement of the earth pulsated through her palms and gently vibrated her bones.

Slowly, the earth's trembling faded away. A vision came to her then — of a cracked, stony, gruesome face deep within the earth, moving toward her and all those she loved, grinning with chipped black rock teeth, opening its mouth wide as if to swallow them whole.

Mephistis.

Lucia snapped her eyes open. Was the goddess of poison air warning her? Or cursing her?

CHAPTER TWENTY-FOUR

TAG

To Tag's relief, Quintus had not shown up for morning training.

"Where's your patrician?" one of the fighters asked as they waited in the pit for instructions.

"He's not 'mine,'" Tag grumbled, kicking at a depression in the sand. "And I have no idea."

"I heard he left for his villa in Herculaneum," a gladiator named Nicodemus said. "But all his stuff is still here — along with one of the slaves he brought with him — so, sadly, he's coming back."

"Nico always knows the gossip," someone laughed.

"The patrician princess probably went home to *Mater* to complain about us mean ol' gladiators," another man added in a pretend-whiny voice.

Tag didn't care what the reason was — he was glad to be free of Quintus, no matter for how long.

The morning's warm-up consisted of running an obstacle course with wooden shield and sword in hand. When it was Tag's turn, he sprinted for the barrels — three of them — and leapt over them, landing on his feet in a crouch. Making sure his equipment never touched the ground, he weaved in and out of the low ropes tied between posts. Next, he dodged a line of sandbags sent swinging in different rhythms, and finally, still on the run, he struck a swinging straw man on its chest. A dishonorable hit to the back would have meant three sprinting laps around the courtyard.

Tag bent over his knees, gasping for air, then got back in line for the next go-round. He looked up when he heard a strange popping sound. A heavily muscled man dropped to the ground behind the barrels, grabbing the back of his thigh, bellowing in pain.

Tag winced. That popping sound meant only one thing — the man had torn a major muscle in two. He ran out to the fighter and could already see the bulge forming where the muscle separated. He cursed under his breath.

The man's red, sweating face was contorted in agony. "You two!" Tag pointed at two fighters staring at their downed friend. "Lift him and take him to the treatment room. *Statim!*"

Tag jogged ahead of them. "Cool clay from near the cistern," he called to a wide-eyed slave standing by. "Two buckets' worth. Now." The young man took off.

When Tag applied the cool clay to the man's back thigh, some of the fighter's curses eased. He reached for a poppy tincture to relax the man, mostly because he wanted him to be still. The worst thing the fighter could do now was to continue moving that muscle, and getting a gladiator to stop moving — no matter the pain — was no easy task.

When the man's breathing eased, Tag headed to the herbal room for additional supplies, Castor trailing on his heels. Inside, he took a deep breath and thought about his next steps. He would reapply the cooling clay, maybe adding crushed mint to the mix. Then he'd wrap the leg tight, holding the muscle together so that it could reattach and heal. Perhaps calendula paste applied before bandaging would —

"Lady Lucia," Castor cried, running over to her as she stood in the doorway.

Tag's heart jumped. Lucia never came into the medical rooms because it meant walking among the gladiators, which her father strictly forbade. "Are you ill or hurt?" he asked.

"No," she said.

"Look, *Domina*," Castor said before she could say anything else. He pointed at a row of terra-cotta containers. "I marked the medicine jars."

She touched the top of one wax-sealed jar. "How do you know which one contains what medicine?"

Castor traced a grimy finger over the Greek letters scratched onto the surface of each jar. "I can read letters now! If this letter is the first one," he said, indicating the *alpha*, "then it means *A*, for *apple tree bark*. And if that letter is *tau*, it means *T* for *toadflax*."

"That is impressive, Castor!" she said, looking up at Tag through her lashes. Her gaze lingered for a moment before she smiled down on the boy, and Tag felt the weight of it like a physical caress.

He cleared his throat. "Castor, I need you to go and check on the injured gladiator. I want you to make sure he hasn't moved."

Castor stuck his lower lip out and crossed his arms. "I don't want to go. I want to show *Domina* all that I've been learning."

Tag raised an eyebrow. "Are you going to misbehave *in front of Domina*?" he asked in an overly surprised voice. He knew that was a low blow — Castor adored Lucia.

The boy's face grew blotchy.

"Go," Lucia said gently to the boy. "After you have finished your healing work, bring a wax tablet to the atrium and show me then."

Castor nodded, gave her a shy grin, and raced out of the room.

Then Lucia's eyes met Tag's, and they stared at each other in silence. It was all he could do not to rush over and press her against him.

One of the gladiators walked by the door, and she quickly spoke. "My nurse has been feeling poorly, and I wondered if you could recommend a tonic."

Tag struggled to remember the proper response. "Uh . . . Tell me her symptoms."

"Metrodona is fine," she said in a low voice, coming closer when the gladiator had passed. "I just wanted to talk to you."

Gods, how he loved her warm, clean scent — like blooming citron trees drenched in sunshine. He would not look at her mouth. Or the silk of her neck. He needed to keep his head. "What did you want to talk about?"

She twisted her fingers together. "I miss you. I wanted to see you."

"Your ankle is well enough to go out into the woods?"

She nodded. "But you are usually training in the afternoons."

As the sound of footsteps approached in the hall, he said loudly, "Perhaps this salve for tight muscles may ease your nurse's backache."

"Thank you, healer," she responded in the same overly loud tone as the footsteps disappeared.

She walked over to the shrine of Asclepius and he moved beside her. Standing close with their heads bowed in front of the shrine was the only way such proximity would be allowed. Tag let his arm brush hers, and even at that innocent touch, his heart raced.

"I can come this afternoon," he whispered, glad that Quintus's sudden absence gave him the freedom to sneak away.

She smiled. "Good."

"In the future, I'll send Castor with a message when I think I can get away."

"You can't — then he will know."

"It will be in code."

She released a breath. "What will the code be?"

"How about, 'The *medicus* is out on an errand,' " he said.

She looked at him disbelievingly. "That's a *terrible* code. It's too obvious."

He grinned, embarrassed. "All right. You come up with one."

"Send Castor with some salve for Metrodona's back. When he delivers it unexpectedly, I'll know you will be free and heading for the woods."

"All right. But how will you get free of Metrodona?"

"I'll figure out a way."

He smiled. She placed her fingertips on a clay foot votive. "Is this for the stable boy? How is he recovering?"

On an impulse, he ran his finger lightly over hers, tracing slowly down and around the curve of her thumb. It made no sense that such an innocent touch could cause him to nearly vibrate with desire for her, but it seemed to have the same effect on her, judging by the way her breath hitched. They both stared at their hands in silence as he continued stroking her skin.

"I will . . . I will find a way to get out there today," he promised.

She shivered and pulled her hand away. "This afternoon, then," she said in a shaky whisper and rushed out of the room.

By the time Tag bound the hurt gladiator's leg and got him to his barrack room to rest, the morning training had ended. He stared at the sun over the trees, calculating how much time needed to pass before he could head out to the woods to see Lucia. Either way, it couldn't come soon enough.

"Healer! Pontius wants to see you," one of the men called, startling him. "He is in the weapons room."

Whatever it was the overseer wanted, Tag hoped it wasn't something that would take up the afternoon. He *needed* to see Lucia.

He entered the weapons chamber, momentarily blinded by the shift from the bright courtyard to the dark and dusty room. As his vision adjusted, shelves crowded with gladiator helmets came into view. When he blinked, he had the uneasy sense that all of the bronze heads — as one — had turned to look at him with silent menace.

"Who's there?" Pontius called from the corner.

"It's me, Tag."

"How is Brutus?" the overseer asked as he inspected the dings on an old shield.

"Severe tear of the major back thigh muscle."

Pontius growled irritably. "What is going on lately? Our injury rate is ridiculous. The latest rumor is that Spartacus himself has returned to the mountain and is punishing Pompeii."

"What?" Tag laughed.

"His ghost, anyway," Pontius said. "And that his fury at not being avenged is causing the mountain to shake."

Tag shook his head. "That makes no sense. Spartacus and his men died in the fields of Lucania, not here!"

Pontius waggled his eyebrows. "Yesssss, but they never found his body, so some of the men believe he came back to Vesuvius to die." He rolled his eyes. Every slave knew that Spartacus and his army of slaves — many of them from Pompeii and the Campanian region — had defeated at least two Roman legions from their Vesuvian stronghold. "Everybody's uneasy. Haven't you noticed all the overwhelming offerings to Hercules lately?" continued Pontius.

Tag had noticed — the niched shrine on the main barracks wall overflowed with flowers, fruits, small statuettes, coins, and other gifts to the muscular son of Zeus.

"The master has heard some of the talk," continued Pontius. "He wants me to shackle all of the gladiators at night so they don't get any ideas about running away and joining Spartacus's ghost."

Tag swallowed. "Is . . . is the master increasing the number of guards around the compound, then?" he asked. *Gods*.

"No, costs too much," Pontius said, picking up an angled Thracian sword. He cut his eyes at Tag. "Any particular reason that's a concern, boy?"

"No, no. Not at all."

"Because it never ends well when a slave tries to run away."

"I am aware."

"Ye might even say new fighters have a greater chance of winning their freedom in the arena than slaves have surviving a run," he continued, inspecting the tip of the sword with one eye. "Which is to say, barely any chance at all."

"I know," Tag said.

Pontius put the blade down and grinned at him. "Good." He slammed the trunk lid, clasped Tag by the shoulder, and ushered him out of the room. "Now, take me to Brutus and let's talk to him together about what he's gotta do to heal that bum leg."

CHAPTER TWENTY-FIVE

Lucia

(Five Days Before)

Lucia leaned against Tag's chest in the shade near their enclosure as he rhythmically stroked her arm. Normally, she found his touch soothing, but now she shifted once again.

"What's the matter, *deliciae meae?*" he asked sleepily. "You are as fidgety as a boxer before a fight."

"The wedding is so close, Tag," she said. "I can't marry that old man. I just can't!"

He stopped his stroking. "We should run," he whispered.

She pushed herself away. "Don't say that if you don't mean it, because I will do it, Tag."

His pupils looked huge. She had never seen him so serious. "I can't bear to lose you," he said. "I dream about running with you all the time."

"I do more than dream," she said quietly.

"What do you mean?"

"I have come up with a plan."

"Tell me," he said, leaning forward.

"I pack up a hoard of money and jewels and —"

"You have a hoard of money and jewels?"

"Well, maybe not a hoard. My mother put away some of her things for me, and in one of the compartments, I found a secret stash of coins and jewels. Anyway, you and I sneak out into the night and head to Nuceria. We don't travel on the main road, because people might recognize me and turn us in. So we travel in the woods *parallel* to the road."

"If you're worried people might recognize you, shouldn't we avoid Nuceria altogether?"

She understood his point — the gladiator schools from both cities were closely intertwined. She and her father often stayed with fellow lanistas in Nuceria and vice versa. "Nuceria is only our first stop. Once there, we purchase supplies and maybe even rent a donkey to travel on to Thurii."

He made a noise in his throat. "Thurii? Why?"

"The city is not very important to Rome, so it's mostly left alone. I don't think it would occur to my father to look for me there. And although I would miss the mountain, Thurii is on the sea, like Pompeii."

Tag swallowed, his eyes shining. "And then?"

"Well, we would use whatever money we have left to buy you medical supplies so you could set up shop as a healer. I am guessing they do not have a lot of options there."

"Possibly. But what if I can't make enough money right away? We could starve."

"No, see, *I* would let it be known in the wealthy side of town that I could teach girls in both Latin and Greek. Richer families always want to act like their Roman counterparts, and once they hear that the higher classes in Rome educate their girls, they'll see it as an opportunity for advancing their own households. More than likely, they would prefer a female tutor to the male tutor they hire for their boys."

Tag nodded, smiling. "That's good, yes. I could see this working."

He could see this working. A swell of joy filled her chest. She closed her eyes and took a deep breath. "I want to do this, Tag. With you."

"I do too," he breathed. "I've imagined running away before, but I couldn't envision a life that made the risk worth it. But when I'm with you, I feel like I can do it — that *we* can do it. As long as we are together."

She grinned. Her dark future had cracked open a little, revealing a small, tremulous light of hope.

"When?" he asked. "We need to act soon."

"Within the next several days, when my father is most distracted with preparations for our trip to Rome."

He nodded and kissed her again.

When the edge of the sun neared the tops of the pines, they knew it was time to return. They walked toward the broken wall holding hands. She noticed that he had begun to drag his feet. He stopped, scowling in the direction of the wall. "I hate this part," he murmured. He drew her into him.

"I don't hear Minos barking, which means Metrodona hasn't started calling for me yet," she said, snaking her arms around his waist. "We have a little more time."

"Did I tell you that you haunt my dreams?" he asked, kissing the top of her head.

"No. But I like the sound of that," she said, burrowing into him.

"Tell me what you dream about," he said. "I'll even interpret it for you."

She sighed, not wanting to tell him the dreams she had of her mother, of her desperate attempts to talk her out of killing herself. Nor did she want to reveal the dreams of the little sisters who looked like her, who begged for her help in hiding from her father. "Hide us, hide us!" they always cried. "He is coming for us!"

So she told him of her other nightmare. "In this dream, it's daytime, but I am looking for you. The woods and forests begin to shake and shudder, and I try to run, but there is nowhere to go, and I begin to shake with the ground too. Suddenly, there is a great sound like thunder coming from deep in the earth and the world explodes in a burst of flame and ash. Then there's nothing left."

She was a little surprised at how silly the dream sounded when put into words. The sense of terror and despair always left her gasping for breath when she awoke.

He was silent for a moment. "I was sort of hoping you'd say you dreamt about me all the time too," he said, laughing.

"Oh," she said, reddening. "It's just that —"

"I am teasing, Lucia. But you've been reading Strabo again, haven't you? About that black mountain in Phrygia?"

She nodded.

"You have to stop reading that. The earth does not spew fire in Pompeii," he reminded her. "We Etruscans were here *way* before the Romans crawled out of their mud huts by the Tiber, and there have never been any records, stories, or legends of anything like that happening here."

"I know," she said, sighing. "I know." Reluctantly, she disentangled herself from him. "I should go —"

"Wait," he said, reaching into a small, worn cloth bag tied to his rope belt. "Put your hand out," he commanded. "I have something for you."

She smiled and obeyed. He placed a small, round piece of terra-cotta in the middle of her palm.

Carved on the front was the serene face of a goddess, her hair piled high. The back was scored with etchings of wings. "It's beautiful."

"It is Turan, the Etruscan goddess of love," he said quietly. "Like your Venus. She is known for helping lovers. For keeping them safe."

She examined it curiously. "I thought it was Psyche at first, because of the wings," she said.

"She is also like Psyche, the soul," he whispered. "You hold my soul in your hands."

She closed her fingers around the little clay votive. "I love you, Tag," she whispered. And they lost themselves in each other again until they heard Metrodona call.

The next morning, in a shaded corner of the atrium, Lucia guiltily rolled up the Strabo scroll that Quintus had loaned her. Maybe Tag was right. Maybe she needed to stop reading about Strabo's "earth-born" fire.

She was leaving with Tag, so she shouldn't worry about Pompeii, right? Yet somehow she felt as if she were betraying her city if she didn't continue trying to figure out what it all meant. Others had clearly grown uneasy too. The city was emptying out.

Many part-time residents had returned early to Rome. Metrodona told her the marketplace was sparser than usual, as some farmers had started avoiding the city in case an earthquake hit. They felt safer out in the country.

Lucia again wondered what Pliny would have made of all these signs. But, she reminded herself sadly, she would never meet the man now. She hated that whenever she thought of Pliny, it was tinged with the shame of discovering what her best friend's husband really thought of her.

Maybe if she studied something else for a while, those feelings would dissipate. She would need to start reading the old Greek masters if she was going to tutor students in Thurii. Her mind drifted to the only philosophical topic that she and Tag had ever discussed — the nature of freedom. What was freedom, anyway? To Tag, it was simple — freedom meant not being owned by another man.

But what did it mean to her? Creating a life she wanted with Tag was a form of freedom, wasn't it? Choosing one's own husband would have been a kind of freedom, but had any woman in the history of the world ever enjoyed such independence? She'd heard women in Egypt could own property and make their own marriage decisions, but those were likely just tall tales from the mysterious east. Metrodona swore that some of the women in lower classes also arranged their own marriages. But the poor were enslaved in other ways too, weren't they? After all, they were bound to toil endlessly just to have enough food for the next day.

The rich seemed freest of all. They could choose where they wanted to live and how. But even they were tied to the need to eat, sleep, and clothe themselves. And if you had children, then you were tied to taking care of all their needs. So was anyone ever really free? Maybe only the dead achieved true freedom.

She was startled out of her thoughts when Cornelia was announced.

"Cornelia, what are you — gods, you're huge!" Lucia blurted out as her very pregnant friend waddled toward her.

"Thank you, darling, I hadn't noticed," Cornelia said dryly. "Since you won't come to me, you have forced me and my tremendous bulk to come to you."

Metrodona cleared her throat, reminding Lucia of her duties as hostess.

"Oh. Yes. Welcome, Cornelia. Please, come and sit. Metrodona, have the cook send us some watered wine," she instructed. "Make sure he uses the cool water from the well."

Cornelia sat heavily on a pillowed stone bench next to her. "Ah, thank you, that sounds lovely."

They stared at each other in silence for a long moment. Cornelia finally said, "I have missed you, Lucia. Why have you not given me a chance to apologize after that dreadful night?"

Gods, how could she explain how ashamed she'd felt? "Why should you apologize? You did nothing wrong."

Cornelia rubbed her belly. "I owe you an apology for tricking you about Pliny. Once I saw that's who you thought was coming, I should've explained. But I was afraid you wouldn't come if I told you it was Quintus. And I was right, wasn't I? You wouldn't have."

"Probably not," agreed Lucia.

"I wanted you to do *something* to get out of marrying Vitulus and moving to Rome," Cornelia said. "And trying for Quintus just seemed too perfect. After all, the gods put him in your path — in your own home — for a reason, didn't they?"

Lucia looked down at her hands, unable to admit to Cornelia that she *was* doing something about her horrible impending marriage. She was going to run away with Tag. "Why did you never tell me Antyllus hates me so much?" she asked instead.

Cornelia released a breath. "He doesn't hate *you*, Lucia. He just doesn't like what your father does."

"Has he always felt that way?"

She nodded, looking away.

"Is he . . ." Lucia paused, trying to figure out how to delicately ask the next question. "He is not that difficult with *you*, is he?"

Cornelia shook her head, staring at the clear water of the *impluvium*. "I wish you could see the Antyllus that I know."

"Has he ever forbidden you from seeing me?" Lucia asked.

Cornelia laughed. "He tried. Once. He didn't try again."

Lucia's throat tightened. Cornelia had risked her beloved husband's disapproval to stay friends with her, even though he considered her way below their social station. Until that moment, she had not contemplated what would happen to their friendship if she ran away with a slave, but it came pounding home now. She would never see Cornelia again. She would never hold her friend's baby. Her eyes filled.

"What?" Cornelia asked, leaning forward. "Why are you crying?"

"Because you are such a good friend. And . . . and when I go away, I will miss you."

"Well, you will just have to make sure your husband allows you to visit often. Your father lives here, which should help, right?"

Lucia nodded and smiled through her tears.

"But I haven't given up on Quintus yet. Has he shown more interest?"

She shrugged noncommittally. It wouldn't matter if he had.

Cornelia shook her head in frustration. By the time the wine arrived, they had moved on to discussions about her birthing room. After a while, Lucia asked the question that had been haunting her ever since she learned the truth about her mother. "Cornelia, have you thought about what will happen if you have a girl?"

Cornelia put down her cup. "The midwife says I'm carrying a boy. I urinated on bags of wheat and barley and only the barley sprouted, so definitely a boy."

"But if the midwife is wrong . . ."

"If the midwife is wrong, then I will enjoy having a little girl."

"But what will Antyllus do?"

She laughed. "Well, he will be impatient to try again for a son, that's what!"

"No, I mean . . . do you think Antyllus would insist that you expose the child if it was a girl?"

Cornelia's eyes widened and she made the sign of protection against evil. "We've never discussed it, but no! Gods, he would never force me to do such a horrible thing! Why are you asking?"

Lucia considered telling her what she had learned about her mother, but then realized that the story would only make Cornelia more anxious. At this stage in her pregnancy, it would be cruel to add to her fears and worries. So Lucia smiled and dismissed the topic with a wave of her hand. "Of course he wouldn't. Antyllus is a good man, despite his disdain for me."

Cornelia slapped at her playfully. "Stop it! Now," she said, lowering her voice, "tell me about you. Are you still seeing your amazing kisser?"

Lucia prayed a blush wouldn't creep up her neck. She should have been more worried about her smile.

"And you still won't tell me who he is?"

She shook her head.

Cornelia huffed. "You promised me you would stop seeing him." She gave Lucia a sly look. "But then again, if I had to marry a man like Vitulus, I'd probably try to find a young, handsome, amazing kisser for myself too."

Lucia grinned at her friend and squeezed her hand.

"Only, *I'd* tell my best friend who it was," Cornelia added with an arched eyebrow. "Unlike some people I know."

CHAPTER TWENTY-SIX

TAG

Tag looked up from crushing thyme root as Castor ran back into the medical room. "Did you give the salve to Lady Lucia?"

"No. But I saw Metrodona, so I gave it to her."

Tag groaned and dropped the pestle. "You're not supposed to give the medicine to Metrodona. You're only supposed to give it to *Lucia*."

Castor screwed up his face at him. "I don't know why you are mad. It's Metrodona who needs the medicine, not Lady Lucia!"

Tag rubbed his forehead. Was that why Lucia hadn't come to the woods when he'd sent the salve the previous day? The household was in a flurry of preparation for her wedding, and they were supposed to run *the next day*. Not seeing her had fed the flames of his fear — what if she changed her mind? What if she refused to go through with it? His muscles clenched at the idea of losing her and the future they'd imagined for themselves.

"Anyway, Metrodona told me to take it back," Castor continued. "She says she doesn't want to see any more salve from me." He pulled the small clay container from his tunic belt and placed it on the worktable.

"Castor," Tag said through gritted teeth, "pick that salve back up, and this time deliver it directly to Lucia."

"I can't," he said. "She is not at the house."

"Did her nurse say where she was?"

"Metrodona said she and *Dominus* and the other man went somewhere."

"What other man?"

"The one you fight with."

Quintus. She was on an outing with her father and *Quintus*? He hadn't even realized the patrician had returned from Herculaneum. Tag picked up the pestle again, knocked it against the stone side to clear it, and resumed pressing and crushing the stubborn plant with renewed force. Lucia and her father were probably just running an errand together, and Quintus joined them.

The best thing to do was to stay focused on making sure he had everything he needed to practice as a healer in Thurii. He began mentally riffling through the small bag of medical supplies he'd packed — bandages, herbs for purging and cleansing, leeches, honey. . . . The pack was bulging as it was — he might have to leave the honey. He would need room too for the new set of surgical tools Quintus had given him. His father believed that the kit belonged to the school. . . . Tag pictured Damocles's reaction upon learning that he had run away — *and* taken the "master's" surgical kit with him.

A deep, hot bolt of shame contracted his gut. How was it that he hadn't even *thought* about what would happen to his father when he ran away? He swallowed a groan, imagining what Titurius would do to his *apa* when he discovered that Tag had disappeared with his daughter. Damocles would not survive

Titurius's rage. He could not subject his father to that. He couldn't!

The pestle clattered onto the table and Tag put his head in his hands. Maybe they could take his *apa* with them . . . but he knew his father would never agree to go. And they couldn't very well drag him away. They'd get caught immediately.

Yet *not* running away and never seeing Lucia again . . . no. He couldn't do that either. Tag's chest tightened as if there was a great vise squeezing his lungs. Why had the gods trapped him in this way?

He stood so abruptly, his stool slid with a bang against a wooden chest of supplies. Castor jumped.

"Go find my father and help him with whatever he is doing, Castor," Tag ordered.

"No, I am tired of being sent awa —"

"Go. NOW. Do you hear me, boy?" he roared.

Castor stared up at him, his face reddening, but he obeyed.

Tag needed to spar with someone. And he needed to do it now.

"Let's go!" Pontius shouted outside the pit. "Next pair, up now!"

Sigdag sauntered onto the sand as a heavily armored *hoploma-chus*, or Samnite fighter, wearing a plumed helmet. As the school's champion, he exuded a confidence that bordered on arrogance. One of the newer fighters tentatively approached as *murmillo*.

"Meanwhile, Tag, you fight as *thraex*," Pontius said. "Nicodemus, challenge him as *hoplomachus* — get prepared."

Tag frowned. He'd only been paired with Quintus, which, he

realized now, meant he hadn't gotten any practice adapting to others' fighting styles. But he needed this.

Once outfitted with metal greaves, helmet, and a small rectangular shield, Tag walked out to the edges of the pit to watch Sigdag fight. The house champion forced his opponent to his knees three times before the overseer called the fight.

"Wake up, Tag!" Pontius yelled. "You two are next."

Tag slipped on his helmet, thankful that the *thraex* one had only a small grille covering his mouth, leaving his vision clear. Nicodemus, however, had to contend with the fish-eye holes and closed-off mouth of the *hoplomachus* helm.

Nicodemus was about the same size as Quintus, Tag realized. And when his face disappeared under the metal, it was as if he was squaring off against the annoying patrician. Quintus, whose wealth and status allowed him to only "play" at being a gladiator. Quintus, who could destroy Lucia in the morning and then laugh about it over wine that evening. Quintus, who stood for every arrogant, insufferable Roman who'd stolen his family's wealth and honor. Tag's breath quickened as a surge of hatred flooded his limbs.

As Pontius approached with the referee stick, Tag leaned into his left front leg and held the angled Thracian sword up in the ready position, his fingers tightening on the grip of his shield. A desire to kill — no, *annihilate* — pounded in his blood, sharpening his vision and hearing. It took an age for the referee to lift the stick, but when he did, Tag lunged with a roar.

He forced his opponent onto his back foot, even as the man thrust forward with his sword. Tag easily punched the weapon away with his shield. With all his might, he lunged at the man, aiming a sidearm slash to exposed flesh. Nicodemus blocked that attack and several more in quick succession.

Tag's opponent backed away and the two men circled each other. Tag could hear the man's labored breathing and smiled with malice, remembering the misery of the closed-off helmet. He pictured Quintus's weaselly face suffering.

Tag suddenly feinted left and his opponent thrust his shield out, exposing his neck. Tag aimed for the opening. Nicodemus barely got his shield up in time to stop the blow, which would have killed him if they'd been fighting with real swords. Still, the force of Tag's attack sent him sprawling. Tag threw one knee on his chest and heard a distinct crack. The man roared in pain, but Tag pressed the wooden sword hard over his throat. Ignoring the touch of Pontius's cane on his shoulder, he growled, "Give me an excuse, Quintus. I know what bones to break in your neck so you'll never walk again. . . ."

"I'm not Quintus!" Nicodemus grunted. "Damned lunatic!"

At the same time, Pontius hit Tag again and again with the cane. "Enough!" he roared. "When the cane touches ye, ye *back off*, got it?"

Tag blinked, and it was as if he had suddenly emerged from the bottom of the sea. He became aware of Nicodemus's cursing, the hoots of the watching fighters, and the trainer's reddened face yelling at him. He jumped back.

"I think my wrist is broken," Nicodemus complained, holding it up, and indeed, it was bent at an awkward angle. "I fell on it and he jumped on me," he hissed as someone removed his helmet.

Tag took off his own helmet. "I . . . I am sorry —"

"Never apologize," barked Pontius.

The healer in Tag took over. "Get me a splint from the medical room," he called to one of the slaves. "And some strong bandages."

"No," Nicodemus cried. "I don't want you helping me. You'll probably break the other wrist."

"Don't be a baby," Pontius said. "Tag, why don't you escort him —"

"Call the older healer to attend to him," someone interrupted them from behind. "I want to fight this boy."

Both Pontius and Tag turned to look up into the face of the straggly-haired German, Sigdag. "You want to fight *me?*" Tag asked.

Pontius looked from the German to Tag and back again, then grinned. "Fine. But don't kill him," he said to the *primus palus.* "We need him as a healer." He turned to one of the attendant slaves. "Take Nicodemus to Damocles," he commanded.

"Why do you want to fight me?" Tag asked Sigdag.

He shrugged. "Skill can be taught. The body can be trained. But pure rage and hatred — that is either in a man or it's not. It's not something I see often in this *ludus.* But I see it in you."

Tag didn't know if he should be insulted or proud. Worse, he worried that all of his rage had been spent on Nicodemus. He felt like a deflated wineskin.

As if he could read his mind, Sigdag showed brown teeth in an ugly smile. "Just because you think it has leaked away doesn't mean you can't call it back." He moved in close to Tag. "That is what a champion does — learns how to focus his hatred on the face of his opponent."

Tag nodded. The German signaled to a slave to bring his shield. He would fight — as he had previously — as the heavily armed *hoplomachus*, which was convenient since Tag was outfitted as a *thraex*.

Tag looked Sigdag up and down. The German had to have at least three inches and fifty pounds on him. Tag's only saving grace was going to be his lightness and speed. "So who do you hate when you are fighting?" Tag asked.

"You should be focusing on who *you* hate right now, boy, but I will tell you," Sigdag said. He closed his eyes for a second. "I hate the Roman who didn't kill me at the battle outside my village. I *hate* that he robbed me of the honor of a warrior's death. I hate the Roman doctor who stitched me up and kept me alive. The slave trader who put me in chains, and Lucius Titurius for working me like an ox in the field. But you know who I hate the most?" he growled. "I hate my gods, for being weaker than the Roman gods. For dishonoring my village and my people and my family by letting us lose to these Roman wolves. For doing nothing to stop the Romans from raping and killing my wife and murdering my infant son. And the Romans themselves for setting my village on fire and making me watch. Should I keep going, boy? Because I've got plenty more. But I think you get the idea. When that cane is lifted between us, I will no longer see you, but every Roman and weakling god who has ever failed me."

But I am not Roman, Tag wanted to say. *I am Etruscan, of an ancient line of priests and healers.* He knew it would make no difference to the big man. In a flash, he remembered how his mother often complained that gladiatorial combat started with the Etruscans as a holy rite, and the Romans defiled it by turning it into entertainment.

"Now," Sigdag said. "I will give you a minute to call up your own hate."

Tag swallowed. Could he find his fury over Quintus again? It didn't take much to try. All he had to do was imagine him using Lucia and laughing about it later. Imagine himself never seeing Lucia again. Imagine having to spend the rest of his life being owned by a man like Titurius and sneered at by a spoiled worm like Quintus.

Even so, terror outweighed anger. Sigdag was huge and strong. Why had he singled Tag out? He tried to slow down his breath by blowing through his cheeks. Fear, he told himself, could be just as motivating as anger, as long as he didn't let it overwhelm him.

The German covered his face in his *hoplomachus* helmet, and Tag bent his knees in preparation. Perhaps he could outlast him or aggravate him into making a mistake. That was all he had, so it would have to do.

The cane between them went up, and they circled each other. The German feinted to one side and Tag threw up his shield. Sigdag swung overhead, clanging him on his helmet at the same time that he put his leg behind Tag's heel. The next thing Tag knew, he was staring up at the sky. Sand irritated his ears, which meant his helmet had flown off.

"Again. Up," commanded Sigdag.

Tag shook himself off, replaced his helmet, and readied for another round. This time when the cane lifted, he threw himself into an attack, figuring Sigdag was used to rattled assailants always on the defensive. The big man blocked his strike, and Tag danced out of the way of his sword thrust. Tag went at him again and again, always barely escaping the sword. Then he heard a strange, hollow sound coming from the German's helmet. It took him a moment to realize it was laughter.

Sigdag was laughing at him? A blinding rage surged up his

center and he came in close again, batting away the man's weapon with his shield and reaching underneath his arm with his sword.

He felt it — the give of wood on flesh. Yes! He'd gotten Sigdag in the side. Not a hard blow, but enough to surprise him. Tag threw his weight into a shield strike —

But the next thing he knew, he was staring at the sky again. How had a man as big as Sigdag moved so quickly?

"Again," the German said.

Three more times they sparred, and three more times Tag found himself flat on the sand. "Ready to give up, little healer boy?" Sigdag taunted.

"Never."

"Good."

On the sixth round, Tag aimed for the midsection after feinting high, then slammed his curved sword into the German's wrist. The man grunted and released his spear. Then Tag attacked hard, slicing up backhanded from the wrist for the neck — but Sigdag blocked him with such force, he went flying. Yet he didn't fall. He scrabbled for balance, found it, and crouched low, noticing that Sigdag had his spear again.

He must have irritated the German, because the champion came at him with a force he'd clearly been holding back. *Block. Block. Block.* That was all he could do. Sigdag's overhead attack was so forceful, Tag knew his shield wouldn't take the weight, so he bent with it, balling himself into the sand and rolling over his shoulder to get away. The German hadn't expected the loss of resistance and staggered forward. In the same moment, Tag sprang up and slammed his wooden sword into the back of the German's knees. At least, he intended it to be a slam — it was more of a chip. But it was enough to send Sigdag down into the dirt.

Now behind him, Tag drew back, readying for a winning blow. But somehow, the German whipped around and used his shield to slam him in the stomach, throwing Tag into the air over him. This time he did not see sky but got a mouthful of sand instead. His forehead clanged against the metal of his helmet, and he felt blood trickle into his left eye. The German pressed his dagger into the back of his neck, and Tag put his hand up in defeat.

Gradually, awareness of sound came back to him, and he heard the men chanting, "Mercy, mercy, mercy," and laughing.

Sigdag removed the dagger and grunted at him. Tag turned over. He spit out sand and sat up. The German held out his hand and Tag took it. Sigdag lifted him up with little effort and leaned toward his ear. "Finally, you came in low, boy."

Tag looked up at him, confused.

"Many make this mistake. They come at me high because I am big. But that means they are not paying attention to what I am *doing*. If your opponent goes high — which I tend to do — you must aim low. Watch your enemy more carefully."

"I . . . I wasn't even aware of whether you were going high or low. I was too scared," Tag admitted.

The German laughed and pointed to his head. "That is part of the game too. But you must pay attention — where is your opponent lunging? Once you understand his preference, you can attack the weak spot."

As Pontius approached, Sigdag called, "I tell you I see something in him."

"Maybe so," Pontius said. "But obviously, he needs a lot more training. And bulk."

Tag should have been insulted, but he wasn't. It had been ugly and possibly embarrassing, but he had gotten a couple of jabs in. That was more than he thought he could have managed.

Even so, the relief and excitement of holding his own with the German didn't last long. With one long release of breath, the bitter reality of his situation flooded back in. He was going to lose Lucia because he couldn't bring himself to condemn his father to a violent death. And even if he got the training he needed, even if he managed to find a way to convince the master to let him fight in the arena, even if he survived long enough to be freed, he would still never see Lucia again.

"You have the speed, boy," Sigdag said, using his massive bear paw to give Tag a small shove. "You could turn into something."

To no end, he thought, and walked away.

CHAPTER TWENTY-SEVEN

～～

Lucia

(Two Days Before)

The air was thick with the musk of frightened animals as they entered the colonnaded courtyard of the Temple of Venus Pompeia. Portable wooden pens overflowed with bleating lambs, snuffling pigs, and pecking chickens. Vendors shouted promises that their animals were "perfect, unblemished, and fit for the gods." Lucia had never seen so many creatures at the temple on a non-festival day. She thought the strange rumblings of the earth must be driving those who remained in Pompeii to increase their attempts to appease the gods.

As they neared the temple itself, Lucia tried to remember a time when it wasn't under some sort of construction or renovation. Empty scaffolding, broken ladders, and unhung friezes leaned against the temple's outer walls. Perhaps the goddess was angry at the slow pace of her temple's reconstruction.

On the walk through town, Lucia's father had not answered her questions about the reasons for this trip to the temple. He only smiled at her and exchanged a look with Quintus. Quintus had insisted a slave hold an *umbraculum* over her to protect her from the sun. She couldn't imagine why it mattered to him, but she went along without complaint. Once inside the courtyard, her father joined the long line of supplicants waiting to purchase sacrificial animals.

"Come," Quintus said to her. "Let us walk among the goddess's gardens while we wait for your father."

He took her elbow, and Lucia felt a deepening sense of dread. Something was going on. She couldn't remember when, if ever, her father had made a special sacrifice to Venus Pompeiana. And why were they doing it now instead of planning their trip to Rome? Had he begun to worry about the signs from the earth too? Yet he hadn't seemed concerned — he'd been relaxed and smiling on the walk over.

Lucia and Quintus threaded their way around the side of the courtyard toward the goddess's garden. Sacred myrtle bushes abounded. Tag had told her that crushed myrtle berries were excellent for use as a wash for wounds. She swallowed a sigh. Everything made her think of Tag. She was so frustrated about not being able to see him that she'd left a secret message on his shrine to Asclepius, telling him they needed to meet that very night to make their final plans.

Lucia noticed that only a handful of other worshippers shared the garden with them, giving them plenty of privacy. Her heart beat faster as she realized the implications.

"Let us sit under this arbor," Quintus said, leading her to a small alcove. He sat. She remained standing. So he took her hand and pulled her toward him on the bench.

"No," she murmured. "I cannot."

"You will have to get over this adorable shyness of yours when we are married," he said.

She froze. "Wha — what?"

He grinned up at her. "Yes, that's what your father and I have been discussing all morning. I went to Herculaneum to convince my father to allow it. He has agreed, and that is why we are here to sacrifice to the goddess of love and fertility."

The shock of his words was so great, she almost grew dizzy. "I . . . I don't understand."

"I have convinced your father to break your arrangement with Vitulus and betroth you to me instead."

"But the wedding is only days away. How did you manage —"

He pulled her down next to him and shifted to face her. He was beaming. "Convincing my father was hardest of all, but he has agreed, mainly because he'd like to see me marry and feared I never would. Your father has sent a messenger to Vitulus this very morning to cancel the betrothal. Aren't you happy?"

"But . . . I am the daughter of a lanista," she said, dumbfounded. "Won't there be a scandal?" After the disaster with Antyllus, she understood more keenly how nobles viewed her father's livelihood.

"Yes, well, apparently, your status is less horrifying to my father than my drinking, gambling, and refusal to marry. Besides, I think he recognizes the business potential as Vespasian's great amphitheater nears completion. And as long as he is not personally associated with the school, he does not care if I invest in it." He searched her face. "Also, I plan on spending most of the year in Herculaneum, to be sure that you can stay close to your friend, Cornelia."

Lucia stared at him, wide-eyed.

"Are you not pleased?"

She swallowed and nodded. It didn't matter what Quintus and her father planned, she reminded herself. She and Tag were running away. In the meantime, she must play the part of the rescued bride and act happy.

The smile she put on seemed so genuine, only Tag and Cornelia could have seen through it.

He clapped, delighted. "See, this will work out perfectly. Your father has agreed to all my demands."

"Demands?"

"You do not need to worry about those. All you need to know is that everyone is pleased, especially your father, who will get the new infusion of coin for which he has been so desperate."

Lucia continued smiling, repeating to herself, *It doesn't matter. None of his plans matter — Tag and I are running away.*

"Your feelings for me are a great balm to my heart," he continued. "I have no doubt that I will come to love you, especially when you bear me sons —"

She blinked several times. He didn't love her? Then why was he pushing for the marriage?

He took one of her hands in both of his. "You must agree that this is a much more suitable arrangement than any one your father planned for you or my father planned for me."

Of course, he was right. Not that it mattered anymore. But she smiled up at him as if it did.

Quintus chuckled and embraced her. "You are a sweet one," he murmured.

The *umbraculum*-carrying slave interrupted them. "Many pardons," he said. "But the master's turn for the sacrifice is near."

As they passed out of the maze of gardens, Lucia touched the foot of the small statue of Eros marking the exit, asking the son of Venus to protect her and Tag when they ran.

Her father grinned at them when they joined him. "Well? My besotted daughter, are you happy?" he asked.

"I am speechless," she replied, continuing to smile in what felt to her a grotesque mask of exaggeration.

"She was quite overcome when I announced the arrangement," Quintus said.

"Well, I do believe the curse is finally lifted," her father said, beaming.

Curse? What curse?

"The gods are at last smiling down upon us," he continued. "Now everyone has reason to celebrate. You, my daughter, will be with the man you love, and we will finally have the means to build up the school and earn the respect we deserve."

Lucia stared at her father. He assumed she "loved" Quintus? Because Quintus told him that was the case? Why had it not occurred to her father to ask *her* how she felt?

She already knew the answer — because anything the rich patrician said was more valuable to him than anything she might say, think, or feel. Sighing, she reminded herself to play along.

Father's attendants held both a lamb and a rooster. "The lamb is my sacrifice," Quintus whisper-bragged into her ear. Of course it was. It was more expensive.

The priest, head covered by his toga, said the prayers while slaves deftly handled the lamb on the altar. Within moments, the beast was limp and bled out, the first blood's catch held aloft in a gleaming bronze bowl. The air was thick with the smell of blood, wool, and the animal's emptied bowels.

A priest quickly cleaned the altar in preparation for the rooster. A young slave took the bird and laid it on the altar. A second slave stretched its neck over a special board with a curved bronze hand to hold its head in place. The priest's sacred ax came down on the bird's neck with a thwack —

At that very moment, the earth rumbled and rolled beneath them.

People screamed. The earth stopped vibrating almost immediately, leaving the young priest holding the sacrificed bird by the feet as blood trickled on his tunic. The small chicken head lay on the altar.

But the bird's wings continued flapping fiercely and angrily, long after it should have stopped moving. The startled young priest let go of the rooster, which flew up into the air, then landed with a thud near the altar bearing its own mangled half head. It began running straight toward the steps of the goddess's temple. Everyone gasped.

"It was not a killing blow," one priest hissed to the other. "The goddess has not accepted the sacrifice."

Murmurs and cries of fear roiled throughout the courtyard. *The goddess is angry. . . . She will hurl her temple upon us. . . . What do we do?* Some people began to run; others called out for family members. Throughout it all, Lucius Titurius stood frozen.

Lucia looked at her father. His face was ashen and his eyes wide. "Father?" she asked, touching his shoulder.

"The curse . . . Her shade has convinced the goddess to reject my sacrifice," he mumbled. "She has made the gods truly turn against me."

What curse is he talking about? And whose shade? "No, no, Father, it is fine. The priest will make it all right."

The bird's flapping caught her attention. It still lived! How was that possible? The strangeness of it chilled her to the bone.

Quintus made the sign against evil, and most of the others watching the drama followed suit.

"Father?"

She followed his gaze. Two priests and an elderly priestess talked and gesticulated in a panic while watching the bird flap against the stairs of the temple. Finally, the young priest picked up the bird and handed it to the priestess. She bustled away with the still-struggling body under her arm.

The elder priest called those who remained in the courtyard to him, his arms stretched out wide. The crowd quieted.

"He who provided the sacrifice that has angered the goddess must step forward."

Her father advanced on the priest. Quintus moved to stand beside Lucia. For a wild moment, she imagined that it was Tag coming to comfort her, and she fought the impulse to curl into him.

"The goddess has spoken!" the priest announced in a deep, sonorous tone. "She has rejected the last sacrifice. Lucius Titurius must spend the night at the temple fasting and purifying himself in appeasement. Before dawn, he will offer another sacrifice to see if the goddess accepts his penance."

He lowered his arms. The crowd began to disperse, murmuring and whispering to one another about portents, staring at Lucius Titurius with scowls of fear. Despite Lucia's own alarm and confusion, she wanted to run to her father and protect him from their judgment. He stood, head bowed, listening as the priest lectured him. He looked so small and, suddenly, so *old*.

Quintus pulled her away. "He is with the priests now," he said. "They will purify him and appease the goddess. There is nothing more we can do."

"But — I'm frightened —"

"There is no reason to fear," Quintus interrupted. "The omen affects your father, not us. The lamb was accepted. Our marriage will still go on."

Lucia groaned silently. *Gods, how has it come to this?* But maybe it *was* a sign. Maybe the gods were removing her father from the house for the night so that they could escape once and for all.

CHAPTER TWENTY-EIGHT

TAG

After lancing a boil and sewing up a fighter's collarbone gash, Tag cleaned his instruments, put them neatly away in his surgical case, and slammed it shut. The sound made Castor jump. The little boy had been squatting on the stone floor of the medical room, practicing writing small words in Greek.

"Maybe you should fight again today," the little boy said.

"I wish I could," Tag murmured. He could have used the release, but he had to cover for his father instead. Damocles had had a very bad day, jabbering anxiously about when Tag's mother might return from the market. Tag finally made him take poppy wine so he would sleep.

Rumors had roiled throughout the compound all day — that Lucius Titurius had angered the gods and was not returning to the house lest they smite it. That the priests were keeping him in the temple against his will. That Lucia and Quintus had just barely gotten away before the priests grabbed them too. It was mostly nonsense, Tag knew, but he wanted to hear about it from Lucia herself.

More important, he needed to talk to her about the bind he was in — how the very idea of running away and abandoning his father to the master made him feel like a murderer.

Quintus Rutilius entered the medical room. Tag heaved a silent groan. "Are you injured?" he forced himself to ask. "Or fallen ill?"

The patrician grinned at Tag. "No. I am, in fact, in the best of health and in the best of moods."

"Ah. Good. Well, if you would excuse —"

"Don't you want to know why?"

"Yes! Tell us why," Castor said, jumping up, face alight.

Quintus blinked at him, then turned to Tag. "Why does this little rag boy think he can speak to me without being spoken to?"

Tag opened his mouth to explain, but Castor jumped in. "I am Castor, and I will grow up to be both a *medicus* and a gladiator!"

Quintus raised his eyebrows at Tag. "He is always with you. Is this your *son*?"

"No," Tag said. "But he is a bright boy, so I am teaching him to be my assistant."

Castor beamed.

"Interesting. Tell him to go, please. I do not like his filthy presence here."

The little boy's face crumpled. Tag gritted his teeth and contemplated telling him to stay, but he didn't want the boy punished for his own obstinacy. So he cupped Castor's shoulder and whispered, "Go check on Xrixus's boil. Take some bandages with you in case he needs them."

"By myself?"

"Yes. Don't remove his bandage without me, but he may need some more strips to put over it. Then check on my fathe —" He caught himself. "Then go into the pantry and count out twenty-five mustard seeds and bring them back. But you must count them three times and get the same number every time. Understand?"

Castor nodded, grabbed a handful of linen strips, and left the room with his head down. Out of the corner of his eye, Tag saw Quintus sniffing small containers of honey-based salves and holding up the little blue glass containers of tinctures. Gods, he wanted to pummel the man for his patrician arrogance. When Quintus reached for a bag of herbs, Tag said quickly, "I wouldn't if I were you."

Quintus stopped and looked at him. "Why?"

"One touch and your bowels will turn to liquid for a week."

Quintus backed away, alarmed. Tag swallowed a smile at how easily the patrician bought his lie. When he made no further move, Tag prompted him, "I am busy, so unless you need something . . ."

Quintus reached for small amphorae covered in wax. "What's in here?"

"Leave it," Tag said. "It's a mix of crocodile and lion fat. We need it for some of our salves. It's very expensive."

Quintus wrinkled his nose. Watching him touch his things as if he owned them — as if he owned *him* — made all of Tag's muscles clench. He forced himself to uncurl his fingers from fists.

"So you have heard that the lovely Lucia and I are betrothed, have you not?"

There was a moment when the words that came out of Quintus's mouth made absolutely no sense. They sounded so foreign, so strange, Tag simply could not understand them. But when they coalesced into meaning, the room tipped slightly and a buzzing filled his head.

"Wh — what?"

Quintus, as always, was watching him very carefully. "Lucia and I are officially betrothed. That's why we went to the Temple of Venus. We will be married soon. Aren't you going to congratulate me?"

Tag's stomach roiled. He was joking. He had to be. "But she is betrothed to —"

"It turns out my future father-in-law was beginning to question the wisdom of tying his little girl to that bitter old man. And we've worked out a very advantageous deal. So he is breaking the betrothal to Vitulus and handing her to me."

"And *Domina*?" He was surprised to hear his voice sounded so normal.

"Oh, she is thrilled, of course. Overcome. Do you know that sweet, shy girl has fallen desperately in love with me? It's quite charming. Her sweet kisses have totally seduced me."

There was a thick paste clogging his throat. He forced himself to swallow and to breathe. Every action seemed to require conscious thought.

Quintus crossed his arms and smiled at him. "I know your secret, boy — I know you fancy yourself in love with her. I have seen your face change when you watch her."

Gods. He knows? "No, I am not . . . She is *Domina* —"

"Oh, it is all right. I understand. Probably most of the brutes here think that they are in love with her too. It is quite common for slaves to moon over their masters. In fact, I'm gambling on that."

Tag put a hand down on his wooden worktable so that he wouldn't sway. So Quintus didn't actually know, but had just guessed at how he felt about Lucia. He needed to think. To be alone. To talk to her. To make some sense of all this.

"Ah, your little shrine to Asclepius," Quintus said, drifting over to it. "I can see you honor him regularly." He picked up the head votive. "A whole *head*? Who got their face clobbered recently?"

Tag breathed shallowly. "Put that down, please."

Quintus rolled the head from hand to hand. Tag wanted to lift him by his finely woven green tunic and throw him out of the room. The patrician raised his eyebrows, smiling. Everything was a game to him.

"You do not want to anger the god of healing," Tag finally managed. "To . . . to have him turn his back on you calls the Fates to send you suffering of the highest order."

Quintus gingerly put the votive piece down. "What is this?" he asked, pointing to a strangely shaped piece of clay. "It looks like a wing. What, are you working on chickens now?" He laughed. "If so, your master could've used your help today."

Tag swallowed again. The wing hadn't been there that morning when he performed the rites. "Mocking gifts to the god is also an offense," he said. "I must ask you to leave so that I can purify the shrine from your dishonor."

"You are much too serious, Tag. Has anyone ever told you that?"

He did not answer, but only stared coldly at the patrician. Quintus stepped away from the shrine, throwing his arms up in mock supplication. "Fine. Well, since I have some extra time now, I believe I will go to the baths. Would you like to join me?"

Tag looked at him with irritated disbelief.

"Ah, well," he said. "There will be plenty of time for that later."

When he was sure the patrician was gone, Tag rushed to the shrine, looking for the oddly shaped votive Quintus had laughed at. His heart raced when he spied it. It did look like a wing. He picked it up and turned it over in his hands. Small, carved Greek letters caught his eye. His heart leapt to his throat when he decoded the tiny message.

Need to see you. After prima vigilia noctis. L.

He closed his fingers around the wing, surprised Lucia wanted to meet so late in the night. Quickly, he calculated how long until then. Seven hours. He had to wait seven hours to see her again. The noise in his head turned into a buzzing in his whole body. Pontius had canceled training because of Titurius's absence, yet Tag *needed* to do something physical or he would explode.

He decided to run in the woods, so he changed into the extra-thick sandals he'd scrounged up and stripped to his loincloth. He was almost out of the gate when he heard someone drawl, "Where are you headed without your tunic, young Apollo? Have you decided to join me in the baths after all?"

Gods, he hated how Quintus talked to him. How he seemed to be mocking him all the time. He was a rich patrician. Why did he have to mock a *slave*?

"I am running up Vesuvius," he said.

Quintus raised his eyebrows. "Perhaps I should join you —"

"You despise running."

"Yes, I do. But I might reconsider."

"But I am also going to collect spiderwebs for wound dressings, and that is sticky, boring work." Tag tightened his fist around the clay wing. The buzzing in his muscles was turning into a roar. He cleared his throat. "So, if there is nothing else . . ."

Quintus hesitated, then shrugged his assent. Tag turned and began trotting out of the gate. He could feel Quintus's gaze on his back like a weight. But he had to act natural. Not like he wanted to scream until all the tendons in his neck snapped. Not like he wanted to pull a tree up at its base and throw it over the top of the mountain. And definitely not like a slave in love with the man's future wife.

Once out in the woods, he began to sprint. He pushed himself until his lungs burned, until his whole body felt as if it would break apart. Without even realizing it, he veered off his usual path and found himself crashing through the underbrush toward the Mephistis altar. Fire crisped his lungs and shot daggers through his legs. But he could not stop, or else the thoughts that hammered through his mind would overwhelm him: *I've lost her. It's over. I'm trapped forever.*

He drove himself forward until he could see the broken columns. Then he collapsed to his knees, wheezing, near the crumbling altar and reburied curse tablet. His lungs heaved as he curled over himself, holding his middle as if someone had slammed him in the stomach with a shield. Finally, his gasps for air tore through the tightness in his throat, and he wept with frustration at the foot of the altar of the forgotten goddess.

CHAPTER TWENTY-NINE

⚊⚊⚊

Lucia

Metrodona was snoring well and hard when Lucia swiped the small oil lamp and snuck out into the night. It was risky going to see Tag like this, she knew, but they could not wait any longer to act. Besides, with her father spending the night in the temple, the watch slaves were likely to be more relaxed than usual. Tonight, in fact, was the best night to run. She hoped he was ready. Silently, she changed into one of her graying *tunica*s and grabbed her hoard of goods.

As she stepped over Metrodona, she said a prayer of well-being for her elderly nurse.

Minos was so excited by this late-night surprise, she couldn't get him to stop whining with excitement as she unchained him. He would serve as good protection when they ran.

To her great relief, she spied Tag standing outside their enclosure, staring up at the stars. Her heart soared. "Tag," she called. "I'm so glad you're here. I was worried you couldn't come."

She raced toward him, put the small terra-cotta lamp and her treasure on a stone, and threw her arms around his neck while Minos bounced around them. She expected him to embrace her, to sink his face into her neck and swing her around as he usually did, but he didn't move. "Tag? Is everything all right?"

His coldness was like icy needles pricking her skin. She wrapped her arms around herself.

"I understand you've been betrothed to Quintus," he said.

She waved her hand as if dismissing Quintus and everything else that had taken place earlier that day. "It just means that we must run away *this very night*. Do you have your things ready?"

He made a strange sound in his throat. "Lucia. We can't. We need to stop."

She lost her breath. "I don't understand."

"Lucia, we've been fooling ourselves. You're going to get married and not even remember me in a few months. This is nothing but torture for me." His voice sounded as raw as if he had swallowed jagged pieces of glass.

"But . . ." She didn't know what to say. She took a strangled breath. "But I love you," she managed. "We're going to get away. *Together.* Tonight."

Tag released a small, strangled groan.

Lucia's airway felt even tighter. "What's happened?"

He made another strange sound in his throat. Why wouldn't he look at her? Her own throat clogged with tears of fear and frustration. She couldn't bring herself to ask what she prayed wasn't true — if he had changed his mind about running away with her. Instead, she asked, "You got my message, though, yes? That is why you are here?"

He opened his palm and held out the wing votive. The pointed edge of one end had scraped the flesh under his thumb almost raw, as if he'd been gripping it for a long time.

"Quintus thought it meant we were treating chickens now," he said dully.

She grabbed his hand with both of hers. "The wing means

freedom," she said quietly. "For *both* of us." When he didn't respond, she repeated, "Which is why we have to act this very night."

He closed his eyes as if he was in pain. She wanted to smooth his furrowed brow, to make everything go away. "Look at me," she whispered.

He opened his eyes. They looked dark and haunted. "Loving you . . . is destroying me," he whispered. "We are fooling ourselves about this. It's better to end this now. To spare ourselves the torture."

"Why are you saying this? Do you not understand what I'm telling you — that we must run —"

"I can't run away, Lucia," he said.

She stared at him, dumbfounded. "What?" she finally managed.

"It was a beautiful fantasy, but I can't do it. I can't leave my father to be murdered for my actions. I can't abandon him to your father's wrath."

Gods, she'd never even thought about Damocles. "Well then, we'll just take him with us."

He laughed humorlessly. "He'd never come. And if we forced him, he'd give us away in his confusion, or we'd be caught because we wouldn't be able to run quickly enough with him. Do you see? I'm trapped."

"But my father wouldn't *kill* him! I know it."

Tag closed his eyes again. "He would beat him, which would kill him, Lucia. Especially once he discovered that we ran off together *and* I'd stolen medical supplies."

Was he right? Was her father capable of killing Damocles? There was a time when she would have deemed it impossible, but that was before she learned about the exposures. When she imagined his rage at losing Quintus's financial backing, she could see him ordering the old man to be beaten. And that *would* kill him.

"Tag, please," she whispered as the impossibility of the situation became clear. How could she ask him to deliver his own aged father to a brutal death? She loved him for his essential goodness; she would never forgive herself — *he* would never forgive her — if she insisted he act *against* it. Hot tears rolled down her cheeks.

Her mind whirred with ways around the situation. They couldn't give up now, could they? But no matter how she turned it over, there was nothing either of them could do. It would ruin them to do this thing with the knowledge of the consequence to his father.

It was done, then. They were both trapped. He would continue as a slave, and she would marry Quintus, a man she barely knew and could hardly tolerate. She closed her eyes against the bleakness of it.

"I'm sorry," Tag said, his voice breaking a little.

"I am too," she said. Through the tightness in her throat, she added, "I love you, Tag. I always will."

He took her in his arms then, and they held each other in silence. After a time, he bent and kissed her forehead, her cheek, the wetness under her lashes. When he reached her mouth, his kisses were soft and gentle, the tip of his tongue tasting the edges of her lips as if they had been dipped in honey crystals.

"I love you," he breathed into her. She swallowed the words into herself and breathed them back into him so that they could share the sweetness of it together.

For the last time.

CHAPTER THIRTY

TAG

Something woke him up. Another tremor? He did not know, but the sky looked different, as if someone had lit a large fire and then just as quickly put it out. He had finally fallen asleep, alone, outside the enclosure after Lucia left — long after she should have, but neither one seemed to have the strength to release the other. She'd taken her hoard and the small lamp, leaving him in the inky black. It suited his mood.

He rubbed his face, grateful that she hadn't insisted — or even asked — that he consider abandoning his father for her. Because if she had, he would have said *yes*. He would have done it. He would have run away with her, and then never forgiven himself for it. She'd saved him from himself.

But that didn't mean he wasn't still considering it. The idea of never seeing her again hollowed him out. It left him wondering if maybe his father *could* manage whatever happened if they ran. Tag had been away in Rome for three years, and he'd handled everything then, hadn't he?

Yet deep down, he knew Titurius's rage at losing Quintus's coin would be lethal. And he couldn't take that risk with his father's life.

The light on the mountain changed yet again, and Tag wondered if it was closer to dawn than he thought. Either way, he figured he might as well go back to the compound.

When he reached the broken city wall, he was stunned to see Lucia and Minos climbing through it toward him. With her hair flowing down her back, she looked so beautiful and lost, his heart lurched.

"What are you doing?" he asked. "It's almost dawn. People will be getting up."

"I don't think I can do it, Tag," she said, almost desperately. "I don't think I can just walk away and pretend I don't love you."

Gods, he hated to see her so miserable. "Did you sleep at all, *deliciae meae?*"

She shook her head, her eyes filling. He moved to her and scooped her into his arms. "What if . . . what if we . . ." she began.

"Shhhhh," he said, trying to soothe her. He could feel her heart racing.

"What if . . . what if I could convince Quintus to bring you *and* your father into his household? What if —"

He froze and held her out from him. "What? Are you suggesting that Quintus 'buy' me and my father?" It felt as if she had punched him hard in the chest.

"Then, when we run, we could be sure he would not be killed. Quintus said patricians treat their slaves better than people like my father."

"And you believe him? You would leave my father with that man? Who would then sell him or throw him out into the street? No."

Her eyes looked wild. "Tag, I just don't want to lose you."

He blinked, trying to understand. She hadn't slept all night. She was not thinking straight. "Lucia, you cannot possibly think that this would be all right. I would rather run away and abandon my father to Titurius than be owned by Quintus. And to have to watch you go to his bed? Impossible." Too late, he thought about lowering his voice.

She dropped her head into her hands and began to cry again. "I know. I shouldn't have thought — It's just that I don't think I can do this, Tag. I would rather die than —"

Rustling came from behind her, and she stopped talking.

"You would rather die than what, my dear?" came a lazy voice that brought a chill to the deepest center of Tag's bones. "Please, do tell." Quintus emerged from the shrubbery.

Tag stared at the patrician, unable to move, unable to think, unable to speak. Minos bared his teeth and growled, but Quintus seemed not to notice. His gaze traveled over both of them. "Well, this explains so much. So, the lovesick act for me, it was all a lie, Lucia? Is that right?"

"It is not what you think, Quintus," Lucia said in a rush. "We were just talking —"

"A lovers' spat?"

"No —" Lucia began.

He flicked his eyes over to Tag. "I was right, then, wasn't I? You are in love with your mistress. Only it never occurred to me that she loved you back. Well, hopefully you will fall for your *new* master soon."

Silence. Tag clenched his fists and swallowed. He had no idea what Quintus was talking about. The bigger question was, what would the patrician do? Would he insist Titurius torture and kill Tag for this?

"How did you find us?" Lucia managed.

"A strange light woke me up, so I went outside. I saw you release your dog and hurry away. I was curious, so I followed."

"What are you going to do?" she asked.

"I don't know," Quintus mused. "I am hurt, of course. I thought you loved me. I found a surprising amount of solace in that. But this could work out to everyone's benefit."

"How is that?" she asked cautiously.

"Your father refuses to give me the young *medicus* as part of the marriage deal until he finds a replacement, but now he will have to give him to me in order to avoid an outrageous scandal. I am sure I am not the first to stumble upon this secret affair."

"There is no affair," Lucia said. "We have not —"

"I was to be part of the marriage deal?" Tag interrupted. *"Why?"*

Quintus turned to him. "Because I insisted."

Tag exchanged a confused look with Lucia.

"Look, I know that you don't care for me much, but over time, I believe that you will learn to like me," Quintus said to him. "Maybe even love me. That you both will."

Tag shook his head, hearing the words, but not understanding them.

"Don't you see?" Quintus said, a pleading note creeping into his voice. "I don't care if you love her as long as you're with me. You'll come to care for me. I know you will."

Tag took a step back, confused. "But —"

"My feelings for you . . . They are a surprise?" Quintus asked, his face flushing. "Since the day you saved me from the other gladiators, I felt . . ." He swallowed. "I thought you knew. I thought you were only pretending not to notice or respond to me. But once you are part of my household, you will see. I will take care of you. Of both of you. You will come to care for me. I know it."

"Quintus," Lucia said. "If it's not me you want, then why marry me?"

The patrician's face flushed even more. "I was not lying. I do — did — find your love for me a balm. And I appreciate your beauty and intelligence. I thought this was a good solution for everyone. With this arrangement, you do not have to marry old man Vitulus. My father is pleased that I agreed to marry at all. I will have children, and I will finally have the chance to show you, Tag, that I am worthy of your affection," he said, turning to him and putting his hands out in supplication.

Minos growled again.

Tag looked at Lucia. Her eyes were wide, one hand at her throat.

Quintus released a shaky breath. "I will give you some time to think about this," he said. "You will see that it's the best possible outcome for all three of us." Nervously, he extended a hand to Tag's shoulder.

This time Minos lunged. Quintus screamed as the dog's teeth pierced the flesh of his forearm. Lucia yelled, "No, Minos. Down! No!" Tag tried to grab the dog's collar.

In the commotion, they did not notice the two people rushing toward them from the compound.

"What in Jupiter's name is going on here?" roared Pontius. He grabbed a stick and began smashing it against the dog's back.

"Stop!" Lucia screamed as the overseer landed a blow on the dog's spine. Minos released Quintus and yelped in pain.

"Minos, NO!" roared another voice, and the dog cowered on his belly, ears back in fear.

It was Titurius.

CHAPTER THIRTY-ONE

Lucia

At the sight of her father, Lucia shrank back. "Father, what are you doing here? I thought you had to stay at the temple."

"The goddess accepted my predawn sacrifice — and then I come back to find this?" He turned to Tag. "Why were you attacking this patrician, boy? A *guest* of this household?"

Tag blanched. "I wasn't attacking him. I was trying to get the dog off of him."

"That is not what it looked like," Titurius said.

Lucia glanced at Quintus. Pontius was helping him wrap his bleeding arm. Gods, how would she explain this? And then it came to her. "I was with Quintus, and Minos thought Quintus was hurting me, so he attacked," she cried quickly. "The dog was only protecting me. And . . . and the *medicus* rushed out to see if he could help Quintus."

It seemed to take her father a minute to register her presence. "What are you saying?"

"I was with Quintus and the dog got upset. Tag was merely trying to pull Minos off of him."

Titurius looked at Quintus. "Is this true?"

She begged Quintus with her eyes to go along with her story.

He seemed to understand, nodding almost imperceptibly. "Yes, it is true," he said. "The dog attacked me, and the boy was only trying to help."

Lucia had barely let her breath out when she felt the crack of her father's backhand across her face.

"You whore," he growled.

"But . . . but we are to be married in days," she stammered, flicking her eyes to Quintus. "There is no harm done."

"That is correct. I believe I am allowed to sample the merchandise before the final event," Quintus said.

Titurius glared at the young patrician. Lucia saw Tag clenching his fists just behind him and shook her head at him in warning.

Holding his injured arm, Quintus nodded toward all of the servants and slaves who had heard the disturbance and come running. "Given how this looks, the rumors are probably already spreading about your daughter. I believe I can make this . . . er, scandalous situation go away."

Titurius frowned. "How?"

"Send the *medicus* to me right away. Problem solved."

"I told you, I'm not releasing him until I have a replacement *on hand*."

"You have the elder slave until then," Quintus said.

"Not for much longer," Titurius retorted.

Tag released a breath in almost a hiss.

"What do you mean, Father? Is Damocles all right? What are you planning to do?" Lucia asked on Tag's behalf.

He turned to her. "We both know he is failing." He did not answer the last question.

Lucia caught the look of dread on Tag's face.

"Well, I'm afraid I will have to insist," Quintus said. "I believe the arrangement we have made will adequately cover costs for an interim healer until you are able to purchase another slave."

"I need a *medicus* who is used to working on gladiators and dealing with their injuries," Titurius said. "They are not easy to find."

Quintus shrugged. "My father knows a lot of former military medics. We'll find you a *medicus* from the legions who has done his time and wants out."

Her father still looked unconvinced. "Marry her today before sundown," he said at last, "to avoid the scandal. And it's a deal."

"Fine," Quintus said, looking at Lucia, then at Tag.

Pontius took the patrician by his uninjured arm and said, "Let's get the elder healer to look at that bite."

Quintus nodded. "I will leave for Herculaneum as soon as my arm is treated. Bring them both to me later today and we will have the ceremony before sundown. Agreed?"

Titurius made a noise of assent.

"Meanwhile, you are not to hurt either of them. No whipping the slave. No bruises on your daughter."

Titurius would have none of it. "You *dare* tell me how to manage my own slaves? My own daughter?"

Quintus straightened into his usual posture of nobility. "Our deal is dependent on you pretending to be civilized for this one day, which I know must be hard for a butcher such as you. However, I insist that you somehow manage it."

Titurius's face reddened in rage, but he said nothing.

Quintus looked at Lucia and then Tag one last time before allowing Pontius to lead him back into the compound. Tag gave him a small nod of acknowledgment, as close to a "thank you," Lucia imagined, as he could muster for the order that kept him from being whipped. But the set of his jaw told her he was still fuming over what the patrician had planned.

When Quintus was out of hearing, Titurius turned to one of his freedmen. "You — lock him up with the imprisoned gladiators."

The man grabbed Tag by an upper arm.

"But he has done nothing wrong," Lucia pleaded. "And you heard Quintus —"

Her father raised his arm as if to hit her again and then lowered it. His face was almost purple with rage. "You have caused me enough trouble. Start packing your things. I will not lose this opportunity. And I will send this slave on," he added, pointing at Tag's retreating back, "*only* when I see the ceremony concluded and not one moment before."

He stomped back toward the house. "Go back to work, you lazy idiots!" he yelled at everyone who had gathered to watch.

As the morning wore on, Lucia paced in her small *cubiculum*. They could not follow through with Quintus's plan. It would crush Tag's spirit to be taken away from medicine and gladiator training just to satisfy another owner's passing whims. And even if Quintus fancied himself in love, it wouldn't change the fact that Tag and Lucia were both being bartered away for a price, to be used against their will. She couldn't — wouldn't — allow that to happen.

She heard Quintus announce to her father that he would have everything prepared for the ceremony in Herculaneum by the ninth hour. She and Tag would have to sneak away long before that. But how?

Think. Think. She would tell her father she was going to Cornelia's for a bath. Yes, he'd allow that. And . . . and she'd tell him she needed Damocles to attend her, because Cornelia wanted to consult with him about her upcoming birth. And Damocles would bring his medical things because he might need them.

They would proceed toward Cornelia's, and then she'd slip out a different city gate with the old man. He probably wouldn't even notice at first. Then Tag could get away through the Vesuvian gate, after which they would find each other at the abandoned shrine of Mephistis. It would be hard going with Damocles, but they could then get him to Nuceria, where they could hire a carriage to Thurii. Nobody would think to look for them there.

Best of all, if her father thought she was bathing and preparing with Cornelia, it would be *hours* before their disappearance would be discovered. She could send a note to Cornelia asking her to pretend that they were there and further delay her father's summons to leave. Her friend would do that for her.

Her heart began to beat faster. They really could do it. If the gods were willing, and she got Tag released from the gladiator cells, they could make it out and protect Tag's father too.

Once she was certain Metrodona was nowhere in sight, she drew the drape across the opening to her *cubiculum* and unlocked the chest where she'd hidden her hoard. She piled all the treasures into an old shawl, including the golden coins from her mother's things.

A ring clattered on the floor and she picked it up. It was a man's ring — her dead brother's citizenship ring, she realized.

She remembered when her brother had first received it, after his manhood ceremony, where he exchanged the *bulla* necklace protecting his child self for the traditional ring of an adult Roman citizen. *Mater* must have gotten the ring back when the officers came to tell her about his death. It gave Lucia a pang to think of her mother holding her firstborn's ring to her heart in grief. She would have had nothing to hold on to for her lost, exposed babies.

She put the ring in the center of the pile and then reached under her mattress for the votive of Turan that Tag had given her. The small piece of clay fit perfectly in the palm of her hand, and she closed her fingers around it.

Keep us safe from harm, she begged the Etruscan goddess of love. *Protect us from our enemies and we will honor you for the rest of our lives.*

When she heard voices, she hastily put the votive with the other treasures and wrapped it all up to look like a small stash of laundry. Then she hid it under the bed. They were going to do this. And they were going to have to do it right away. It was just a matter of figuring out how to get Tag unshackled.

She wandered out to the atrium, where slaves had hung the laundry to dry. At the ends of the lines flapped the slaves' own tattered tunics and unraveling shawls. Carefully, she slid off a few pieces that looked about the right size and rolled them up. She dashed back into her *cubiculum* and changed. Even though everyone in the compound knew her, she gambled that she would appear invisible to the guards as long as she covered her hair and slouched like a tired slave.

Once dressed, she looked around her room. Metrodona had

left some bread and fruit for her earlier. Perfect. She would pretend to bring Tag food from the kitchens, and they could make their getaway plans then. She put a shawl over her head, hugging the bread to her chest, and peeked out of her *cubiculum*. All clear.

With her heart thudding in her ears, she walked toward the barracks.

CHAPTER THIRTY-TWO

TAG

The cell in the barracks reeked of sweat, urine, and fear. Tag sat with his head leaning back against the wall, his wrists and ankles shackled to the stone. He closed his eyes. He could not fathom how it had come to this. It was as if the gods had conspired to torture him in the worst possible way — to be sold to the man who was going to *marry* Lucia? What had he done to anger them so?

He thought of what this meant for his father. Gods, he would be left alone in the Titurius household, the very destiny Tag had been trying to avoid for him. The master clearly knew that he was losing his faculties — "failing," he had said. What would Titurius do to him?

Metal clanged in the cell next to him and a man muttered in Iberian. Hamilcar? What had the hotheaded gladiator done now? On the other side, a voice with a lilting accent asked, "Why is the healer in chains?"

"Long story," Tag mumbled.

"We have nothing but time here."

"Don't want to talk about it," Tag said. "Tell me about you."

"My name is Taharka from Nubia."

"Rome has no outposts in your land. So how did you end up here?" Tag asked.

The man laughed, a heavy yet melodic sound. "They have no outposts in my land because Romans know better than to engage our warriors, for we would conquer the conquerors."

"Yet you have been conquered."

"Only by greed," said the Nubian. "I was trading gold with the Roman governor of Numidia. He claims I tried to cheat him, which I did not. So he had me arrested and sold into slavery — the profits of which he took, along with my entire cache of gold. The bastard."

"A greedy Roman magistrate sold my family into slavery generations ago," Tag said. "I am sorry."

"I have always been strong, but now I will be stronger," Taharka said. "I will fight in the arena and win my freedom, and then go back to Numidia and take revenge on that crooked Roman. Then, and only then, will I return to my beloved Nubia."

Tag kept silent. Did *every* gladiator believe that he would survive the ring and win his freedom? He could hear the desperation of the dream — and how unlikely it was. A deeper despair sank into his bones. He never would have won his freedom as a gladiator. Nothing would have enabled him to live freely. And even if he could, he would never be able to be with Lucia anyway. So what was the point?

The iron doors clanked and rattled. Someone was coming.

"Slave girl to see the healer," announced one of the guards in broken Latin. He escorted a hunched girl covered by a shawl into his cell, winking at Tag as he left.

"Tag —" came a familiar whisper.

His head shot forward, his eyes wide.

"It's me," Lucia whispered. "I . . . I brought some bread for you."

He stared at her, openmouthed. "What are you doing here? You can't —"

"I am preparing for us to run away," she whispered.

He laughed and choked back a sob all at the same time. Gods, he loved her. But how could she still think they could do this?

"Don't laugh," she scolded in an undertone. "We are both going to run away. As soon as I —"

"Luc —"

"Don't use my name! Listen to me. As soon as I can get you unshackled, we will go." She explained how she would take Damocles with her and how they would link up at the abandoned shrine.

As insane as her plan sounded, Tag still felt hope beginning to stir in his chest. She sounded so convinced that they could escape, that they could actually make their dream of creating a new life together a reality. Was it truly possible? Could he protect his father *and* be free?

Voices and feet came thundering down the hall. Lucia covered her head.

Tag's cell door swung open, and Titurius's form filled the doorway. "You little tramp!" he roared. "You've been fooling all of us, haven't you?" He swiped at Lucia's shawl, exposing her face. "You think I would be so stupid as to not have you watched? You think you could outwit me?"

He grabbed the back of her neck and pulled her up, and she uttered a small cry of pain. Tag scrabbled against the stone wall to stand, his chains clanging as he raised his fists.

"And what are you going to do, *medicus*? What a waste! Even after I sent you to Rome to train! Well, I don't care what Quintus says, I'm going to beat you blind and —"

Titurius stopped as the earth began to tremble. They heard sharp cries from outside as the intensity of the shaking grew. Instinctively, everyone crouched and covered their heads as the ground rolled and shuddered under them. The air was filled with the sounds of crashing columns and buckling walls.

Earthquake, Tag thought. This was no tremor; this was the real thing. The earth bucked under their feet and the movement seemed to go on and on.

The ground finally stopped undulating, though the creaking of settling walls and joists continued. Clouds of plaster dust hung in the air. The sounds of people running and women crying drifted into the room. Titurius looked dazedly around, and Tag saw with relief that although cracks had appeared in the cell walls, the building itself seemed intact. The roof held.

Lucia rushed to Tag's side, and Titurius caught the movement, which seemed to bring him back to himself.

"You are the curse-bearer," he said, pointing at Tag with wide, almost crazed eyes. "This is all your fault. You made this happen." He grabbed Lucia by the upper arm and dragged her outside. "The curse will be broken when you marry Quintus," Tag heard the master say, and he couldn't tell whether Titurius was trying to convince himself or Lucia. "The priest assured me of this! I am taking you to Quintus's house *now*. You must marry right away to keep more evil from befalling us."

"No!" Lucia cried, trying to wriggle out of his grip, looking back at Tag through the open doorway.

Titurius roared for his steward. "Prepare the horses for me," he commanded. "We leave for Herculaneum now."

"But, sir," the steward said, running to meet Titurius just outside the doorway, "the damage to the compound . . . We don't even know how bad it is yet. You can't leave now! You are needed here!"

"Do as I command!" Lucius roared.

"Dominus —"

"The gods have spoken," he said. "I must get her married now to save us all. I'll be back before sundown. Pontius, you're in charge of the barracks and the gladiators. Keep an eye on them. I don't want anyone running away in this chaos."

Pointing to Tag, he added, "And as soon as things settle, I want that boy crucified for defiling my daughter. Do you hear me? I want to see him hanging by the beams when I get back."

"No, Father! You cannot. Quintus said —"

"He doesn't have to know until *after* you're married. Everything will be fine as soon as that takes place. And finally I will have my revenge on the curse-bearer."

Tag watched Lucia disappear into the light as her father dragged her after him. For one brief moment, he had dared to hope again that maybe — just maybe — they really could steal away. But now, it was all over. How many times would he lose her?

Then he heard people crying out in pain, and the healer in him made him sit up straight. People were injured. Maybe even trapped under rubble. The stone cells and barracks had withstood quakes before, but what about the old house? And Damocles? Was he all right?

"Pontius," he bellowed. "Let me out! Let me check on my father!" Then he added, "Some of the men may need medical attention!"

He hoped that would work. It did. Pontius rushed into the cell, ashen-faced. "It's bad," he said, hands shaking as he unlocked the chains at Tag's wrists and ankles. "The master must be desperate for Quintus's money to leave now." He grabbed Tag's arm. "Don't do anything stupid — we need you as *medicus*."

"Let them out too," Tag said, nodding to other men shackled in the adjoining cells.

"Can't risk it. They're not hurt, so they stay."

"But the walls could fall on them!"

"This building has withstood worse. I'm going to round up the other gladiators to see who is injured. You must attend to them first, do you understand? I can't find your father, so it will be my only excuse for sparing you from the beams. Make an effort."

As soon as he was unshackled, Tag shot out of the cell.

"Where are you going?" Pontius shouted.

"For medical supplies," he called back. But he was lying.

CHAPTER THIRTY-THREE

———

Lucia

(The Day Before)

Even as the earth continued to spasm with aftershocks, Lucia's father refused to let her out of his sight. He sent a girl to get a change of clothes and pack up her things for the trip to Herculaneum, then dragged her out into the garden, waiting for the horses to be calm enough to ride.

Then the earth rocked yet again and terra-cotta roof tiles crashed down around her. People screamed and ran. Others called out names, desperately trying to find one another. Lucia worried about Metrodona. And Cornelia! Gods, she hoped she was unhurt.

"Father, Herculaneum may have been hit too," she said. "I don't think we should go right now. We should attend to the house here."

But he ignored her, his jaw set.

She tried another tactic. "Father, you cannot crucify Tages. It will only enrage Quintus, and you need his —" She was about to say *money*, but quickly changed it to "patronage."

"He can get a *medicus* replacement easily enough," Titurius said. "He has no right to tell me how to treat my own slaves." He turned to her and lowered his voice. "And I don't want him to find out how you demeaned yourself with a slave as well!"

"I did not demean . . . Nothing happened —"

He made a disgusted noise in his throat and marched away from her to talk to his steward. She turned to run to her room and get her hoard, but one of her father's freedmen emerged from the shadows to grab her arm.

"Not so fast, miss. I am to watch you until you are on the road to Herculaneum," he said. "We're going to the stables now."

She wanted to scream in desperation. She had to save Tag, but how? How?

In the chaos, two horses were brought to them outside the stable. One horse pulled a small cart, while the other was saddled up.

"*Dominus*, the horses are still agitated," the stable master cried. "I do not recommend taking them out now. I do not know that they can be controlled. Nor do we know what the roads are like."

"I don't care," Titurius said through gritted teeth. "Besides, we'll be safer out on the road than inside the compound. We can walk the horses around any blockages. Now let's go."

The stable boy finally put blinders on the horses, which helped a little, but not much. As if in a dream, Lucia climbed into the rickety cart, and they rolled out of the compound gates.

When she thought about Tag, despair swallowed her like a giant wave. At least she knew he hadn't been crushed in the big quake. But what if the walls collapsed as the earth continued its small shudders? How was she going to get back to him? She closed her eyes at the thought of the pain and agony he would endure if Pontius did crucify him as ordered. Death did not come right away with crucifixion; after a couple of days of misery, the victims usually died of asphyxiation when they lost the strength to lift their heads.

Then the implications of that thought made her sit up. Even if Pontius crucified Tag that afternoon, he should survive for at least a few more days. He would still be alive! She could save him! Someone would help her get him down. And then they could still run away.

She started paying close attention to what was around her. The road to Herculaneum was crowded with Pompeians fleeing the earthquake. Yet some people were moving against the horde, *toward* Pompeii, which was puzzling. Then she realized that many of the servants who worked in the giant villas on the coastal roads probably had homes and family in or near Pompeii. That gave her some hope. If the throughways remained in such chaos, that might provide enough cover for her to steal away back to Tag.

After what seemed like forever on the crowded road, her father saw a man he knew. She pretended drowsiness as her father dismounted from his stallion and then caught up with the man, who welcomed him into his covered litter with a bejeweled hand through the drapes. In the midst of an earthquake and after sentencing a man to crucifixion, her father *would* still break for business.

Her carriage driver stepped over to the woods to relieve himself. Lucia climbed out of the carriage and walked carefully toward her father's stallion, which was nibbling grass on the side of the road. She could tell that the animal was still on edge and ran her hands over it to calm it. She'd never ridden him before, and she hated to try while the creature was so nervous, but she had no choice.

She brought the animal close to her carriage and used the large wheel as a step. Quickly, she bunched her tunica up to her thighs and mounted. The horse made some noises and sidled about, but that was it. With one last glance at the litter, she turned the horse around and walked it off the main road, where the bottleneck of people was greatest. She didn't want to draw attention to herself by making any sudden movements, but the sight of her exposed legs drew looks of scandalized astonishment. She covered the tops of her thighs with her *palla*.

I don't care what they think. Just as long as Father doesn't see me. Don't let him see me, don't let him see me, don't let him see me. . . .

She was almost away when the carriage driver emerged from the woods and spied her. "Hey!" he yelled. "Stop! Stop!"

She kicked her legs hard, urging the horse to run. It took off in a frenzy, and soon the woods and scrubs blurred past her as she flew back toward Pompeii. Toward Tag.

CHAPTER THIRTY-FOUR

TAG

Tag ran toward the house. "*Apa. Apa!* Where are you?" he called.

His heart dropped when he saw thick black smoke billowing from the herbal room. His father often worked by oil lamp, even during daytime. Stuffed with dried herbs and papyrus sheaves, the room was particularly vulnerable to fire.

He burst in. "Father? *Apa?*" Flames crackled over the worktable where the oil lamp had spilled. He could barely see, and the noxious smell of the burning herbs made him cough. He squinted. There! His father had fallen. Putting his tunic over his nose, he ran to the corner of the room.

"*Apa?*" Tag shook him. No response.

The smoke was starting to choke him, and his eyes stung with the acrid smell. He dragged his father out of the room by the armpits. Slaves ran past him into the herbal room, carrying buckets of water and blankets. Once safely in the courtyard, Tag turned Damocles over and gave a strangled cry at the sight of his father's empty open eyes. His mind divided. One part turned medical as he noticed the gash on his father's crown. He felt his chest — no pulse. *The patient appears to have fallen and struck his head on a sharp surface. The trauma, combined with the toxic smoke from the herbs — some poisonous — caused his heart to stop beating. . . .*

But the other part was so young it couldn't even form words. All it could do was cry for the one constant force in his life — his *apa*.

Tag became aware that someone was shaking him. "Healer! Healer! You must help us." Through wet eyes, he saw one of the house slaves, wide-eyed and panicked. "In the kitchens. Boiling water everywhere. You must come!"

Tag stood. "My supplies are in there," he said, stupidly pointing to the still-smoldering herb room. How could he help anyone without salve and bandages and needles and flax to stitch up gashes? And his father! His father!

"Please come!" the man cried as he pulled Tag's tunic desperately.

"Let me cover him," Tag said. With a shaking hand, he shut Damocles's eyes, grabbed a discarded cloak nearby, and placed it over his father's face. He appealed to Februus, the Etruscan god of purification, asking that his father's spirit be cleansed even though he couldn't treat his body in the ancient ways.

At another insistent call, Tag turned to follow the desperate slave. A dog howled in terror nearby, and he thought of Minos. He should free Minos. Lucia wouldn't want him hurt. He would save Minos for Lucia. . . .

But before he could act on that thought, they were in the small brick kitchen. The hearth with the iron cauldron had toppled in the earthquake. An old woman stared with shocked yet vacant eyes at the bright red skin that peeled from her arms like the casing off of a boiled sausage. A girl crouched under a broken wooden chair, her arm dangling at a strange angle.

Tag felt paralyzed. Who should he help first? Pontius had released him so that he could treat the gladiators, but so many people seemed hurt. He could hear moans and keening throughout the courtyard. How could he do any of this without his father?

Grief and fear tightened his throat. Someone tugged on his tunic. Castor stared up at him. "Are you all right?" Tag asked the child.

Castor nodded. He looked terrified, but at least he wasn't injured.

"Can you help me? As my assistant?"

The boy nodded again, the thought of having something to do seeming to strengthen him.

"Good. I need you to find wine. Bring up as many amphorae as you can. Then have her drink as much undiluted wine as she can manage," he said, indicating the burned woman. "This will help dull her pain. But you must hold the cup for her, do you understand?" Castor nodded a third time. "Then bring me as much clean water as you can find. We need to wash the cuts and burns."

The boy scampered toward the cellar and Tag looked again at the old lady. He'd never seen anybody with such deep burns survive the pain and fever that would inevitably follow. But he had to try. He went over to the old woman, who had begun shivering, and found some flour sacks to wrap around her shoulders. She wailed when she tried to put her hands down on her lap. He murmured platitudes, but what could he do until some pain relief came? How would he treat her?

He caught the eye of the young teen girl still crouching under the chair. "My *mater*," she said, pointing behind her. "Can you help my *mater*?"

With a sense of dread, he looked into the corner of the ruined room. A woman lay crushed under a large wooden beam, eyes open in death. He recognized the face. It was Castor's aunt.

"I am sorry," he said softly, crouching to face the girl. "Your *mater* is gone."

The girl, although about twelve or thirteen, sounded like a little child. "No, she is not! She is right here!" She began to cry.

"I am sorry," he whispered again, and felt hot tears prick his eyes. "My *apa* is gone too. Perhaps they are together, chatting as they always did in the afternoons."

The girl sobbed.

Time disappeared as Tag and Castor tried to treat the old woman, who vacillated between screaming in another language and passing out. After wrapping her arms as best he could with wet bean sacks, Tag turned to the girl.

"Now I need to see your arm," he said, looking around at what he could use for a splint. A broken wooden stool leg looked about right. As he bound the girl's arm, he heard Pontius bellowing for him.

"*Medicus!* Where are you? We need you!"

He froze. Pontius didn't know where he had gone or what he was doing. In the chaos, Tag could run. But where? Did he really want to go to Thurii without Lucia? Maybe he could find her on the road to Herculaneum . . . but then Castor decided for him.

"He is here!" Castor yelled. "The healer is in here!"

Tag groaned and closed his eyes.

"Come out here right now!" Pontius ordered. "I've got men for you to treat."

"I'm coming," Tag called with a resigned sigh.

CHAPTER THIRTY-FIVE

—∞—

Lucia

Lucia prayed the horse wouldn't lose its footing as it flew away back toward Pompeii. She heard yells commanding her to stop, but she couldn't have halted the beast if she wanted. The horse seemed wild with terror as its hooves thundered along. She held on, barely breathing, begging the horse not to throw her.

Had her father followed? Even if he unhitched the wagon, that old nag wouldn't be able to match the stallion's speed. Still, she was too terrified to look behind her. She prayed to the goddess of the hunt for help — *Let me escape, let me go free. . . .*

She felt the horse slowing as they approached Pompeii. The clog of people seemed overwhelming at the Stabian Gate, so she steered it around the perimeter road, heading for the Vesuvian Gate.

The horse had dropped to a walk by the time she could see the gate at a distance. People streamed out of the city there as well. She slid off and began leading the stallion through the knot of people.

The horse was sweating and huffing with its head lowered, and Lucia wondered if she'd hurt it somehow. Then the horse made a frightened sound and began rearing in terror. She looked down to see what had set him off. When she saw it, she gasped and pulled the horse back with her.

A swarm of snakes — gods, she didn't know snakes *swarmed*! — slithered out of their nests in what seemed like a mad panic. Ribbons of black and yellow moved past them and disappeared under a brush of dry, dusty leaves. And they continued slithering farther from there, the leaves moving like small waves rushing toward some unknown shore.

Gods! What could scare *snakes*?

A sense of dread filled her belly. Maybe something worse still was going to happen. At least she could find Tag first. She resumed walking the nervous, exhausted horse toward the crowded gate.

"Where is everyone going?" she asked a group of slaves and freedmen streaming out of the city. Some of the faces looked familiar, but she couldn't place them.

"My patron's farmhouse in the vineyards," said one man.

"The countryside is safer than the city right now," another one said. "We are getting out before more walls collapse."

Animals brayed, and carts loaded with crying children and squawking chickens in wicker baskets pushed past her. One woman balanced a woven basket of goods on her head. Another man carried an elderly man on his back.

She recognized a man who sold figs and grapes at the market. "Sir," she cried. "You are going back to your farm?"

He nodded, squinting at her.

"Can you take this horse with you?" She held out the reins. "It is the property of Lucius Titurius, and if you keep it safe for him in your stable, there will be a reward for you. You can bring it down to him when it is safe again."

He nodded again and took the reins.

People jostled, elbowed, cursed, and kicked her as she pushed against the flow to enter the city. But she did not care. Once inside the gate, she skirted around the knot of people waiting their turn to exit and went along the stuccoed wall to the left. Within a block, the crowd thinned. She lifted her *tunica* and ran.

Even as scared as she was for Tag, she noticed a new strangeness in the air: The world had gone silent. The dogs that had been howling moments before had quieted. Even the ragged chickens in the streets had stopped their infernal clucking and squawking. Her sandaled feet slapping on the cobblestones and her rapid breaths sounded unnaturally loud.

Then a boom erupted around her, through her — *in* her — with such ferocity she fell to the ground in a crouch, covering her ears. The force of the explosion rattled her teeth and bones. She felt a blast of sudden heat, like someone had opened an immense kiln in her face.

As if in a dream, she watched the cobblestone street ripple at the top of the lane, then hurtle toward her like an ocean wave. The ground heaved as the wave passed under her, and she fought for balance, still trying to cover her ears against the immense roar that filled the skies. Weblike fissures crackled on the city's stucco wall, following the wave like a fisherman's net being dragged through sand. The roaring was so otherworldly, so shocking, she curled her head into her body in an instinctual crouch of protection. Her breathing came in gasps as she scrunched her eyes tight against whatever evil was hurtling down upon the city to destroy them all.

After a time — she could not say how long — she raised her head and saw a naked toddler wandering alone in the street, wailing with a wide-open mouth. But she could not hear the child. Everything was dreamlike and strange. Even the light had changed, growing somehow thicker, browner. Something had happened. But what?

Slowly, she stood, looking around her. People stepped out of their homes and shops. Lucia saw the people across the *via* look up at the mountain, which was hidden from her view by the city wall. They registered wonder, then a horror so intense, it was as if their faces were melting into grotesque tragedy masks before her eyes.

Haltingly, with a sense of heavy dread, she moved toward them and tipped her head back to see.

Vulcan had punched a hole through the mountaintop with his anvil. The top half of the mountain had disappeared, and a towering column of living, breathing gas, smoke, earth, and rock shot into the heavens. Within the monstrous column, red lightning bolts tore up and down the great, swirling mass, illuminating what seemed to be the enraged faces of demons ready to burst out of the plume and attack the city.

Lucia stared stupidly up at the roiling tower, remembering her theory about a new life erupting into being. But this didn't look like life. It looked like pure destruction. It sounded like death.

Well, if death was coming for them all, she was not going to spend her last moments with strangers in the street gawping at the sky. She *had* to find Tag. She lifted the hem of her *tunica* and sprinted toward home.

By the time she reached the compound, the sky was black and raining ash and rock. She protected her head with an abandoned cloak she found on the road. If Tag had been crucified, he would likely be in the training arena near the barracks, to remind the other slaves and gladiators that they should fear their master. He would be stripped and probably beaten, hanging defenseless against the rain of rocks. . . .

Please, Diana, Jupiter, Mercury, let him be alive.

In the middle of the arena's sandpit, she whirled around, her eyes taking in everything around her — the crumbled walls, the fallen wooden supports. But no crossbeams. No Tag.

What did that mean? Would he have been hung someplace else? The courtyard, maybe? No, she'd be able to see the cross soaring over the roofs. So perhaps in the chaos, Pontius hadn't gotten to him yet. Or maybe he never intended to carry out her father's orders. Her heart leapt with hope. It would be much easier for them to escape without having to figure out how to get Tag down.

The rocks started coming down more heavily from the sky. She ran for cover under the eaves of a crumbling roof. When she last saw Tag, he had been chained. Could he still be in the cell?

She turned toward the holding cells, but then hesitated. She would have to find the keys to unshackle him, and then they'd need to run. *Think, think.* The best thing for her to do would be to salvage the money she'd put away earlier in preparation for their escape. Then, once she freed him, they could take off. They'd have to find Damocles too and convince him to run with them. The chaos of the explosion would provide cover.

She raced to her *cubiculum*. It was only then that she thought about Metrodona. Poor Metrodona! She must be terrified.

"Have you seen Metrodona?" she asked one of the slaves running past.

"Hiding in the cellar," the woman said as she clung to a man

Lucia did not recognize. "*Domina!* I thought you were in Herculaneum," she cried, stopping to stare at her with wide eyes.

Lucia recognized her — the head laundress. "I came back. I am looking for the *medicus*. Do you know where he is?"

"His body is with the other dead in the courtyard," the laundress said, making the sign against evil. "He died in the fire."

Lucia swayed.

"Lady, you must come with us! We are going to the marina to escape by boat. Come. We must leave now!"

"No," Lucia managed when she could breathe again. The old slave was mistaken. She'd just grab her things so they could run as soon as she found him. And she would find him. He had to be alive. He *had* to.

The slave followed her into her room, still begging Lucia to come with her. Lucia grabbed a blanket off her bed and threw it at the woman in a fury. "Leave me! Save yourself! I am not going until I find him!"

The woman clutched the blanket, shook her head, and left.

CHAPTER THIRTY-SIX

TAG

Tag bent over the gladiator they'd pulled out of the collapsed latrine. With a rag, he cleared out the dust over the man's nostrils, wiped out his mouth, turned him on his side, and pounded on his back, trying to clear his lungs. The man began to cough. At the same time, Tag checked his ribs and limbs. He seemed fine.

"Take him to open air," he told the gladiators who had helped remove the rubble.

"Take him at once," cried the little boy beside him. Castor had taken to shadowing Tag and echoing his orders. Any other time, he would have found that both charming and irritating. Now he barely paid attention. He only became aware of the boy when Castor grabbed his hand and held on tight as they were led to different parts of the compound by the cries of the injured. It appeared that very few were badly hurt, except the kitchen women. And his father.

His father. *I need a coin*, Tag realized. He should put a coin in his father's mouth for Charun, the Etruscan demon who would ferry him across the river to Pluto's realm. His father had kept a stash of coins behind one of the walls in the herb room, he remembered.

The room was still smoking, but he went in anyway. Castor stayed outside, biting his lip, too afraid to enter the charred room but clearly unhappy about having even that much separation from Tag.

Tag found the small leather pouch inside a burned terra-cotta jar. The money had miraculously survived. He took a coin out and then tied the small leather bag to his belt. It occurred to him then that there might be other useful things that escaped the blaze, including bandages, herbs, and potions. He dug around the rubble, rescuing what he could.

That's when the world exploded.

At the unearthly boom, Castor ran to him and buried his face in his hip. Tag bent low, covering the boy's head with his body, sure that the remaining walls were about to come crashing down around them. The roar that followed vibrated in his bones. Castor wouldn't release him, so Tag picked him up and ran into the courtyard.

Where had the mountain gone?

The top of it seemed to have shot into the air in a flashing column of smoke and fire. It roared, rumbled, and spit like a gigantic, furious beast. Some of the slaves dropped to their knees, wailing that it was the end of the world. Others ran in terror, calling for those they loved. Tag could only stand and watch, awed by the force and horror of the display. Castor trembled in his arms.

After a while, the massive column slowed its ascent and began spreading like a thickening storm cloud. Tag remembered the coin for his father. He went over to Damocles, but Castor refused to budge when he tried to put him down. Tag sighed and bent with the boy to wedge the coin between his father's cold lips. Castor put his small hand on Tag's wrist as if to help him. After, he replaced the tattered cloak over Damocles's head and said a silent prayer over his body.

"Is . . . is the world ending?" the boy finally managed between hiccups.

"I don't know," Tag said, and realized that had been the wrong answer when the boy's trembling increased. "I mean, no, no. Of course not. It is . . . it looks like there is a fire inside the mountain," he said, trying to sound bland and unconcerned. "That is all. Soon it will burn itself out."

He remembered his discussions with Lucia about the "earthborn" fires in Phrygia. She had been unnaturally preoccupied with that passage of Strabo. Had some part of her sensed that Vesuvius was like that black mountain? He and everyone around her had told her it was impossible.

Lucia was gone. His father was dead. Tag had been sentenced to die. And now the mountain was turning itself inside out. He would just stay here by his father until the end. What was left for him anyway?

Castor still clung to him. He patted the child's back. "We need to find your people," he said.

The boy shook his head. "My auntie died in the kitchen."

Right. Tag groaned. "There are other women who have helped take care of you. We need to find them."

"No, no, no. I stay with you."

Tag closed his eyes wearily. When he opened them, he saw that the giant plume rocketing from the mountain had spread its ash-brown cloudy fingers wide across the sky. Day began turning into night as the strange mass blotted out the sun. People screamed. Newly lit torches hissed. Somewhere, a baby wailed.

With the darkening sky came the pinging of what sounded like hail on the villa's terra-cotta roof shingles. *Hail?* Tag caught a handful in his palm. It stung but did not hurt, and it looked less like ice and more like tiny pieces of frothy, gray, pitted rock. Impossible. The sky did not rain rocks!

Castor began to cry again, so Tag ducked under the eaves of the courtyard. He caught sight of an abandoned water jar. The little rocks *floated.*

"What is happening?" the boy cried.

He had no answer.

Soon, larger black rocks began crashing onto the roof and ground. They came out of the sky with such force, it was as if Jupiter himself was hurling them. Somewhere nearby, a dog yelped. Minos!

"I've got to untie the dog," Tag said. "You stay here. I'll only be a minute."

"No, no, no!" Castor cried, plastering himself even harder against Tag.

"Fine, but we're going to feel the rocks."

"I don't care," wailed the child.

Tag ran as fast as he could to where Minos was still chained up. The poor animal looked terrified and was panting heavily. "Good boy, good boy," Tag murmured as he unchained him, crouching over Castor as he did so to shield the child from the rocks pelting his back. Minos bolted as soon as he was free.

"We have to leave! This place is cursed!" a woman cried.

"The stables," someone yelled. "The master's horses should get us to Puteoli!"

With the child still clinging to him, Tag rushed back under the porticus for coverage from the rock fall. Already, his feet sank to the ankle in the accumulation of lightweight stones. He dragged his father's body under the eaves to protect it from the pelting rain of rock.

A group of slaves with torches saw him and the boy. "Come with us! We are going to the marina to escape by sea!" one of the men called out to him. "The roads out of the city are too crowded!"

"Can you take the boy with you?" he called back.

"No!" Castor cried.

Tag followed the bobbing lights of the group heading to the marina. Once there, he decided, he would hand the boy over and head back to keep vigil by his father's body. And if the mountain wanted to take him, it could, but at least Castor would be safe. He felt a measure of peace at the thought.

The group entered the street and began moving along the cut-through to the marina almost in single file. Everyone's arms but Tag's were laden with possessions. Some carried pillows or cloaks over their heads for protection. As the rain of rocks increased, Tag hunched his shoulders and put his arms up, trying to keep the worst of the deluge off his and Castor's heads. It did little good. His face was coated in ash, and he had to keep blinking to stop the strange powder in the air from burning his eyes. His lungs blazed as if they were being singed from the inside. Occasional bursts of sulfurous air — which he guessed came with the rain of rocks — made his stomach roil, and he fought against the hot bile that climbed up his throat.

He pushed on, wondering about Lucia. Where was she? Had she made it to Herculaneum? His chest clenched with a familiar ache at the thought of losing her forever. The earth and sky both seemed to reflect how he felt on the inside — black and bitter and hopeless.

A large rock bounced off a roof and tripped an elderly man in front of him. The woman with him fell to her knees beside him.

"I'm fine. I'm fine," the man said, looking more embarrassed than hurt as Tag helped him up. "I'm fine." The woman gave a half sob of relief as she clutched the man's arm.

"Come, we must catch up," Tag told the pair. "I can still see the torches." But were the lights he saw those of their group? Many others had streamed into the streets carrying lamps and torches too. Either way, they were headed in the right direction, he figured.

"Thank you," the woman said. She looked vaguely familiar, but he couldn't tell exactly who she was in the darkness with her face covered with ash. "Here," she continued, handing him a blanket. "Cover your head!"

He accepted the blanket. As soon as he threw it over himself and the boy, the scent of it almost made him lose his footing — lemons and flowers and woods.

The woman turned back to him. "Come," she said. "We must keep moving."

"This is Lucia's," he said hoarsely.

"Yes!" the woman said, sounding exasperated. "But no matter how much I begged, the young *domina* would not come with us!"

Tag blinked. "What do you mean, you begged . . . ? You talked to her? She is *here*? In Pompeii?"

The woman pulled him by the elbow. "Yes, she returned for some reason. She would have been safer far away from this place. Foolish girl!"

Tag stopped. "I have to go back."

Again the woman grabbed his arm. "No, you must come with us. It is certain death at the villa! Don't you see the mountain falling on us?"

"You must take the boy," he said. "Please."

"Nooooo!" Castor cried.

"I'm going back," he said to the child. "You'll be safer on the boats with these people."

"No, no! I want to stay with you!"

"I'm sorry," he mumbled. "This is safer for you." Roughly, he pried the boy off of his side and shoved him at the woman. The child thrashed and screamed. Gods, he hated the look of terror and betrayal the boy gave him. But he wasn't abandoning him — he was putting him in the hands of people who could take care of him. He had to keep telling himself that.

"Keep him safe, please," he yelled as they continued toward the marina. He was going back for Lucia.

CHAPTER THIRTY-SEVEN

Lucia

She saw a body under the eaves covered by an ashen cloak, and the words of the laundress repeated in her head: "He died in the fire." *It isn't Tag, it can't be Tag*, she chanted as she approached it, as if her fervent wishing could make it true.

The mountain roared in her ears — along with her thundering heart — as she lifted a corner and peeked. She sobbed in relief, releasing the cloth. It wasn't Tag, but his father. She gulped acrid air until she could calm herself, and then prayed to Damocles's shade for forgiveness for the insult of her reaction. He'd understand, she knew. She also prayed to him for help in finding his son.

But his father's shade gave her no message, so she retraced her steps back through the house, stopping in every room and calling for him, just in case he'd been released to treat the injured. Not surprisingly, most of the rooms were empty. As she passed a hallway, though, a slave popped his head out and called to her. "In here, girl! We are in the cellar. You will be safe with us!"

She shook her head. "Is the young *medicus* in there?"

The slave's eyes widened as he recognized Lucia. "No, *Domina*. Last I saw, he was treating the injured in the kitchen."

Her heart soared. That meant he was free and unhurt. But where? "And Metrodona? She is safe in there?"

He nodded. "Yes, but she worries for you."

"Tell her I am fine," she said, and continued going room to room. Could Tag have returned to the barracks? Perhaps that was where he had taken the injured. She headed toward the gladiator complex.

A flickering light in one of the cells in the stone barracks told her it was occupied. She called out, "Tag. Tag! Where are you?"

A door opened and light spilled out into the thick, sulfurous blackness. "Lucia?"

Her heart leapt. But as she ran toward him, she saw it wasn't Tag calling her name at all. It was her father.

She slid to a stop amidst the growing accumulation of rocks.

"Get in here now!" Lucius Titurius ordered. "I have been searching for you!"

"Is . . . Tag in there?" she asked. "Is he all right?"

There was a pause, then, "Yes, he is here. Come inside."

"The *medicus* is not here, miss," someone with a thick African accent yelled from inside the building. "He is lying!"

"He has chained us all!" another man yelled. "He is going to make us all die in here!"

"Shut up!" her father yelled, his face red with fury as he turned toward the men inside and made a threatening gesture.

She stopped. "Father, you have chained them? Why?"

"The ungrateful sots were running away! I will not lose my investments. Not now." He held up a sword with blood on the blade. Had he attacked his own weaponless fighters?

"Is Tag in there or not?" she said.

"By the gods, you get in here!" he roared. "Or I swear, I will hunt you down and drag you in!"

Tag wasn't there. Lucia turned and ran. Her father roared after her in frustration, and it was as if the mountain itself spewed her name.

CHAPTER THIRTY-EIGHT

TAG

Tag had barely turned away from the couple taking Castor before he was swallowed up by blackness. He needed a torch. He spied a lit one across the *via* and headed toward it. But his hands shook as he struggled with its rusted pins. How could the mountain continue its unholy roaring? How could it be *night* in the middle of the day?

Once he finally freed the torch, he looked around him, trying to understand where he was. He knew the city well, but suddenly everything looked foreign and strange. And, as if in a nightmare, he heard the disembodied wails of hurt and frightened people.

"Fulvia!" cried one man. "Fulvia, where are you?"

Someone coughed between wracking sobs.

"Have you seen my baby?" a woman wailed. "I can't find my baby!"

He couldn't see them, couldn't help anyone. Children cried-out for their mothers. Sometimes he heard them being comforted, but one cry reverberated in his chest.

"Don't leave me! Wait for me! Please, wait!"

It was a boy's hoarse, pleading voice. Tag thought of Castor's wild-eyed thrashing when he'd foisted him on the slave woman, and he closed his eyes against the guilt. But he *had* to do it. He hadn't *abandoned* Castor! He'd left him with people who would take care of him. Yet the sound of the boy's anguished cries seemed to follow him through the streets.

Maybe he was imagining it. Still, he turned around, peering into the darkness. "Where are you?" he called out. "Tell me where you are, and I will help you!"

"I'm here! I'm here," sobbed a familiar voice that made his heart sink into his belly. "Wait for me! Wait for me!"

It was not possible. Not possible. But there it was again.

"Healer! Wait!"

"Where are you?" Tag cried. "Can you run to me?"

The sobbing was different this time. More hopeful. Tag moved in the direction of the noise. Then he saw him in the small light of his torch. Castor was stuck up to his thighs in the drifts of pumice, tears carving black furrows through a layer of ash on his face. He held his arms up to Tag like an infant.

"Castor! You foolish boy! What have you done?" Tag picked him up, the rocks reluctant to release their hold. The boy wept into his neck. "You followed me this whole way?" he asked. "Gods! Gods!"

"I'm with you," Castor repeated in between hiccups. "I'm with you. I'm not with those people, I'm with you."

Tag closed his eyes and tightened his grip on the boy, relief flooding through his entire body to have him back. "It's all right. It's all right now. Listen. We are going to find Lucia. You will help me find Lucia, yes?"

Tag could feel the boy trying to nod. But exhaustion seemed to have overwhelmed him, and he fell asleep on Tag, grasping at his tunic with hands and toes as he always did — like a little monkey.

Tag tried not to panic at the slower pace he had to take with the boy in his arms. He sank deeper with every step into the layered rocks and ash. But he had a torch, and Castor was safe. He just needed to concentrate on putting one foot in front of the other, following the streets — corner fountain by corner fountain — until he got home.

Lucia had come back. She was here. They could escape together. She had returned for him. This was their chance. He sang it to himself like a chant.

The compound was quiet when he finally made it back. He needed water, and so did the boy. He spied a terra-cotta water jar abandoned under a half-fallen roof, jammed the torch into the accumulated rock, and grabbed the jar. A layer of pumice floated on top, but it was probably all right to drink. He scooped out the top layer and woke the boy.

"Come, Castor, drink this," he said.

The boy fussed but drank when the cool water hit his cracked lips. Tag drank heartily too. He realized the boy needed food as well. Should he risk trying to scrounge up some bread? He slogged toward the demolished kitchen, hoping he could find something.

He found a round loaf someone must have dropped. It tasted of ash, but it gave them both sustenance. Outside again, he grabbed a large garden pillow and handed it to Castor. "Help me hold this over our heads," he told the boy.

At the cellar entrance, the slave guarding the stairs pointed toward the barracks when he asked about Lucia. "She ran that way." The door slammed before he could learn anything more. But he had confirmation. . . . She really *was* there!

As he neared the barracks, he saw light flooding out from an open door. A man stood there, brandishing a bloody *gladius*.

"Pontius?" Tag shouted. "Is that you? Is Lucia with you?"

"Who's there?" the voice roared as Tag came closer.

His heart sank. Not Pontius. *Titurius* — the last person he wanted to see. He must have returned to Pompeii in search of Lucia. Did that mean she was in there with him?

Tag put Castor down. "Listen to me. Do not tell him I am here. But ask him if *Domina* is in there. We must find out."

Castor scrabbled over the pumice toward the light spilling from the open door. "Master, is *Domina* in with you?" he called. "We are looking for *Domina*."

"Who is 'we'?'" Titurius responded.

The boy looked confused. "I mean, just me. I am looking for *Domina*."

Castor froze in fear as the master looked out at the boy with a face like thunder. The child took a step backward.

Tag moved forward from under the eaves. "Do not hurt him," he shouted. "It is me, Tag. I am looking for your daughter."

"Tages?" Titurius shouted. "I should have crucified you myself!"

"Where is Lucia?" he yelled back.

"In here," the master called. "Come inside and see."

But something wasn't right. "Have her call out to me so I know you are telling the truth," he shouted.

Titurius raised his *gladius*. "You *dare* disobey me, *slave*?!"

"Lucia," Tag yelled. "Are you there?"

No answer.

To his amazement, Lucia's purple-faced father stepped out

onto the shifting ground toward him. "I will cut your heart out, boy. I swear it!"

"Go inside with the other men," Tag said to Castor. "Now. They will keep you safe." He needed to run, but not without first knowing Castor was secure.

"Go!" he shouted to the boy again, but Castor could only stare with wide, terrified eyes at the master approaching. Thankfully, the layers of light rock slowed his progress.

Tag caught sight of a long, bright-red shield leaning against the wall. As quickly as he could, he grabbed hold of Castor and pushed the boy to safety under the eaves, shoved the torch into the rocks, and grabbed the top of the long *scutum*, pulling hard with both hands against the accumulation. The shield came free with such force, he almost toppled backward.

From the corner of his eye, Tag caught sight of Castor crouching under the crumbling eaves. "Go to the men!" he repeated to the boy. "You will be safe there."

"No, I am not leaving you!"

Titurius lunged at Tag with the sword. Tag blocked the blow with the shield, which sent him deeper into the bed of ash and rock. He had barely heard the thud of metal on wood over the roaring of the mountain, but he felt the hit vibrate through his arm up to his shoulder. It was as if they moved in a strange dream, where everything was slow and muffled.

Tag concentrated on not losing his balance on the shifting ground as his owner came at him again and again. The master had experience and rage on his side, and pride: Titurius would rather die than allow Tag to live. But Tag had youth and strength; he could outlast Titurius if needed. He kept backing up to draw the master farther away from the room with the light. The man clearly did not like being led into the darkness, and the floating ash seemed to unsettle him.

Suddenly, Lucia's father charged at him like a bull, and Tag barely blocked the swipe at his neck. Titurius bared his teeth in a growl. "Fight, you lily-livered son of a sow!" he roared.

"How can I fight with no weapon?" Tag yelled back. "You have no honor attacking an unarmed man!"

"You are not a man, you are a *slave*! A thing I own!"

They continued circling each other, catching their breaths. Tag's lungs burned as he sucked in the hot, ashy air.

"Leave him be, *Dominus*!" yelled Pontius from the open door. "He will die in the elements soon enough."

"Oh, I'm not going to kill him yet," Titurius said with an ugly grin. "But my fool daughter will come back if she knows he is here, and then I will finish him off in front of her. Call out to her. She can't have gotten far!"

Pontius shook his head but complied. "Lucia! *Domina!*" he yelled. "The *medicus* is here! Come back!"

Lucia was that close? Tag whipped his head around looking for her.

Titurius attacked.

CHAPTER THIRTY-NINE

Lucia

Lucia huddled in the dark under the eaves right outside the barracks. She heard her father's angry voice mixed with the mountain's roaring, and wondered whom he was yelling at this time. Was he sending someone after her? She had to go, but where? Think. *Think.* Could Tag have left with the groups of slaves fleeing to the countryside? Or perhaps he'd gone wherever the laundress was heading. He could be *anywhere*! Despair hovered with every ashy breath.

"*Lucia!*"

She raised her head. Who was calling her?

"The *medicus* is here! Come back!" someone yelled. It didn't sound like her father. Pontius? She trusted Pontius.

She moved toward the sound. "Tag is there?" she shouted back.

"Yes, yes. He has come," bellowed the trainer. "In the cells with us. Come!"

She pushed through the accumulation toward the barracks. As she neared the lit room, she caught sight of shadows moving near a torch set in the ground.

"What is happening?" she called out to Pontius. "Where is Tag?"

"It's a trap!" Tag's hoarse voice emerged from the blackness. "Run!"

She did run, but toward him.

CHAPTER FORTY

TAG

Out of the corner of his eye, he could see a bobbing light moving closer. It had to be Lucia, but he couldn't let himself be distracted. Titurius attacked again, using overhead blows that forced Tag to hold the shield high. After carrying Castor for what seemed like hours, his already-exhausted arms trembled with the effort.

"Stop, Father, stop!" Lucia cried out. "Please! I'm coming."

Titurius turned toward her, and in that moment, Tag remembered Sigdag telling him to go low when someone consistently attacked high. So with every ounce of power and rage Tag had left, he slammed the edge of the shield into the back of Titurius's knees.

The master screamed as both of his legs buckled, but he held on to his sword. Tag smashed the shield down on Titurius's chest and heard the breath go out of him as he sank deep into the bed of tiny rocks. Tag dropped the shield and used two hands to twist Titurius's wrist until he loosened his grip on the sword. With a growl of satisfaction, Tag took it and held it over the man's neck.

"Tag, don't!" Lucia yelled.

"Tell me why I shouldn't," he roared.

"Because he's my father. Because . . . because you're *not* a murderer." She moved closer to him, lowering her voice as if gentling a horse. "You are a healer, Tag. Not a killer."

Lucia was really here? Tag's rage began to dissipate. "He would kill me without a moment's hesitation."

"Let's just leave, Tag. Right now. Take the sword and we'll disappear —"

"Give me the sword, boy," Pontius yelled, coming up behind them.

Tag groaned, still holding the sword to the master's neck. There was no way he could physically overcome the big Samnite. But even as he fought with himself about what to do, Pontius lunged at him and wrestled the sword out of his hand, all in what seemed like a blink.

Lucia moaned. Tag backed up, trying not to lose his balance in the ever-growing accumulation of rock beneath his feet.

"Kill him for me now!" her father yelled.

"No!" Lucia begged.

Tag put his arms up in an appeasing gesture. Pontius had always seemed to like him, but that wouldn't make any difference now — not when the master gave him a direct command. He stopped backing up, dropped his arms, and straightened his spine. It was over. He looked Pontius directly in the eye. *Die with dignity*, he remembered from the gladiator code. He could at least do that.

But instead of striking him, the old overseer announced, "If yer going to run, boy, do it now. This is yer only chance."

Tag released a breath he hadn't even known he was holding.

"WHAT??!" roared Titurius. "You betray me too?"

"Ye will let him go, and ye will unshackle all my fighters," Pontius said, turning to Titurius with the sword. "I will not have them die like penned animals."

"They are my *property*," the master shouted. "I will do with them what I want!"

As the two men argued, Tag ran to Lucia and took her in his arms. "You came back," he whispered, his throat tight.

She squeezed him hard and said, "We need to go *now*."

He nodded. "But I won't leave Castor," he said, turning to look for the boy. "He has to come with us."

A burst of strange thunder rolled over their heads and they all cringed. Flashes of red lightning flickered across the blackness. Castor came running from under one of the eaves. "Why did the master want to hurt you?" he wailed.

Tag looked over at Pontius and Titurius. The overseer had the sword pointed at her father's chest. "Unshackle 'em," Pontius commanded again. Tag sent the old trainer a silent prayer of thanks.

Lucia squeezed his hand to get his attention. "Let's go," she urged.

"We're going to need the torch," Tag said. He scrabbled through the rocks as fast as he could, grabbed the torch, picked up the shield, and ran back toward Lucia and the boy. Castor had his head buried against Lucia's waist, and despite the odds against them, Tag felt his heart lift. They were going to do this. They were finally going to leave. Together.

CHAPTER FORTY-ONE

Lucia

Tag lifted the *scutum*, Castor reclaimed their discarded pillows and blankets, and the three of them huddled under
the rectangular shield for protection as they set off. They
moved as a unit, Lucia holding the torch in front of them, but it
only gave them inches of light in the inky, hot blackness. The
constant pinging of rocks on the shield, combined with the mountain's endless roaring, created an unearthly cacophony straight
out of Pluto's realm.

Like a slow-moving beetle with six legs, they shuffled out of
the compound toward the Nucerian Gate, past the eerily quiet
palaestra and amphitheater in the center of the city. By now, the
streets were mostly empty, though they spied the occasional bobbing light from a torch or lamp.

"Where are we going?" Castor asked several times.

"To safety," Tag always answered.

"Is the world ending?" he asked.

"No," Lucia said. But did she know, really? It certainly seemed
possible.

The little boy began to cry. "It is ending, I can tell."

Lucia took his hand and squeezed. "As long as we are together, the world will not end. I promise. We are going to stick together and make it out."

As they neared the gate, she stepped up on an unusually high crossing stone. To her surprise, it gave beneath her foot, as if she'd trod on an overly filled wineskin. She yelped in shock and fell backward. Tag caught her just in time, though he had to release the torch, and Castor snatched it up from the ground before the fire was snuffed out.

"Did you hurt your ankle again?" he asked.

She shook her head, staring. The thing she had thought a stone was slowly turning into a monster. The ash-coated creature rose on four spindly legs and squealed in outrage.

"It's a pig," Lucia said in wonderment.

The animal grunted and squealed again and worked its trotters in the ash and rock, scattering small stones in its wake as it set off in a panic.

"Why was the pig there?" the boy asked.

"It must have fallen asleep," Tag said to Lucia. "You saved it."

But she didn't see how she helped it at all. When the poor beast tired out and lay down again, it would be covered up just as quickly as before. If she hadn't stepped on it when she did, it probably would have died sooner, more mercifully. She wondered about the other odd shapes she'd seen covered in the layers of tiny rocks. Were they also animals, slowly asphyxiating?

"Oh, gods," she cried out. "Minos! We have to go back for Minos — he's still tied up!"

"No, Lucia, it's all right," Tag soothed her. "I freed him hours ago. He took off. I'm sure he is well away and safe by now."

"He ran off? You freed him?"

"Yes, and we must keep moving, so that we will be free too."

Still, Lucia hesitated. What about Cornelia? Was she all right? Could she really run without ever seeing her again? Without ever saying good-bye?

"What is the matter?" Tag asked.

"What if — what if Cornelia is hurt? What if she needs my help?" Guilt edged her concern as she realized this was the first time since the mountain exploded that she had even thought about her friend.

Tag tugged at her arm. "Cornelia has Antyllus and an army of slaves to take care of her," he reminded Lucia. "She will be fine. Unlike us, if we are caught. We must keep going."

With a pit of worry tightening in her stomach, Lucia knew Tag was right. "Good-bye, my friend," she whispered through a tight throat, and they resumed their slow but persistent plodding. *I will find some way to see you again soon.*

CHAPTER FORTY-TWO

TAG

Tag's muscles trembled with relief, fear, and exhilaration all at once. The world around them had turned into a night-mare, yet it was also giving him the chance to make his greatest dream come true: To escape and live as a free man with Lucia by his side.

He wanted to move faster, to run, but knew it was better to keep their measured pace. Still, he worried about Lucia and the boy. Castor wasn't going to be able to keep walking for long. One of them would have to hold him soon, which would slow them down even more. He wondered if he could create a kind of sling for the child so he could carry him on his back without using his arms.

He was still thinking about how to tie the sling as they neared the Nucerian Gate. He spotted a fresh torch that had been dis-carded on the rocks, and grabbed it. They would need the additional light once their current torch began to sputter.

"Carry this," he told Castor. "We must all do our part."

The boy nodded solemnly and held the unlit torch with both hands.

At the gate, they were surprised to find a small crowd huddled under the tall concrete arches. Some had lamps, and their faces flickered gray with a coating of ash.

"Have you seen my son?" an old man asked them, eyes wide and confused. "His name is Gaius Sabinus."

"No, grandfather. Are you injured?" Tag asked.

"No, no. I . . . I . . ." He looked around as if trying to place where he was. "I am waiting for my son. My son told me to wait for him here. He is fetching a cart for me to ride in. He told me to wait here."

Lucia squeezed Tag's hand. Something wasn't right. He squeezed back as if he sensed it too.

"Perhaps you would be better off on the road. He will find you," she said.

"No. No. No," the man repeated. "He told me to wait at the gate."

"We can't just leave him," she whispered to Tag.

"But we can't take him with us either!" He wanted to help the man, who reminded him of his own dead *apa*, but how could they? And how awful would it be for the son if he actually arrived and his father had disappeared? "We can't help him, Lucia," Tag said. "We must focus on getting out."

She nodded, though he could see it pained her to leave the old man. For a moment, Tag felt a surge of exasperation and frustration. They couldn't save *everybody*! As much as his instincts as a healer told him to do something, he knew that he could not. "His son will come for him," he said aloud, as much for himself as for her. "We must keep moving."

Once through the gate, he breathed deeply. The air still swirled with ash and stank of sulfur, but they were out. Out of Pompeii!

Many of the tombs of the necropolis outside the gate were almost completely covered with mounds of ash and rock. Only the tops of small obelisk-like monuments poked through. The road cutting through the necropolis was only identifiable by the depression in the rocks made by countless Pompeians on the run.

Once past all the graves, Lucia insisted they move off the road.

"Nobody will recognize us in this darkness," Tag said. "We will be fine on the road."

"But we don't know how far this dark cloud extends," Lucia said. "What if someone recognizes me when it clears? They will want to know where my father is, and insist on escorting me to the 'safety' of his friends in Nuceria. And if they don't recognize us," she added more quietly, "Castor is bound to accidentally give us away."

This was true. The boy wouldn't mean to, but he would say something that would let any listeners know who they were — and if Lucius Titurius should decide to follow them, they couldn't take any risks. Tag led them off the main path to the edge of the woods.

"Where are we going?" Castor asked.

"A secret way," Tag answered. This was their original plan — to stay parallel with the main road, but not on it. Only, they had never imagined traveling in such strange and dark circumstances. He looked up at the thin but steady stream of traffic on the road to Nuceria. As long as they kept the flickering torchlights to their left, they would not run into any difficulty.

"It's scary out here!" the boy cried.

"We'll be fine," Tag assured him. "I promise."

CHAPTER FORTY-THREE

Lucia

I t didn't take long after they moved away from the road before Castor began whining. "I'm tired. I'm thirsty."

"We all are, *mellite*," she said. "We just have to bear it until we get to Nuceria."

Tag shook his head. "I should have thought to grab some food and water as we left."

"How could you?" she said. "And from *where*? We had to leave when we did, Tag. Do not blame yourself."

He slowed. "All the same, maybe we should go back on the main road. People are bound to have something to drink with them. We can trade for some —"

She stubbornly shook her head.

"Lucia, we are covered in ash. None of us is recognizable. Maybe staying on the main road is safe enough under the circumstances."

She pointedly looked at Castor and then back at Tag. They simply couldn't risk it, not when they were so close to freedom. Tag sighed, and something about his expression reminded her of Damocles.

"Tag," she said, pausing and looking up at him. "I'm sorry about your *apa*. I saw him. . . ."

He swallowed hard and nodded. After a moment, he said, "Come, we must push on."

Fatigue filled her bones, and she wished she'd slept some the night before. Time seemed to shrink and expand. They could have been walking in the nightmarish world of thick black air for moments or hours. Was it possible to sleep while walking and holding a torch? How else could she explain not noticing that Tag now carried the boy on his back, even as he held up the shield? When had Castor climbed up?

"How did you do that?" she asked.

"Do what?"

"Get Castor on your back?"

Tag furrowed his brow at her. "We stopped and shifted because he was fussing so much. . . ."

She remembered none of this. They trudged on. Slowly, she became aware that Tag was breathing heavily.

"We need to stop and rest," she said. He was clearly exhausted.

He shook his head.

"Let's just go to the edge of the woods and let the shield down for a few minutes," she said. "The trees will give us some protection from the falling pumice."

"But I don't like it in the woods," Castor whined. "I'm scared."

"It's all right," Tag said as he led them to the trees. He put Castor and the shield down and shook his arms out, then jammed the end of the torch into the ever-deepening carpet of rocks, ash, and stone.

Castor plopped down on the carpet of small stones. "Ouch," he mumbled.

Lucia winced when she leaned back against a tree. She'd forgotten the shawl she'd bound to her back. She lifted it over her head and placed it in front of Tag.

"What is in here?"

"The money I had put away for us," she said. "You know, the hoard. I went back for it before I started looking for you."

"Smart girl," he murmured.

She smiled up at him. "It should be enough to pay our way to Thurii, I think."

Tag sat next to her, suddenly looking stricken. She leaned toward him. "What is the matter?"

"I . . . I didn't grab any medical things. I started to, but then the mountain exploded, and I was only thinking of getting Castor to safety. But I can't start treating people without supplies."

She touched the scowl lines breaking through the caked ash on his forehead, then caressed his cheek. "We will just buy some with my savings. It will be all right. There is enough here to get us through."

"I'm sorry," he said.

"Do not be sorry. We are together, and we're going to be free."

He leaned forward and kissed her. He tasted of ash, salt, and sweat. She closed her eyes.

"Ugh," Castor said. "You look like statues kissing."

They grinned at each other, and a sense of giddy exultation hit them both at the same time.

"I love you, Lucia, my heart," Tag whispered, kissing her again.

"And I love you, Tages the Etruscan Prophet."

"Can I play with the treasure while you kiss?" Castor asked, untying the shawl and digging his hands into the pile of coins and jewels.

Lucia smiled. "Just for a moment," she said.

"Oooh, what is this?" he asked, holding out her brother's ring.

"It was once my brother's, but now it belongs to Tag," she said. "It means he's free."

Castor tipped his head slightly and frowned. "Is it a magic ring?"

She looked at Tag, whose expression of surprise made her grin. "Put it on. Put it on and never take it off. Nobody will ever treat you as a slave again while you wear this."

"But how does the magic ring make him free?" Castor said.

"It's not magic. It marks him as a citizen," Lucia explained.

The boy continued frowning. "But . . . but who freed him?"

"No one —" she began.

"She did," Tag said.

Castor looked more confused than ever. Lucia took Tag's wrist and slipped the ring onto the fourth finger of his right hand. "Never take it off, do you hear me?" she whispered.

He nodded and gripped her hand tight.

"Well, can you free me too?" the boy cried.

"All right," she said. "I now declare you free. You are no longer a slave."

"Where is my cizimen ring that says I'm free?"

She chuckled.

"You will get your citizen's ring when you are a man," Tag explained.

"Oh." The boy looked at Tag with a skeptical scowl. "I thought only the master could free us."

"The master is my father, remember," Lucia said. "And that is enough." She didn't want to have to explain that they weren't free according to Roman law, that Castor was right: Only her father could legally manumit them. But they were starting anew, and they would start *free*. All of them. It was the only way.

Castor seemed to accept her answer and went back to digging through the treasure. After a few more minutes' rest, Tag began gathering their things. "Help me pack up," he ordered the boy.

"NO!" Castor shouted with unusual force.

Tag's and Lucia's heads snapped up, and they looked at Castor with wide, astonished eyes.

The little boy crossed his arms. "I don't have to do anything you tell me now that I'm *free*!"

Lucia suppressed a smile.

"You have to do what I tell you," Tag said as he tied up the shawl. "Because I am like your father, your *apa* now. And all boys must obey their *apa*s."

Lucia saw the expression on the boy's face and signaled to Tag, who paused in his packing.

"This is true?" Castor asked shyly. "That you are like my *apa*?"

"Yes."

"*Like* my *apa* or now my *actual apa*?"

"Both. No. Your actual *apa*. From here on out."

She waited for the boy to ask her if she would be his *mater* — but he didn't, which, she had to admit, gave her a pang of disappointment. Perhaps that would come later. Still, she liked the idea of the three of them together, like a family. It felt comforting somehow. More hopeful. And it would provide an excellent cover: Her father would set slave catchers on the lookout for his daughter and a male slave, not for a young family.

"Can I *call* you *apa*?" Castor asked Tag in a quiet voice.

Lucia watched Tag carefully. It was hard to tell with the caked-on ash, but it seemed as if a pang of grief shot through him at the question. He must have been thinking about poor Damocles. She squeezed his hand.

Tag smiled at Castor, though, and ruffled his ashy hair. "Yes, you can call me *apa*."

The beaming smile the boy gave him in return made Lucia's entire being swell with love for Tag.

CHAPTER FORTY-FOUR

TAG

They set off again, with every step like an exaggerated pantomime of walking. The accumulation sucked at their feet, so it felt as if small demons held their ankles until the last possible moment, when they released them with a pop, only to grab them again with the next step. It was slow going.

As they walked, Tag pressed a kiss on Lucia's forehead. His throat grew tight as he thought about what she'd given up for him, about the way she'd looked at him when she slipped the citizen ring onto his finger. He had not known it was possible to love someone as he loved her. It made him ache, and — at the same time — drove him to promise himself that he would devote the rest of his life to making her happy.

And then he grew giddy again. *The rest of their lives. Free!*

They reluctantly moved closer to the main road when they neared the Sarnus River, which roiled and foamed with rocks, pumice, and debris. Crossing the main bridge, along with everyone else, was their only option.

When a break between groups of refugees emerged — which seemed to take an age — the three of them scurried onto the bridge. The wooden pass creaked and groaned, and Tag wondered how long its supports would last under the constant deluge of rocks and people.

Once on the other side, Tag heaved a sigh of relief. They stayed on the main road for some time, which pleased him, but it wasn't long before Lucia suggested they once again move away from the stream of people. "It will be all right," he said. "Truly. Nobody is paying attention to us."

But he spoke too soon. A group of refugees kept looking back at them fearfully.

"We have weapons if you come any closer," one man shouted at them. "And we will use them if you try to steal from us or take our slaves!"

"Gods, why do they think we would do that?" Lucia asked.

Tag noticed several groups gathering together ahead of them. Light from torches flickered on drawn knives and swords.

"What is happening?" Castor cried.

"It's the shield, I think," Tag said, remembering that the name of the gladiatorial school was clearly painted on it. "Maybe they think we're escaped gladiators out to start another slave revolt or something."

"Let's move off the road, Tag, please," Lucia urged.

Without another word, Tag led them away from the road and they resumed their parallel trek.

He noticed Lucia kept peering behind them. "We are well away from the road," he said. "Do not worry, *mi ocelle*."

She shook her head. "I know. It's just that . . ."

"What?"

"I think . . . I think someone is following us."

Fear stabbed through his belly. "Impossible."

"There is a light that has consistently trailed us. It got closer while we waited to cross the bridge, and then it left the road when we did."

He turned to look. She was right. A small light moved toward them in a steady march. Did he imagine the light listed a little, as if the person was limping?

"Perhaps someone got confused and followed us, thinking we were still on the main road," she said, almost hopefully. "It would be understandable in this darkness."

He grunted. That may have been true when they first separated from the main throughway, but not now. Someone had made a deliberate decision to follow their light. Had Titurius sent a slave catcher after them? No, Titurius wouldn't have been able to hire anyone that quickly. Could it be Titurius himself? But her father wasn't physically capable of following them for so long, was he?

Then he remembered how much money was at stake. Lucia's marriage to Quintus meant the survival of Titurius's livelihood. He would never allow that kind of wealth to escape his grasp without a fight. Tag forced himself to breathe.

"We're far enough ahead that we should still make it to Nuceria before whoever that confused soul is," he said in a falsely calm voice. Mentioning her father would only panic everyone — especially Castor.

She nodded, but he could tell she did not feel any easier about it. Without saying a word, they began moving faster. Castor must have picked up on their anxiety, because he did not complain. For a brief time, anyway.

Despite Tag's reassurances, Lucia kept glancing over her shoulder.

"Tag," she said quietly. "Maybe we should put out the torch. He . . . whoever that is . . . will lose us in the darkness if we don't give him a target to follow. Then we can continue with the light after he's gone."

Before Tag could respond, Castor jumped in with a panicked voice. "No, the dark is scary! What if we get lost? Or an animal gets us! We have to have the light!"

Tag breathed out, agreeing. He didn't relish the idea of maneuvering through the inky dark without their torch. "Maybe we should try the main road again," he said. "Whoever that is won't be able to distinguish our torch from all the others."

Lucia shook her head. "No! You saw how those people reacted to us. And even if they aren't hostile, they might recognize one of us. We've gone too far to risk it. Let's just quicken our pace. Once in Nuceria, we'll disappear in the chaos."

Tag snuck a look behind him. They did seem to be putting more distance between themselves and the bobbing light. Still, shouldn't they have been in the city by now? Why was it taking so long?

"Tag, listen," Lucia said after a time.

"To what?"

"The pinging on the shield. It has slowed down."

She was right. They seemed to be reaching the edge of the dark cloud of spitting rocks. They could even see a small lightening of the sky ahead of them. Finally, some indication that the nightmare might be ending! That had to mean they were through the worst of it, didn't it?

Tag stopped and put the shield down. Some small, pitted rocks still rained down on them, but it was nothing like the constant deluge before. He caught a few in his outstretched hand.

"We don't need this anymore," he said, throwing the large shield to the side. "We'll go faster without it."

"Are you sure?" Lucia asked.

"The sooner we get to the city, the sooner we can disappear. At this point, speed is what we need."

He led the way, even faster still.

CHAPTER FORTY-FIVE

~~~

Lucia

(Hours Before)

Tag was right. They did move more quickly without the shield. Still, she felt naked — exposed and vulnerable — without it.

They took turns carrying Castor. When the lightening sky ahead of them disappeared behind a hill, Tag took the boy from her. "Let me carry him during the climb."

He tossed the boy onto his back, and Castor clung to him like a little monkey. She was glad because the climb was more difficult than she remembered. But then, she'd always been in a cart or carriage when she'd traveled to Nuceria with her father.

Tag turned to her and grinned. He'd traveled to Nuceria too, so he knew what the climb meant as well. This was their last challenge. The last hill before the city! She grinned back up at him. Their new life was right on the other side.

Once in the city, she would find the baths, first thing. She looked at her arms, caked with ash, the creases of her elbows cracked and pitted where she'd held Castor. Even her eyelashes felt heavy with debris. *Gods, to be clean again.* She envisioned all the cool, sparkling water spilling from faun fountains on street corners . . . imagined the feel of it slipping down her raw, coated throat . . . conjured the sensation of her newly scrubbed skin, emerging golden and glowing from scented water, and almost groaned with anticipation.

Lucia and Tag were both breathing hard when they got to the ridge. As soon as Castor slid down his back, Tag bent over, hands on his knees. Lucia patted his back as he tried to regain his breath, coughing and panting in the still-ashy air. He stood and put his arm around her shoulders, drawing her in close.

Castor scampered to the edge overlooking the valley. "Is that the city? Is that where we are going?" he asked.

"Yes, that is Nuceria," she said.

The early-morning light glimmered off Nuceria's red-tiled roofs and bronze-edged temples. They stared at the light in wonder. Spiny fingers of the mountain's monstrous ash cloud seemed to reach for — but not quite touch — the shining city. Soon they would also be out from under its darkness.

Lucia squeezed Tag's waist and put her head on his shoulder. "I think amidst all this destruction, the god hid a small gift for us," she whispered.

He looked down at her in surprise.

"We never would have had the opportunity to run otherwise," she said. "I do not understand Vulcan's wrath or why he is punishing Pompeii, but we must make a sacrifice to him and all the gods for allowing us to escape together." She quickly made the sign against evil in case the gods took their success so far as a challenge.

"We must make for the poor section of town right away," he said, as if reminding himself of the plan. "No one will think to look for us in the squalid areas."

It was true, which gave her hope. Even if her father had somehow followed — or sent someone after them — she was sure it would never occur to him to start in the poorest section of town. He might eventually end up there, but by then they'd be gone.

Still, a chill of fear ran up her spine. Would she stand out too much in the poor district? Would she be able to manage the deprivations? She tried to imagine a life with no money for scrolls or papyrus and ink. No fine foods or good wine. No sweet-smelling oils. Only the clothing on her body. Had she inadvertently bound herself to a life of even less freedom than she would have enjoyed with Quintus?

As if sensing her thoughts, Tag cleared his throat. "Lucia, my heart, are you regretting this?" he asked haltingly. "If you've changed your mind, I . . . I could take you to the home of one of your father's friends and —"

No, she wanted this. She'd chosen him and a new life, a freedom of a sort she'd never imagined available to her. Even if it meant their lives would be hard, she would never regret that. "Gods, no!" she said.

He grinned in relief.

"We should go," she said. "We're so close."

He nodded and they released each other. "Castor, let's go," he called.

No response.

"Castor!"

They looked at each other, their eyes widening. Could he have fallen or tripped down the hill? No. It was more likely that he had gone clambering around the other side.

"Castor!" Lucia yelled more loudly. Maybe he hadn't heard them over the incessant rumbling of the still-spewing mountain.

A small sound came from above them. They both raced after it.

CHAPTER FORTY-SIX

TAG

They found him standing on the other side of the high ridge. "Castor!" Lucia exclaimed. "Gods, you scared us! Don't run from us again."

But the boy didn't respond. He seemed transfixed. "What is that?" he whispered as he pointed over the valley.

"Pompeii," Lucia whispered too.

Tag saw what had captivated the boy. As the rising sun warmed Nuceria behind them, their old city was still in total darkness. The mountain's black cloud, occasionally shot through with eerie flashes of red lightning, panted menacingly overhead. Even so, tiny lights emerged from the morass, flickering and bobbing around the buildings. "It looks like people are coming out of their homes to assess the damage," he mused.

"Oh, good," Lucia breathed.

"Good?" he asked, thinking about her father. If he hadn't been the one following them, then he would certainly set slave catchers after them now.

"I was thinking about Cornelia," she said. "This has to mean she's safe now, don't you think?"

"Yes, of course," he said, wondering if that were true.

It was a lovely sight, really, the numerous lamps and torches like stars winking in a wide expanse of black. The city survived. Despite never wanting to see Pompeii again, Tag thought the signs of life were at least a symbol of hope.

"They're like your lights!" Castor exclaimed, grinning up at Lucia.

Lucia blinked. "What?" she asked, but the boy had already turned back to the view.

"He's talking about your eyes again," Tag said.

She laughed and shook her head. He laughed too, kissing her ashy forehead. But he did not want to spend any more time looking backward. It was time to go. "Come," he said. "Nuceria awaits."

At that very moment, a thunderous cracking, tearing sound exploded all around them. Castor ran to Tag, wild-eyed. Tag scooped him up and the boy gripped him tight. Lucia curled into him as well. Tag wanted to run, but the booming crash paralyzed him with fear. Was the mountain collapsing in on itself? On them?

Over Castor's trembling head, Tag peered at the monstrous cloud that had devoured the top half of Mount Vesuvius. A massive, menacing nebula of heat and ash and rock — an enormous billowing monster of gray and red — crashed down inside the giant ash column. It bubbled at the lip of the crater as if gathering strength, then began barreling down the mountain. Fingertips of red extended out from the roiling mass as it hurtled toward Pompeii. Toward the small flickering lights. Toward all those people who thought the worst was over.

"Run!" Tag breathed, as if the people in the streets of Pompeii could hear him. *"Run! Run!"*

With moans of horror, they watched as the immense cloud rolled over the city — like a giant hand pushing a face under water, Tag thought, and holding it there until all signs of life were gone. The land went black, and when the roiling mass hit the sea, the ocean writhed and hissed as if in agony, emitting great billows of steam.

A wall of heat reached them then, bringing with it a whiff of poison and sulfur and death. *Pluto's breath*, he thought. *No, Mephistis's*, and he was awed by the goddess's destructive reach. He pressed both Castor's and Lucia's faces into his chest to keep the worst of it from their lungs. Within seconds, the smell receded, just as the cloud reversed its course back over the city and up the mountain's flanks, like a wave being sucked back into the sea.

He blinked away the burning air. It took a moment for him to make sense of what he saw.

Where Pompeii had been flickering to life only moments ago, there was nothing. Every small winking light had been snuffed out. Every sign of hope had been obliterated. Nothing was left of the city except a sea of smoldering, hissing blackness.

CHAPTER FORTY-SEVEN

Lucia

I don't understand," Lucia murmured. "The mountain . . . It *swallowed* Pompeii."

Castor began to cry into Tag's neck.

"What's happened?" a voice roared. "What's happened?"

She turned, stunned. *"Father?"*

Lucius Titurius was weaving from exhaustion, his eyes wide with horror as he stared at the obliterated city below them. Tag pulled Lucia away as her father lurched toward the edge of the ridge. Tag put Castor down and murmured to him to go to the ridge facing Nuceria. But the boy refused to move, clinging to Tag's tunic.

Titurius threw down the torch he'd been carrying and fell to his knees. "Where did it go? Where?" he cried.

"The mountain took it," Lucia said again. Even as the words came out of her mouth, she could not fully fathom their meaning. How was it possible? And yet the evidence was right there — everything was gone. Their home. The school. The gladiators. Metrodona and everyone else in the house.

And, oh, gods! Cornelia and her baby. She covered her face. Oh, no, no. Cornelia *must* have escaped! Surely Antyllus would've sent them out of the city at the first sign of trouble, maybe even when the earthquake hit. Perhaps they escaped via his boat. Didn't Cornelia say he had one? Yes, they were probably bobbing on the bay that very moment, safely away from the black destruction that swallowed Pompeii.

Yet even as she tried to convince herself that her dearest friend had survived, her heart grew heavy. She knew Cornelia had been too far along with child to run. She would have stayed in Pompeii with her husband and family in the hopes that whatever this was would soon pass. And now she was gone. No one could have survived that.

Her father moaned pitifully.

"We need to run," Tag whispered into her ear.

Lucia stared at the smoking blackness that had once been her beloved city, feeling as if each leg was a block of marble sunk deep into the earth. How could she move when Cornelia never would again?

CHAPTER FORTY-EIGHT

TAG

Lucia's father finally spoke. "It's your fault," he wheezed, rising from his knees, pointing. "*Your* fault."

"No, Father, please," Lucia said. But Tag knew he wasn't talking to her. He was looking at him.

The old man unsheathed his *gladius*, and a jolt of fear flooded Tag's limbs.

"You both need to go down to the other side," he told Lucia and Castor as coolly as he could manage. Castor began whimpering. "Go," he repeated.

Titurius pointed the tip of the sword at Tag. "You. You are the curse-bearer. You made this happen. Everything started falling apart after that day."

"What's he talking about, Tag?" Lucia asked shakily. "Father, what are you saying? What curse?"

Tag clenched his teeth. "Lucia, get away with Castor, please. I will follow," he urged. He lifted his chin at Titurius and called in as strong a voice as he could muster, "No, *you* cursed your family. The gods are punishing *you* for your outrage."

"I should have killed you when I had the chance," Titurius said.

"Stop. This is madness!" Lucia cried. "Father, go back to Pompeii. Perhaps . . . perhaps the school can still be saved. We were on the edge of the city. The mountain may not have reached it. It may not be too late."

She glanced at Tag, and then back at her father. Tag instantly understood. Despite the fact that everything had almost certainly been destroyed, perhaps her overwhelmed father could be convinced to go back to Pompeii and see the devastation for himself, which would give them enough time to disappear.

Titurius hesitated for a moment, but then the mad gleam in his eyes grew brighter. "I will go back. But not without you, daughter, and not before I kill the source of all my misery."

Titurius and Tag began to circle each other. The ridge overlooking Pompeii loomed dangerously close. Tag's right hand twitched in want of a sword to defend himself. "I didn't curse you," he shouted, trying to buy time. "Your wife did."

He heard Lucia take in a breath. Gods, why wouldn't she listen to him and get away?

"I could have had it reversed," Titurius said. "I know I could have, if only you hadn't plunged the iron nail into it."

"Father, what are you talking about?" Lucia cried again.

Tag put his hands up in a calming gesture. "Lucia is right. The school may yet be saved," he lied, grasping at their only hope. "Go back."

"Not before you die," he said, lunging at Tag. Lucia screamed, but Tag easily dodged the blade. Titurius came after him again and again, Tag dancing away every time. The old man was weaving and wheezing. Surely Tag could disarm him. He just had to wait for the right opportunity.

If only he had a weapon. If only he had kept his shield . . .

"Father, stop!" Lucia cried. "Don't hurt Tag. Let him go. Go back to Pompeii and leave us be."

"I am not going without you, girl. Your marriage to Quintus is the only thing that will save us now."

Tag looked beyond the ruined city, realizing that not just Pompeii had gone dark. The whole region was blacked out — even Herculaneum, which meant Quintus was likely gone too. Despite his dislike for the spoiled patrician, Tag felt a pang. Nobody deserved to die in such an awful way.

Lucia pointed at the coastline. "I see no lights around Herculaneum," she said, as if reading his mind. "Quintus is dead. Your only hope now is rescuing what remains of the school. You must go back."

"There may yet be gladiators who live," Tag added. "If they are in the cells, they'll be waiting for rescue as we speak."

Titurius slid his red-rimmed gaze to the still-smoldering city. Tag could tell he was considering it. He really had gone mad if he thought anyone survived the mountain's attack. But if they could convince him it was possible, they had a chance.

Tag felt Lucia's small hand move into his as she gently tugged him back. "Go," she said to her father in a soothing tone. "Pontius will not be able to control the men for long without you. He *needs* you."

Staring into the blackness, Titurius nodded over and over again, clearly wanting to believe it was true. But then he turned, saw their linked hands, and his eyes grew wide with outrage. "You *dare* touch my daughter in front of me?" he bellowed.

What happened next occurred in an instant, yet somehow, at the same time, with dreamlike slowness.

Titurius pulled his sword arm back and lunged. Tag tried to pull Lucia away, but she leapt forward, arms out in appeal. In the space of a blink, the sword thrust meant for Tag's left kidney plunged into Lucia between her lower ribs instead. Tag heard the faintest *clang* as the sword tip stabbed the hoard of coins and jewels slung on her back.

The three of them froze — all staring with disbelief at the weapon sunk deep into Lucia's chest. Black liquid blossomed around the sunken blade. Titurius began to pull the sword back.

"No!" The medic in Tag took over. "Don't take it out!" he shouted. He needed to assess the damage before he could allow the sword to slice backward through her flesh. But he hadn't spoken quickly enough, and in horror, Titurius pulled the sword out of the front of his daughter's chest. He staggered, moaning in shock.

Tag quickly untied the shawl containing Lucia's hoard; the sack fell to the ground with a clattering thump. He cursed at the sight of spreading blood on the back of her *tunica* where the sword tip had gone through. He pressed on the cut, trying to contain the bleeding. Lucia gasped in pain and stumbled toward her father before he could look at the entry wound. Titurius keened and backed away, the sword still dripping blood. It seemed to Tag that they were all moving as if underwater.

With a dazed, uncomprehending look, Lucia stared down at herself. She looked up at Tag with enormous eyes.

"I can fix this," he said. "I promise. It's going to be all right."

Lucia shuddered with pain as he continued pressing on the wound in her back, reaching to apply pressure on the front too. The movement propelled her forward again, which made her father back up even more. Tag gripped her arm, trying to steady her. "No, no, Lucia, don't move. Let me —"

"You," she gasped, staring wild-eyed at Titurius. "You killed all your girls. You cursed us all." Her voice, thick and dry, sounded like it came from the underworld.

"No," her father said, hands still on his head, his expression contorted with horror. "No. I'm sorry," he said. "I'm sorry."

"*I* curse you," she wheezed. "The Furies will haunt you for eternity!"

"No, please," Titurius cried as he continued backing up. His back leg slid on some loose rocks, and his knee buckled under him. He tumbled backward, his arms waving as he tried to catch himself.

But he was too close to the edge of the outcropping. It happened in eerie silence. Titurius's mouth moved, but Tag heard nothing. In a blink, the man who owned him disappeared over the ridge, hurtling to his death, back toward Pompeii, his demolished city.

CHAPTER FORTY-NINE

Lucia

(Moments Before)

Castor began to sob behind them.

"Father?" she managed. One moment he was in front of her, the next he was gone. Had she blacked out? This pain clawing at her side made it hard to concentrate. To think. To breathe. She needed air, but even as she gulped, it wasn't enough.

"He . . . has gone to Pompeii," Tag said, his voice cracking. "Now, I must treat you."

"Hurts," she said, gasping.

"Shhhh, I will take care of it. You must follow my instructions," he said. But his voice and hands were shaking. He sat her down when she began to sway. The movement was excruciating. "You're going to be all right," he chanted over and over again, and she couldn't be sure if he was saying it for her benefit or for his.

Air. She needed more air. Fire flashed through her side. She clutched at Tag's arm as he gently laid her on the ground. "Castor!" he called.

She could see that the boy was crying as he ran toward them. "I need your help."

Castor nodded even as he continued weeping.

Lucia tried to say, "Good boy," to encourage the child, to tell him not to be afraid, but her mouth was filled with a thick paste of hot metal, and when she tried to speak, only a gurgling sound came out.

Poor little boy. He was so scared. But Tag was here. Tag was going to take care of everything. It was going to be all right.

If only she could take a breath. Searing pain tore through her again. Gods. She needed air — the clean air that was *just* on the other side of this hill. The pure air in Nuceria. They could see it. Why couldn't she *breathe* it? She gasped and clamored for it — for *any* air now — dirty or not, but it didn't come.

She heard fabric tearing. Tag was going to wrap her wound, sew her up, and everything would be all right. He was a good *medicus*. He'd often described how he stitched up gladiators. He'd stitched up worse wounds than this. She knew he had.

Then why was he crying?

"Stay with me," he kept whispering. "Please stay with me." Which she did not understand, because she had no intention of going anywhere without him, now or ever again. Her father hadn't hurt Tag. That was the most important thing. Tag said he'd returned to Pompeii. They were finally free. It was going to be all right.

She gasped again for air, yet also felt it rushing out of the opening in her chest. Despite the pain, she tried to press her hand on it, so the air would stay in.

"It's collapsing," Tag murmured. Pain — white-hot and blinding — tore through her. She wanted to scream, but only a dry, desperate gasp emerged.

She forced her eyes open so that she could look at Tag, even as small lights exploded around the edges of her vision. The massive wave of pain threatened to make everything go black. Why couldn't she move her mouth to speak? She wanted to tell him everything would be all right. She wanted to tell him she loved him. And she would, once she was on the other side of the pain. Once she could take a breath. She would definitely say it then. . . .

But the wave hit again, and she went under.

CHAPTER FIFTY

TAG

ods, no, please, no, please, no . . .
His hands weren't moving fast enough.
No no no no no no no.

He'd torn strips of fabric from her *tunica*, but he didn't have enough. And gods, the cloth was so *filthy*, caked with dirt and ash. He pictured the basket of clean linen strips he was always trying to get Castor to roll up for him in the medical room. And his surgical tools. His tools! The ones that would allow him to clamp the bleeding, to sew her up, to keep her with him. But he didn't have them. He didn't have anything he needed.

This is just a bad dream, he told himself over and over again. Yet he knew there was no way around the fact that her father had slashed through both sides of her lung. And that they were stuck at the top of a dark hill, thick with sulfurous air, without water, without medicine.

Still, he would save her. Somehow, he would save her. He would just have to carry her to Nuceria, where he could get the tools to sew her up, where he would find medicine, clean water, and help. It wasn't that far now. He could do it.

Castor made a choking, sobbing sound.

"Castor, you have to stay calm. Now listen, I'm going to pick her up, and you'll have to carry everything else. Do you understand?"

"Her lights are gone," the boy wailed, staring at Lucia's face. "Her lights are gone."

Tag froze. *No, no, no, no, no . . .*

He'd seen death before, seen the emptiness in the eyes, but he refused to believe it. His shaking fingers searched her neck to feel the pulse he always loved to kiss. Even when he confirmed its absence, he wouldn't admit the truth. Because she couldn't be gone. It was not possible. *Simply not possible.* Not when they were so *close.*

As the truth finally pierced him, the pain roared through him with the raw, incoherent force of the spewing mountain. And like the mountain, he felt turned inside out with it. He was beyond speech. Beyond understanding. This wasn't happening. Couldn't be happening. Not now.

Tag could do nothing but curl around her as the rage and grief washed over him, stealing his breath, splintering his insides into endless jagged points of misery. Frightened, Castor wept too, their sounds an echo of the mountain's last thundering act of destruction.

CHAPTER FIFTY-ONE

TAG

(After)

He felt a tug at his shoulder. A frightened, hoarse voice breathed into his ear. "Healer?"

Tag did not respond.

"Apa?" the voice called louder. "I'm scared. I'm thirsty."

Tag didn't say anything. Couldn't say anything. He never wanted to move again. How could he, knowing he had borne a curse that came true? Titurius attacked another innocent of his household and died right after, just as the curse foretold. Had Tag set it all in motion when he pierced the curse tablet with iron so long ago? Was it his fault?

The weight of that possibility immobilized him. He wanted to die here next to Lucia. Death was the ultimate freedom, wasn't it? Let a blanket of the still-swirling ash enshrine their entwined bodies for eternity. They would be free together forever.

But the sound of the little boy's desperate, fear-filled cries broke through his fog. Castor was coughing and hiccupping, and something about his terror reached Tag and shook him.

He needed to help the child.

Tag stirred and looked at the boy. Castor's eyes looked sunken and dull. No tears made tracks down his face, even though he was crying. Tag knew that meant the boy's humors were deeply, dangerously out of balance. Too much fire and earth, not enough water. He needed to get the boy liquids, as well as food and shelter.

But when he thought about Lucia, his will to move, to do anything, fled yet again. His eyes closed, weighed down by grief and ash. Yet he could not block out the sound of the child's weakening whimpers.

It was almost as if he heard Lucia's voice in his ear: *"Tag, this was not your fault."*

He groaned in misery. Would he ever believe that?

"You are a healer," Lucia continued in his mind.

But he hadn't healed *her*! Hadn't protected her. And so what was the point?

"You must help Castor."

Despite his despair, he pushed himself up, sloughing off the ash that had accumulated over him like powdered snakeskin. He stared at the ring on his soot-covered hand, the ring she herself had put on him, the ring that would keep him from ever being a slave again. But he didn't want life — or freedom — without her by his side. Without Lucia.

The boy whimpered weakly. How long had they been out there? Years? Decades? Lifetimes?

The boy needed care. *His* care.

He croaked the boy's name. Castor looked at him, dull-eyed. He needed to carry the child who now called him *apa* to safety. The thought kept him from lying back down. *Castor needed him.*

So, against every impulse, he forced himself up to standing, swaying with sorrow and misery. He took a coin from their stash and began to weep again.

I can't do it. I can't do it. I can't do it. I can't . . .

The boy seemed to understand. He took the coin from Tag's trembling fingers, crawled to his beloved, and placed it between her cold lips as Tag closed her empty eyes.

"Thank you," Tag managed.

He returned to the unwrapped shawl of coins, and with thick, heavy fingers, riffled through it. There. The little votive. He picked up the small clay figure of Turan, the Etruscan goddess of love, and placed it within her curled palm. When he'd first given it to her, he'd said, "You hold my soul in your hands." It would always be so now.

He felt her wing votive still in his small bag at his belt. Should he put it in her other hand? No, she'd given the wing — and freedom — to him. He would keep both.

Unsteadily, Tag straightened her limbs and smoothed her blood-soaked, torn dress. He took the blanket — the one that had connected them back in Pompeii, the one smelling of lemons and pine and *her* — and placed it over her body, moving it toward her head.

He paused at her neck, unable to go on. His hands shook so hard he dropped the cloth. For the last time, he touched his lips to her cold mouth. *"Te amabo in aeternum,"* he whispered against them. *I will love you for all eternity.*

Only then did he find the strength to pull the blanket over her face like a shroud.

He wished he could set her body aflame to release her soul, but he did not have the means nor the strength. So he prayed to

Mercury to escort her gently into Pluto's realm without the funeral pyre.

He gathered their things and picked up the boy, who lacked the energy to cling to him in his usual manner. Instead, Castor's limbs hung listlessly, his head flopping on Tag's shoulder as they set off toward the city she'd promised would lead to their life of freedom.

Pale beams of light broke through the edges of the thinning but still monstrous cloud as they neared Nuceria. Bits of ash hung in the thick, heavy air like motes swirling in dirty water. Would they ever breathe clean air again?

As he walked, Tag forced himself to consider what he needed to do next. He would go directly to the poor section of the city, where no one would question him. He would gather what he needed to set off with the boy to Thurii. And there he would follow through on the plan they'd made together. For her.

"Almost there," he half whispered, half croaked to the sleeping child.

But Castor had not been sleeping. He raised his head and looked up at Tag.

"Are we still free?" he whispered.

It was a long time before Tag could answer through the jagged rock of grief lodged in his throat. He would never be free of the sorrow and regret of losing her. But he knew that was not what the boy meant.

"Yes," he answered finally. "She set us free."

AUTHOR'S NOTE

The History of Pompeii

The original founders and inhabitants of Pompeii were a mix of Etruscan, Samnite, and Greek peoples. After Rome conquered Pompeii in 80 BCE, it was considered a colony of Rome. I based Tages's family history on the supposition that the transition into a Roman city was not necessarily pleasant for all involved, particularly the replaced old guard.

The Eruption

It is hard for us to imagine, but locals did not know that Vesuvius was a volcano. Before 79 CE and the events depicted here, it had not erupted in nearly two thousand years. The Greek geographer Strabo conjectured that Vesuvius may have once burned but that it had long ago ceased doing so. The ancient Romans did not even have the word *volcano*, Strabo called such phenomena "earth-born fires."

Vesuvius's volcanic eruption released a hundred thousand times the thermal energy released by the Hiroshima atomic bomb. It spewed volcanic gas, rock, pumice, and ash in a column that hurtled twenty miles into the air, discharging its contents at the rate of 1.5 million tons *per second*. This type of explosion is called a *plinean explosion*, thanks to Pliny the Elder's description of a massive column that spread out like an umbrella pine. (To us, it would have looked like a mushroom cloud.) The eruption of rock and ash lasted for eighteen hours, with approximately eight feet of pumice stones falling on Pompeii. It was during this period that most inhabitants escaped. The second phase of the explosion buried Pompeii and surrounding cities in avalanches of superheated gases, ash, and dirt called *pyroclastic flows*. There was little or no lava; instead, people and animals were killed instantly by intensely hot (around 500 or more degrees Fahrenheit) poisonous gas surges. These pyroclastic flows then cooled and hardened over the city, burying it for nearly two thousand years. In the novel, I placed Tag and Lucia on a hill overlooking the city so that we could witness the destruction of the killer pyroclastic flow with them.

Most Pompeians escaped to Napoli (Naples), Nola, and Nuceria; we know this because we have letters from officials of those cities, asking the Roman Senate for money for help in taking care of Pompeian refugees. The Roman cities of Herculaneum, Stabiae, and Oplontis were also destroyed by Vesuvius. Scholars believe that most of the people who died in Pompeii were those who did not have the means to escape — no horses or carriages, nor anywhere to go. As in modern disasters, it was likely the poor who suffered the most; indeed, most of the bones found are of women, children, and the elderly (*Resurrecting Pompeii* by E. Lazer).

In the nineteenth century, archaeologists made haunting plaster casts of over a hundred of the bodies of those who died in Pompeii. Close to 1,200 bodies have been discovered in total. Many bodies of animals were preserved in plaster as well, including casts of dogs, horses, pigs, and donkeys. I based Lucia's dog,

Minos, on the heartbreaking cast of a dog who died still chained to his post. But in my version, I made sure the dog was released and ran to safety — the benefits of fiction!

The Date of Eruption

Many readers may notice that I set the date of Vesuvius's eruption not on the traditional date of August 24, 79 CE, but in early October of that same year. Why? Because many leading archaeologists and scholars now believe the August 24 date is incorrect.

Despite what some textbooks may say, there has never been a clear consensus on the date of the explosion. In fact, at the turn of the twentieth century, most believed the volcano exploded in November. The confusion can be traced back to monks who translated (or mistranslated) Pliny the Younger's letters in the Middle Ages. Pliny the Younger was the nephew of the naturalist Pliny the Elder, who died in the eruption in the midst of commanding the Roman navy to rescue as many people from the coast as possible. Pliny the Younger, seventeen at the time, witnessed the event from across the bay and recorded his observations decades later.

Today, most archaeologists believe Vesuvius exploded in the fall of 79 CE. They point to strong physical evidence in support of this claim, including:

• Harvested autumnal fruits have been found in the correct archaeological strata in villas near Pompeii. Pomegranates, in particular, point to an autumn eruption, since, in Italy, they tend to ripen in late September or early October. Dried figs and grapes (both of which would have been harvested in late summer) were also discovered.

- A number of victims appeared to be wearing heavier clothing more appropriate to cooler weather. One skeleton in Herculaneum was discovered wearing a fur cap. To be fair, people may have donned layers of clothing to protect themselves from the rain of rocks, but the fact that so many individuals were dressed this way leads many archaeologists to think the eruption was later in the year.

- According to classicist Professor Mary Beard, a Roman coin that could only have been printed after September 7 or 8 of the year 79 CE was "found in a context where it could not have been dropped by looters" (*Pompeii: The Life of a Roman Town*).

- Mario Grimaldi, archaeologist and professor at the University of Naples, Suor Orsola Benincasa, was generous enough to give me a personal tour of Pompeii's ruins. He asserts that most Pompeii specialists believe that the explosion occurred in the fall. In addition, Professor Andrew Wallace-Hadrill, author and director of the Herculaneum Conservation Project, is also convinced the eruption took place in late September/early October.

Given so much scholarly consensus on the revised time frame, I could not bring myself to write the story based on the incorrect date.

The Characters

All of the characters in this novel are purely fictional. For greater latitude, I placed the Titurius Gladiatorial School in an as-yet-unexcavated region of Pompeii — called "Regio V" — near the Vesuvian gate. Only the naturalist Pliny the Elder is a real person in history. He and his nephew, Pliny the Younger, lived across the bay in Misenum. Everything we know about the volcano's explosion and the fate of the region, as mentioned above, comes from the letters of Pliny the Younger.

Pregnancy and Exposure

According to Roman law, a newborn child was placed at its father's feet. If the father picked up the child, he claimed it as his own. If he refused to pick it up and walked away, the baby was then exposed (left outside the city walls to die). The mother had no say in the matter. No one knows how often exposure was actually practiced.

The novel's exposure story line was inspired by a letter from a Roman traveling in Alexandria to his pregnant wife, sometime in the second century CE. It is a lovely, chatty letter until he writes this about her pregnancy: "If it is a male, let it live; if it is a female, expose it" (Oxyrhynchus papyrus 744. G). The utter casualness and callousness with which that instruction was given struck me hard. It set me to wondering: Had he given that command before? How would the mother react to such a command — one she was duty- and legally-bound to obey? What if the command came every time she bore a daughter?

The rate of infant mortality in ancient Rome was very high. Around 25 percent of babies in the first century CE died within their first year, and up to half of all children died before the age of ten. Many young women also died in childbirth.

The character of Cornelia was inspired by a skeleton of a heavily pregnant woman who died beside her husband and family. The family appeared to be wealthy, and it is conjectured that they did not attempt to escape, as so many did, because of her condition.

Slaves accounted for as much as 30 percent of the population in ancient Rome's slave-labor economy. According to Keith Bradley, professor of classics at the University of Notre Dame and an expert on ancient slavery, "The reality was that, in the highly status-conscious world of historical Rome, no one could imagine a society without [slaves] . . . Slavery in Rome was not regarded as a moral evil that had to be suppressed, and it produced no abolitionist advocates of the sort prominent in the modern history of slavery."

As a result, while it is hard for us to imagine this, no one in the ancient world had any moral problem with slavery, including early Christians. It was only in the sixteenth and seventeenth centuries that people began to frame the question of slavery in moral terms. Until then, owning other human beings was accepted as either the natural order or fated by the gods. There were, of course, slave revolts — Spartacus's is undoubtedly the most famous of the ancient period — but in those cases, the revolts were against abusive slave owners and not against the practice itself. Given that ethos, I had the character of Tag focus on finding his own *personal* freedom rather than on trying to dismantle slavery in general, since attempting to do the latter would have been inconceivable to the ancients.

Household slaves were considered part of the Roman *familia*. It would have been common to have the master's children and slave children grow up as playmates and to have them educated together. Most Romans advocated treating slaves decently. According to Dr. Bradley, "it was recognized that slave-owning could have injurious moral effects on slave-owners if personal restraint were not exercised." In other words, restraint was advised lest the slave *owners* suffer unduly from guilt!

Curses, Superstition, and Religion

- Curse tablets are real objects of perceived dark magic in the ancient world. The ancient Greeks and Romans used the tablets to inflict pain or misery on those who angered or hurt them. They were made by scratching a curse onto a thin rectangular sheet of lead, using a stylus or pointed tool. Sometimes hair from the intended victim was bent or rolled into the tablet to make the magic stronger. According to the Getty Museum, the folded lead "could be pierced with nails to pin down the target, giving [the tablets] the Latin name *defixio*. The curse tablet was then thrown into a sacred pit at a sanctuary, a watery chasm, or a spring or pool . . . ensuring its delivery to the Gods of the Underworld, who would carry out the punishment." I integrated commonly used curse-tablet language in creating the fictitious curse tablets in the novel.

- I based the headless chicken scene on the life of a famous rooster called "Mike the Headless Chicken." In 1945, Mike was meant to be dinner, but his owner accidentally cut his neck in the wrong spot. The ax missed the jugular vein and left the brain stem — the part that controls reflexive actions — and an ear intact. The bird staggered around like most newly beheaded poultry — only, amazingly, he didn't fall over and die. In fact, the chicken continued to live for an additional eighteen months. His owner learned to feed Mike with an eyedropper containing water and grain. Scientists at the

University of Utah verified Mike's continued robustness. I imagine that superstitious Romans would have been greatly alarmed if something similar happened during a sacrifice, especially if it occurred during earth tremors. They would have seen it as a rejection by the gods and a terrible, frightening omen. You can read more about Mike the headless chicken at www.miketheheadlesschicken.org/history.

• Throughout ancient Europe, clay votives of body parts were offered to various gods as requests for healing or in thanks for recovery. Some scholars believe that the Greeks, who colonized the area in the fifth century BCE, introduced the practice to the Etruscans in central Italy. Most often, votives were made of terra-cotta clay, though ivory or bronze examples have also been found.

• Mephistis was a Samnite goddess of poisonous vapors. There is indeed a small altar to the goddess in the old part of Pompeii near the Temple of Venus complex.

• The Romans believed in many gods, and their religious life was integrated into everyday ritual. Each home had a household shrine for the family gods, where prayers and libations were offered daily. Separate shrines existed for specialty concerns like healing or fertility. Additionally, shrines existed throughout the city and in nature — in neighborhoods, alcoves, crossroads, graveyards, and at sacred places such as springs, groves, and rivers.

Gladiators

The enormous amphitheater that we know as the Colosseum in Rome was about a year away from completion when Vesuvius exploded. The ancient Romans called it the Flavian Amphitheater in honor of Vespasian, the head of the Flavian dynasty, who initiated the project. Based on the sheer size of the Colosseum, I imagined that many gladiatorial school owners would have been trying to build up their schools and stables of fighters in anticipation of the greater demand for gladiators. Pompeii had a gladiatorial stadium of its own, but it was small and provincial in comparison to the Colosseum.

Many scholars believe that gladiatorial combat originated from Etruscan funeral rites that later became integrated into Roman culture as entertainment. Despite the popularity of gladiatorial combat, Romans were utterly dismissive of gladiatorial school owners, calling them "Butchers of Men."

The bones of gladiators still shackled in their cells have also been found in Pompeii. Most gladiators were slaves, and they could indeed earn their freedom in the arena — if they survived long enough. Deaths in the arena were not as common as Hollywood movies want to make us think. Gladiators represented a huge investment, and school owners expected to be compensated accordingly if their fighter was killed.

Free men sometimes "sold" themselves into gladiatorial slavery as a way to get out of debt or to gain fame or notoriety. Occasionally, rich Romans also trained and fought as gladiators, though it was rare. Those who did were reviled by the upper classes.

Graffiti

The graffiti quoted in the novel is real and pulled from walls on streets I imagined Lucia traveled on the way to the market. Pompeii's graffiti provides a rich and often entertaining look at life in the city. Many of the scrawls are bawdy, and many were aimed at influencing votes in elections. Apparently, public defecation was a problem in some areas of town, as several inscriptions either bragged about it or warned against it. Near one city gate, there is even a formal notice posted by the local government that says: "[Defecator] — make sure you keep it in until you pass this spot!" I was fascinated too that in between all of the earthy sayings and the political mudslinging, the occasional philosopher carved his or her observation about the nature of life and the inevitability of death. For a look at the graffiti in Pompeii by excavated region, check out the page at: www.pompeiana.org/Resources/Ancient/Graffiti from Pompeii.htm.

ACKNOWLEDGMENTS

A big thank-you to my wonderful editor, Cheryl Klein, for pushing, pulling, and cajoling me into making this story better, even when I thought I couldn't. Thanks too to my brother, Michael Alvear, for taking me by the lapels and shaking the fear out of me on numerous occasions. Bruce, Matthew, and Aliya — thanks for listening to my endless ruminations as I worked out the story in the car or at the dinner table. And, of course, a huge thank-you to my mother, who swept me off to Pompeii when the project became a reality.

Thanks also to my readers, Elizabeth O. Dulemba, Kara Levy Beitz, and Stephanie Dray, as well as my terrific agent, Courtney Miller-Callahan. What would I do without you guys?

Many other people helped with this project, including ancient Roman experts Caroline Lawrence and Irene Hahn. I am indebted to both of them for their kind attention to the work as they searched for anachronisms and errors. Fellow docent and Latin teacher Conway Bracket checked the Latin usage as did Latin teacher Ginger Emshoff. Hank and Kim Siegelson provided medical insight in regard to the sword injury. Thank you all! Any mistakes or errors in the book are completely my own.

Finally, I want to thank Mario Grimaldi, archaeologist and professor at the University of Naples, Suor Orsola Benincasa. He was kind enough to devote almost an entire day to my questions during a personal tour of Pompeii and his excavations. It made my first trip to Italy even more wonderful than I'd thought possible.

ABOUT THE AUTHOR

Vicky Alvear Shecter loves doing historical research almost as much as she loves losing herself in stories of the ancient world. Vicky is the author of three nonfiction books for young readers, most recently *Anubis Speaks! A Guide to the Afterlife by the Egyptian God of the Dead*, and a young-adult novel, *Cleopatra's Moon*. She lives near Atlanta, Georgia. Please visit her website at www.vickyalvearshecter.com or follow her on Twitter at @valvearshecter.